FISH

Also by John Fraser and published by AESOP Modern Fiction:

Animal Tales
Behaving Well
Best Friends
Black Masks
Blue Light / Starting Over
The Beach
The Case
Confessions
The Cure
Down from the Stars
The Ends of the Earth
Enterprising Women
Exploring the Clouds
Fake Fur
The Future's Coming Everywhere
Happy Always
Hard Places
An Illusion of Sun
The Magnificent Wurlitzer
Medusa
Mercenaries
Military Roads
The Observatory
The Other Shore
Paradise
People You Will Never Meet
The Red Bird
The Red Tank
Runners
'S'
Short Lives
Sisters
Soft Landing
The Storm
Strangers and Refugees
The Test
Thinking Scientifically
Thirty Years
Three Beauties
Tomorrow the Victory
True Stories
Unsteady States, Vol. I
Wayfaring
Wisdom

FISH

John Fraser

AESOP Modern Fiction
Oxford

AESOP Modern Fiction
An imprint of AESOP Publications
Martin Noble Editorial / AESOP
28a Abberbury Road, Oxford OX4 4ES, UK
www.aesopbooks.com

First edition published by AESOP Publications

www.johnfraserfiction.com

A catalogue record of this book is available from the British Library.

First edition 2024

ISBN: 978-1-914938-31-3

Contents

FISH

THE BIG SHIP bypassed the quay, going very strong, amazed the welcomers and the lounging land-admirals, hit the shore, ran through the seawall, trod, planed, skimmed – over the crab stalls, the scaly cobbles, the gasping fish on death's row – and paused briefly, very briefly, at Reception, Hôtel des Matelots – checked in and out, in its own fashion ... visited and exited brusquely the dining room, the kitchen, the bins arrayed behind. Stopped.

The hill, of course. Nature built the town on it, to stop the sea.

Ignoring decency, restraint ... making a judgement: anathema. The ship speaks: 'This place is hostile, junk: destroy it, give it to the sea, pulverise its stones, its scrabbling people, sow its stumps with salt, plant the others' fleet on it.'

'They've been invaded,' says Petronia. 'The people who lived here: – and us, just sightseers, from everywhere. How do we behave?'

'There's no one,' says Vinnie. 'Just the ship, with those big headless fish, side by side in troughs, like torpedoes.'

'Do we eat them?' asks Petronia, quite bewildered.

'I could put one on my wall,' says Vinnie. 'Just a skeleton, if you find a kettle big enough to render it.... They'll be full of poison stuff. If they had heads, they could be hunting trophies....'

*

'My advisor says three years of difference is too much to guarantee a lover's constancy,' Petronia says to Vinnie. 'My romance pitted against your reason, excitement versus experience. That means we two should not get together.'

'That's advice, not a command,' Vinnie says, annoyed.

'I trust her, and I don't trust you,' she says. 'I don't know what you're up to. At school we tried each other out, there wasn't anybody there to ask about sex ... there were no teachers. Now, I don't trust other people, nor their ships....'

They laugh. They're very frightened ... in general; and this rampant ship confirms it. There'll be something in the identities of each that makes them suspect, vulnerable, to anybody, anybody on the ship. If, of course, there is a crew.... Now, there's no one you can see.

'Everyone's invaded now,' says Vinnie, trying to calm himself. 'Money, tourists, new build or sports ... smarty robots. Perhaps the ship is ours. We could use it, make it a residence. The hotel's been trashed....'

'Oh Vinnie, how you anger me,' she says. 'You're the boy with too-short legs who fucks the women, every one of them, because they think you are the norm, you must be real because you love yourself and when they split with you, they see you've made them small and silly the moment you two stepped into the bed, because it's just a procedure, a flourish, like urinating, giving blood, or throwing up. You steam off to the next love, you're a train that snorts out grit and cinders that get into everybody's eye....

'Tack a shark's skeleton on the wall? You don't know better, that there are decent things...? You're brutal because you can't think of anything else. The evil, the malicious – they creep into your empty mind because it's cool and quiet in there....'

'Petronia,' says Fritz. 'We've been invaded! Really. The prices are exploding, and I can't get a connection.'

'I've broken with Vinnie, Fritz,' she says. 'I like you more than him, and he's always preferred Nadia to me.'

'Not now, Petronia,' says Fritz. 'Not now.'

They're not in *their* country. They don't like where they are, or where they were. Who does a country belong to? No one, probably.

'It will mean Resistance,' Vinnie says, listening in, unmoved. 'Although the invading ship was ours.'

'Yours? Mine?' asks Petronia, sounding pert. 'And "our" sailors? – they're all from somewhere else, ours and theirs. I saw no one. They've hopped it. It's called "jumping ship". That means the ship is salvage, abandoned – belonging to anyone who seized it, saved it. That's why you must resist pirates, stay on board to the death, if you believe in owner's rights.'

'It doesn't sound good law,' says Fritz, wrinkling his brow, like a comedian.... 'What concerns me is those fish. Were they protected? Or maybe you can catch some, not others, and so off with their heads....'

'You can eat reds, not blues,' says Vinnie. 'Petronia says we should contemplate becoming animals – I suspect it has been done....'

'No,' Petronia protests. 'I said, "Would we take on certain characteristics of animals, like swimming underwater for months, and beeping to our mother half a world away?"'

'That, we have recently learned to do,' says Vinnie. 'Without getting wet, just knowing her phone number.'

'If we thought that being another animal,' Petronia persists, 'might give us better chances of survival, would we take the risk? Would we change our status as top dogs? It's "against nature" if the boundaries are fixed so as to keep the species separate, however inconvenient some shapes may be.... Not being able to sweat except by lolling out our tongues. Monogamy. Cuckoos laying eggs in your baby's bed.... Eating dead flesh and howling.... Of course, some of those inconveniences we already face....'

'If you were a red fish,' says Fritz, weighing it up, 'you would be decapitated, so you'd not show what you are. If a blue one, not: unless you wanted to pass as a red.'

'I think the risk's too great,' says Vinnie. 'Not just decapitation: there's being eaten by a shark or beached.... If we transformed into big fish....'

'Oh, I'd chance it,' says Petronia. 'I can't swim, so I'd want to be furry, of middling size, run fast, and live in holes that someone else had dug. Not swim all day.'

'It's not like that,' says Vinnie, trying to hold her hand. 'You'd be modified, your body, mind – if you have one – changed: but not so as to fly, or spout, eat plankton. Nor roar. Some things come natural – others eternally out of sight.'

'It's not meant to be a fun trip,' says Fritz. 'Changing species; but it's on the cards. There'd be two subspecies – even many more – of modified people, and the ancient, primitives, living side by side. You'd be a carnivore, Petronia, exclusively. I'd dangle from a tree, eat quinces. My life would be much longer than a gorilla's, but I'd be afraid of you.'

'Listen, guys,' says Vinnie. 'If we've been invaded – where are they, the invaders? Where are we, the resisters? Where's the sailors on an empty battered ship that's knocked down the hotel?

'A series of them, puzzles. If we were animals, we'd be the puzzled kind who gawp.'

'Sloths,' says Petronia. 'That's the word. I'm a journalist, and the first – the only – lesson we were taught, to keep our minds full but fresh, is: "take the concrete evidence, ignore the rest, the inferences, hypotheses, the background. Take what you can see and touch, and follow it, like it was a silken thread. It leads you on to more, more concrete scenes ... and ultimately, truth....”’

‘It leads you down to hell then up, and then the furies turn on you, rip you apart, and you are dead,’ says Fritz, and laughs uncertainly: ‘Torn to bits. Your head torn off, the tongue – wagging on. Your partner’s too.’

‘The only real thing, apart from the empty ship gone mad and on a rampage – is the headless fish,’ says Vinnie. ‘They’re huge. Like little submarines.’

‘You’re undecided, Vinnie,’ says Petronia. ‘About what you can see. It’s the spirit of the age. Frontiers – species ... too many for the patrolling guards. We’re on the cusp – maybe the brink, the teeter-totter. Think *Overkitsch*, think Galia Salimo, working the smokers’ room on Sundays in the Casino, where the colonels hang out, filling the spittoons with their depleted spermatozoa, and preparing for the omni- or the bi-sex who’ll take off their kit onstage ... all fluid and in flux....

‘High kicks, Vinnie: you’ll love those. It’s the comradeship, the promiscuity – that’s what those headless fish proclaim. Eat, everybody! Together! The hugger-mugger ... enjoy!

‘Combat, Vinnie! Fight for what you think is yours. Fight for what you think is theirs. Take it.’

‘It’s true,’ says Fritz: ‘All boundaries are up for grabs ... they melt and merge, like jello ... land, sea, bird and feline.... All of us, we come from mixed families. We’re rain and snow, hail and drizzle, we fall to earth, we’re ice and then – we’re lichens, peat.... Invasions – they impale, infect, ingratiate – they are your murderer, your seducer and your administrator. They’re your grandfather, they write your constitution, police your market.’

‘Everything’s invasion in your eyes, Fritz,’ Petronia says. ‘A change of season, of rhythm, of your temperature....’

‘It’s so,’ he says. ‘You sleep, hallucinate – your sex, the colour of your skin, your eyes – all seep into the shimmer. You understand what you once were, the life in trees, amid the scarlet rocks, black sand....

‘It’s like the Russians; true Russians, not like us. One day they all wake up and lo! They understand – they’re Mongols, every one, have always been, since when they thought they were something else. There’s a revelation, liberation – new identity you might explore: yes, understanding what you were, will be – that’s acknowledging invasion, undeniably and everlasting ... submit and welcome....’

'Mongolians have an unmatched sense of humour,' Vinnie says, hustling them along, 'Stick to the fish. Petronia is right – they're all we have ... since we can't board the ship....'

'We might even climb up,' Petronia says. 'There might be....'

'People. A prison hulk?' asks Fritz. 'Strange people, refugees, or pirates ... our sailors, sleeping, drugged or drunk. Bewitched – infected and incapable: "full ahead", the vessel, hoping to hit and stick....'

Fritz swarms up a rope that's dangling down. The ship is smaller, now they're near. Metal, rusty, a leaf-mould brown.

'Monkey-tricks,' says Vinnie. 'I can't climb ropes – call Nadia, she's worked in a circus, that's how they pass their time....'

'Ships full of cash,' says Vinnie, 'or just abandoned – once were full of precious things, of drugs, but those must be cut and marketed. It must be things that's easier.... Ships not worth a dime ... unusable but traced.... Seas are packed with them.'

'How do you tell the blue fish?' asks Petronia. 'Is it whiskers, or do you need a test? And if there's drugs – how do we sell them? Suppose there's corpses....'

'All these possibilities,' says Fritz, looking down. 'Have answers. There won't be drugs. If there's corpses, we'll run away and phone in from afar. As for the fish – we've eaten all the reds, the blue ones are decapitated so they're not identifiable, and we can eat them.'

'Yes,' says Vinnie. 'History never stays stuck and motionless. Everything shifts on. Remember – "and yet it moves". Remember the pictures – they were all fixed in "flat earth", one-dimensional: then science came along ... and it was round and round. Now it's the whole world in a thin black box.'

'For an empty ship, it's already full ... we're not able to deal with so many possibilities. We'll cut corners, drop bundles,' says Petronia.

'There's clothes,' Fritz shouts up, from down, in the hold: muffled, 'Lots and lots of clothes. For every kind of person, every shape – it would take me years to describe them to you – you must come up and see it – like the Titanic, but no risk: still afloat, all the luggage left....'

'If we're interested, naturally,' says Vinnie. 'Nadia wears all kinds – tutus: sand camouflage for when the elephants do their gavotte.... The circus ring requires you play everything, and no one should see what you really are.'

'Is that style?' Petronia asks. 'I've always shied away from that, but I may have misunderstood. It sounds like gloss. I like the substance. Let it shine, words trumpeting out – no matter what language people speak, or none; none properly.'

Petronia – a Roman look. A nose that's lightly squashed – said thus to be noble: a look daring, adventurous- but also vacant, knowing she's in the wrong company, but never knowing right ones ... where she'd be bored, uncomfortable. Clothes that swirl, unserviceable except for ceremonies – she's much taller, more robust than she appears. She would defer, retreat – but can't ... a presence dominating, on the brink of an escape. A prey desirable, but impossible to carry off, unthinkable to butcher....

*

'We know there's no one there on board,' Vinnie shouts up. 'Find clues, Fritz. Or is everything a clue?'

'A proclamation? A threat?' asks Petronia. 'It could be pirates ... or Islamic State. I'm terrified. Nothing stands still, nothing is stable, there's danger all around and we – I – have no answer, not to anything. Other people – they have qualifications, work that satisfies....'

'It makes no difference, no difference at all,' says Vinnie, firmly. 'War comes; poverty precedes and follows. You see the money you don't have, building towers and military roads. You hug your little telephone, it's like a tiny tiny future world, where you are not. Get used to it, don't be afraid, it doesn't help. We know – we're eating everything, there's less and less each year. If people don't know that and take some care – it's not surprising there are pirates of all kinds ... there's remedies that no one takes, and we, who stand here peaceful on our shore—'

'Nadia will know,' Petronia interrupts. 'She has control. Her body – she can make it float and fly, wear any kind of clothes and make a spectacle. Besides – the ship has nobody on board. That's good. We're safe. Fritz can't follow indications, clues – it's all a heap, a mound, to him. The sailors will have dumped the refugees, and kept their clothes: no mystery....'

'Let's follow him,' says Vinnie, pushing Petronia towards a dangling rope. 'Climb up, I'll catch you if you fall.'

'We could call the Prefecture,' she says. 'I've only ever climbed a rope that's knotted, for your hands and feet,' but nonetheless she struggles up, and Vinnie waits till she's on deck, and follows her. 'You were a refugee, Vinnie,' she says. 'You must know how it works. Escaping....'

Vinnie stands beside her. 'I came by land,' he says, 'by bus. No fishing, and no one drowned at sea, for sure. I came out from war, that everybody said we'd win, and then I came here and everybody says *we*'ll win, but there's no sign of that, no sign at all. I wonder why they say it, if they know....'

'I've never heard you sound so patriotic, Vinnie,' says Petronia. 'We're all different, of course. You were a militiaman. Irregular. And now we're all friends. Just friends, nothing more.'

Fritz appears – he wears a captain's hat. 'These are the orders,' he says, waving a clipboard. 'I can't read them, but it's too late now. And – it's a writing I don't recognise ... who knows if they were following them....'

'Nadia can read,' says Vinnie. 'All alphabets. You look for place-names....'

'No, no,' says Fritz, 'It's all in figures, and some letters. Somewhere there'll be a steering-wheel....'

*

'Most of what I do every day,' says Nadia. 'You couldn't do. You couldn't dream of doing it. The fear, the trembling. All lived with, and overcome. I could write my memoirs. Now – this boat....'

She climbs the rope in quick quick time, and Petronia nods to Vinnie, saying 'see – she's here to save us'.

'It's clear,' says Nadia, 'whoever's clothes these were – if they were made to leave, they left butt-naked....'

'Is that all?' asks Fritz. 'Where do the clothes come from – either there were no tags, or every maker's name was scissored out? And were the people thrown into the sea – or left for better lives....'

'How should I know?' Nadia asks. 'Those fish – they're rotting. What a waste!'

'Your animals would love them,' Vinnie says. 'We'd give them to you, though it might be theft ...'

'Oh Vinnie,' Nadia says, with bitterness. 'We are the animals now. We do the tricks. Who else?

'The dogs especially – they loved the show, and then the state stepped in....'

'You do the tricks now,' says Petronia, 'without machinery. It must be good.'

'We had a little zoo,' says Nadia, crying softly. 'Then we let them go. The big ones – in the end they went as dog-food. They ate too much, and took up all the space. The dogs – they were cute and delicate – I think they went into the fields, where there were bigger dogs.'

'In the end,' says Vinnie, 'they served a purpose. But human cadavers – they're no use at all.'

'I'm sure there was a good end here,' says Fritz. 'We have to work it out.'

*

The fish begin to stink. Vinnie finds a kind of diver's suit, it protects him as he throws them over the side, and the group sets fire to them with kerosene, as they float near. They smell fresh, as if they're cooking – oily and pungent – it's years since there was such rich smoke from massive bodies. No one knows what was their right name.

'It gives you appetite,' says Fritz.

How had it all happened? Maybe – everyone – crew, passengers, pirates and prisoners, immigrants, refugees – saw that their old world, of friends, prosperity, peace – had come swiftly to an end. Leaping naked in the sea. Leaving the engines of the ship full on – a liberation – into the waves. Acceptance that the old ways were over. Not a start, but a search beginning, unencumbered.

It sounds improbable.

Each thinks this might be the scenario, none shares the fleeting thought, that it's too far-fetched, fantastic. It fits what little facts there are, that's all; it doesn't convince, but seeing a vast panorama, where present is already history – it's fashionable. Plausible.

... Except – for the fish.

The ship came to hunt the fish. If, casually, it became a slaver, or a saviour – then the revolt ... and overboard the crew, and all the rest from fear and threat – why leave the clothes? A fishing vessel that did a trade in clothes? The crew – mutinied or mad and drugged – abandoned everything, the last aboard – set the engines at the maximum, and left.

Bewitched? A Circe and her gang – seduced the crew and all the passengers, took them as slaves of passion, or as pigs, hid them along with all the other pigs ... everyone on board, stripping off, men and women ... would account for all those clothes, the suits, the uniforms, the feathered caps, the underwear, the white lace from Djibouti ... dishdashas and djellabas, Bermudas, panamas, jeans, denims, paisleys, cardigans ... all thrown off, and the ship, set adrift with engines whirling – pointing towards destruction, explosion in the open sea, or carelessly pointed as it was – towards the group of friends, just friends, who saw, dismayed, the smouldering carcasses – roasted now, black hunks of flesh stuck to the bones. 'We should have boiled them,' Vinnie says, 'But how?'

*

Where did all the others go? Why are they alone?

These four – are the only ones exposed, without a bolt-hole, a cover, a refuge where you go when there's a bang. Vinnie – a volunteer militiaman, a mercenary, in other words. They're used to catastrophe, dressed up as photo-ops. Petronia – writes pieces for the papers, asking not to be paid, and sometimes they are published: representing life-style. Everything is that.

Fritz is a paragon of fussiness, precision, failed the accountancy exams, too soft to join the cops.

Nadia – tried the hi- and slack-wire, almost made it, but she aged, and now she's grounded, holds the stay-rope for the acrobats, incites the crowd to clap. Yes, my lookalike, my brother, sister – just like you and me. Nearly made it, now has a stack of years to live.

All the others, the population – heard the alarm, went to the shelters or ignored it, knew there'd be trouble, witnessed nothing or hoped they hadn't ... they don't appear again, unable to add a detail, even an emotion ... emotions get too big when there's the new and unexpected – you roam, eyes like plover's eggs – staring and unfocussed.

'We should resist invasion,' Vinnie says. 'For sure, they're fascists. Even if you're one, Petronia, *our* fascists wouldn't be so gross….'

'I'm not up for this,' says Nadia. 'There's no co-ordination. I live by that, and if it isn't planned, we all fall down. You can't resist the ghosts, who let go the ropes, or were dropped. They stand between you and the net, the safety – putting out their tongues, and mocking. No, I'm not with Vinnie – he's a soldier – soldiers wait until they're ordered. By themselves, they smoke and lounge....'

*

'Clothes,' says Fritz. 'Worn all over, second-hand or third- ... burkas and dishdashas, Givenchy and Dior: when it's been worn, trailed in the dust, all looks the same. It's culture, everybody borrows and repeats – art is fashion, fashion is the rags you wear ... Then, there's the fish – protected, travestied. Too big to eat, too small to sell ... no story there, the eternal march goes on, down with the weaker species, only scorpions and mambas have a chance....'

'And ants,' Petronia says, not following, but anxious to be heard.

'My point is, dear,' says Fritz, trying to hold the upper hand, 'we could take the ship. Make it our home, travel ... go wherever. Everywhere is home, and nowhere's where we stay. None of us has reasons to stay here – or there! No one came to save us, help, inform. We're always on our own, the couples split but they are always one and one, who do not ever add together, making a three or five....'

'Good try, Fritz,' says Vinnie. 'What would be the point? A permanence, a home? We're not classified that way – we're emblems of the incompatible. Even the four of us encapsulate a variegated species.... Nadia would be the matriarch, climbing trees, swishing her tail ... mating with Fritz, the alpha warrior, then there's Petronia, the compliant female, screwed by everyone and carrying babies up and down the tree until they slip and fall ... and me, self-pitying, despised, hovering on the edge and made to sleep alone on deck.

'We make societies, Fritz. Some have their insurmountable obstacles – like us, the ship: no food, no destination, short of people ... a foundation myth that's curious ... clothes provided, but no people, a smell of fish, no carcasses ... try to make sense of that, ye true believers!' And he laughs. 'Of course, to understand, we'd need a box to clip on to our heads, to give our brains a boost – it doesn't solve the problem of the food, but still .... intelligence is all, we're sure.'

He takes Petronia aside – 'Forgive me, value me for what I am – I've nothing, nothing at all to give, I know – only to take what is irreplaceable ... your abundance, your ingenuity, your freshness. Imagination is the word – or, better – fantasy's the colour most people cannot see, the critics do not recognise – you paint the world, Petronia! Your touch....'

'Don't, Vinnie,' Petronia says. 'Don't give a "touching" speech. You were a soldier and escaped – there's nothing humble there. Until you're hit – it's risk. There is no balance when you aim at guys: – you threaten. And you risk.... It's precarious. Threat and risk – that's what you have, and what you offer, with a grudge – now you are here, quite unrecognised and under-valued ... When people know where you came from, they turn away; it isn't fair, perhaps, it's prudent, though.'

There's a long pause.

'Why did we come, Petronia, why come here?' Vinnie asks. 'We reasoning creatures – why come to this complicated, unsettled place, unstable and unpredictable. I suspect, it's unproductive too. It wobbles, and destroys itself. Why did we land here, start to eat and kill, exterminate, start on each other, eliminate, invent the best way to murder generations, never asking "Why? Why did we take the ship, and come to colonise this savage place?" It must be true – there's no return. We've been abandoned here. Abandoned by a force unknown, and by ourselves.

'Perhaps it was within us from the start, the day we landed on this world, this globe ... all of us, full of hope, incontinent and stumbling – to fear, suspect each other – getting rid of those who are indifferent or hostile, each against all, until the enterprise is dead as well. What enterprise is that? ... Like colonists who kill the people that they find – and then succumb – starving, poisoned, disoriented by the strangeness of what they see, don't understand, and can't digest....'

'The ship?' Petronia asks. 'The ship you think you came in? There's no other ship but what you see. Is it seaworthy? Impossible to know. The fear of falling, sinking, always with you.... You come by ship from space? It explains everything, but it's impossible as well. You hit land – is that where your mission starts? You've no idea. What mission?

'It isn't so, nothing, none of what you say. You fantasise. That's poetry, a cartoon strip. We climb aboard this rusty monster, we've seen how it rampages on its own, undirected and unfathomable. Are you with me, Vinnie? If you want my presence, you must take this other risk, and come aboard ... taking the risk from me, my friends, and taking it again upon yourself.'

'Fine talk,' says Vinnie, sharply. 'Each bears their risk, you can't transfer it. I wanted you, you don't want me, and so – I don't want anything.

'Our Fritz has usurped the captain's hat. For him, that ends the game. It leaves the rest of us subordinate, prey to his whims....'

THE PASSENGER LIST

They're all quite young. Fritz has started his first big beard, finished his studies, looking for a humble job in some ambitious professional scam. Nadia is older, ended her physical work, seeking a place to sit and give tough orders. Missing the animal acts all her life. Vinnie has been a soldier, volunteering to avoid conscription, joining a cause he's quite indifferent.... Like his mates, all terrified and boasting, ready to play the pacifist or the warrior; and Petronia – thinking to drift high, but really barely off the ground, so, no hurt when she falls ... she often will.

*

'If we go on board, and make the ship move,' Vinnie says, 'we shall be anonymous. Like the people with the clothes. Without the clothes.'

'We shall be like them,' Petronia says, warming to him, just a little, 'Not dead and not alive. Not belonging, not to the ship, nor to anywhere.'

'There is a radio,' says Vinnie. 'There always is, they're everywhere. You can say exactly what you like to anyone who's interested. Somewhere, people might be interested in me.....'

'In the ship,' says Petronia, 'there's nothing else for someone to be interested in.'

'There will be flags,' says Fritz. 'Those tell you who you belong to....'

'They tell you who your enemies are,' Petronia says, 'if you can do anything at all about it.'

'You don't think you matter,' Fritz says, 'because you don't, and so anything, any great statement can be wrong and you don't need defend it or explain. If you don't kill, give orders, disturb daily routines – do as you wish, what's left. Follow the trends, ignore them.... When I get on the ship, I'll make it matter – where we are, what we signify, and how we can escape the cops. You others – you'd just drift. Nadia. Hmmm. Mentally, she's on an ark, of course – alas, there are no animals to train. She'll be disappointed. A sad woman, Petronia, is no use to any man. Sad men – can be turned around, they're waiting for it, hoping for a laugh. Petronia expects happiness – it's a mistake ... it's not contagious, though hoping for it, will cast her down.

'Nadia, though ... is trouble to herself, to us, to any polar bear we meet adrift on dwindling ice-cubes....'

'So, we must accept you as the boss?' Vinnie asks, squaring up, and laughing.

'We all had parents, one at least,' Petronia says. 'We've cut the ropes, away we float, like hot-air balloons.... Some will rise, over the mountains, away, away, some slump to the ground, and wait for something to pump us up. But will there be room, in the basket, for children? Somewhere, something, that seems a little permanent?'

They stare at her. Vinnie says, 'I have children. If you care.'

'It doesn't seem *you* do,' says Nadia. 'I thought you were a warrior, signed up for a term of it....'

'You volunteer,' says Vinnie, 'more risk, perhaps, but shorter service, better, lighter stuff to carry round. More pay, rewards for daring....'

'And you dared to have a child?' Petronia asks, disbelieving.

'Several, I believe,' he says. 'There's killing, death, and with that comes a wish to live, perpetuate, do what seems normal....'

'Throwbacks,' Nadia says. 'Who plump up the numbers .... With perpetual war, the population is assured ... replacements and annexations, all paid....'

'Oh,' says Vinnie, committed to go forward, embarrassed and confused – 'Conscripted for six months, with "no criminal responsibility". Breeding? The consequences – they don't interest. It's a kind of duty, like begging passes when you can, then coming back to barracks when you're due, however drunk you are. Sex *a piacere.*'

'Paternity like that, I understand. Maternity, a bigger bind....' Nadia wonders.

'Oh,' Vinnie says, pushing ahead, 'procreation is a duty. And ancestral reactions coming out.'

'The ship,' says Nadia. 'A hostel? For lady sailors? Not a rest cure, for sure. Petronia's mind's already quite adrift, and for me the ship's a hulk, a prison. Forever painting, the constant up and down – it gives me nothing except fumes and motion sickness. The hi-wire's paradise, compared.'

'You'd be at home,' says Fritz. 'The ship tosses like a slack-wire; fall from the ship, the sea's a net, but won't protect – it heaves in sympathy – put a foot on it, down you go, and drown. Balancing, not looking down: your profession, Nadia, teaches all a sailor needs to know ... balancing....'

'I don't need challenges, don't want risks,' says Nadia. 'The captain doesn't guarantee you anything – instead, commits you to a destination you can't see, where you won't stay, has nothing for you but some squalid days with feet still pitching from sympathy with waves....'

'I agree,' says Vinnie. 'Think a little, and everything life brings is wallpaper. At best – a screen. Hand-painted, but to designs already in the book – a new edition published every year. The thing to do is hope there'll be surprises. If it wasn't contradictory, I'd say – "plan for them," surprises.'

Petronia rounds on him – could it be a ploy? A provocation, to see reactions? 'You're quite attractive, Vinnie, but your stories, true or false, finish you off. You're cooked, and burnt. Attraction – sex – it wears, wears off, it's a patina, at most, it's horn-silver. That takes longer to soak off – the acid leaves a stain, sometimes a hole.'

It's all true, there's no response – Vinnie wants something for tomorrow, possibly today, Petronia wants to skip what's close to, seeks a look down the road where all is obscured by dust and clouds.

Nadia says, 'You guys – make up your minds. What do you want? Solve the mystery of the ship, the clothes? Calculate the heights, the age, of those who lived in them? Choose leaders – Fritz for sure. I organise, Vinnie's a warrior, Petronia's a wimp ... we are a microcosm, a crew. Or do you just want to float the ship and set off, no regrets, into the unknown?'

Fritz will be boss, though no one's said as much.

THE UNKNOWN

Everything's unknown, the past, the future – the present zips by too fast for knowing. The books? They're Brownie snaps, not rules for living: Mann, Tolstoy and Proust – perish the thought, to follow them, or try to learn ... so – don't think about them, not at all; and perish all the same. Petronia's taken many a course in culture, civilisation – and keeps quiet, so as not to shame the other three. They're pig-ignorant of everything except that they've learnt to balance on the rolling ball like Nadia, receive applause, fall off, pretend it's all intended, part of the act.

Ah! The tide! Here it comes, ready to jog the tale along. They're all aboard, no one can swim, and so they float, the ship along with them;

apologetic, bows off the shore, arse backwards, into the world ... 'Hit the red button!' Nadia shouts. 'Or we'll end broadside and be wrecked.'

The motor starts. To end the world or start the ship – hitting the red button's the good recipe.

Soon, they're far away, nothing to see but distances, all around, no clues.

The courage rises, soon, all four are prancing in the billowy clothes they've found. 'Hey,' Vinnie shouts. 'I found a food store – all Nutella – we can last on that for centuries....'

That is true – in part. It gives you buboes and dissolves your gut – taken in quantity, of course. Maybe that did for all those other passengers.... The four new ones, pirates, thieves, adventurers, or just castaways – they speculate: 'Maybe the crew binged on this stuff,' says Nadia. 'And they fell overboard. It's plausible.'

'Anyway, there's eats,' Petronia says. 'And – I bet the motor runs on nuts. Now, without a care – we can get drunk and fuck each other....'

'Like we could before,' says Nadia. 'Though – it's true. We're a green paradise. We trust: we trust in something that will steer us to a destiny we never dreamt ... call it nature, destiny....'

'We could be benefactors,' Vinnie says. 'Redeem ourselves if we've done wrong, and pile up credit if we have no sin ... to guarantee us, in the event it all goes bad.... Be philosophers, in short.'

'Or we can pick up stranded guys,' says Fritz. 'Take them on board and clothe them in their local togs.'

'Fish,' says Vinnie. 'Bigger than we can eat, but for a change, we turn their livers into marmite, fuel, coast along awhiles like that ...'

'You missed it, Vinnie,' says Petronia, admiring. 'Your vocation. Your vernacular has a literary whiff....'

'Of course,' says Nadia, ignoring her, 'if we rescue, we could enslave. That is the classical way, the sequence. Down below – all those machines, the blunted scissors, sparkling cloth from Abidjan ... I bet the rescued, then enslaved – they'd have been enrolled to fix the rolls of cloth, and when the job was done ... over the side....'

'Maybe it wasn't that at all,' says Fritz. 'Enslave and rescue – that would be the classic turn. Take on a cargo, have them make the goods, then drop them on an island to be free, wait for another ship ... free, enslaved, and so it goes....'

'But why?' Petronia asks, the question hovering over her.... The clothes....

'The plan, the ship –' says Fritz, 'the wreck without a crew. No doubt there was a battle, both sides lost and walked respective – figurative – planks.

'Or possibly – the island where the slaves were to be left to settle was so attractive, that the slavers landed too. They planned to open factories – and so, the ship, it drifted off....'

'Perhaps,' says Vinnie, drily. 'They forgot they had to push the button. Or, it's temperamental, didn't work, and so....'

'We're desperate,' says Petronia, 'we shall be forgiven, whichever scenario we decide to feature in.... It reminds me of the song of the shirt, except we're the subject, not the author. "Stitch, stitch" – a life sentence. I hope someone else is found to do it, I have wobbly fingers.... This is the big chance, that I choose to miss....'

'Most people are desperate,' says Fritz. 'You must prepare, and hope. Be unique. How are you spotted? The toffee in the jar that stands out, and gets selected.... The frog who's born to wear the crown ... just spawn among the spawn. The toffee in the jar, selected, stands out, and wins a prize.'

'Oh,' laughs Vinnie. 'Toffs again! You're sure you're chosen, Fritz! Where, exactly, are you taking us?'

'There's nothing,' Fritz says. 'Nothing to see. And the wheel – not easy to master it. But – everywhere looks exactly identical. It's wonderful – like water-lilies all the same – see the pink, the lilac, colours of diamonds, the spray pearls grey and rose.... There's nothing to choose between any course. It's sea. So, it's plausible not to make a move....'

'Take us somewhere, Fritz,' Nadia says, poking him with a marlin spike.

'Look,' he says, pointing all round, 'there's nowhere to go. It's all the same. If there's anywhere, it will come to us.'

And so, in a way, it does. The little boat, with Walid and Jakob. 'There's lots of us,' Walid says. 'Behind. We went too fast, were out in front – and now, we're lost.'

'No,' says Petronia, wearily – repeating a truth as she had often done before. '*We*'re lost, *you*'re found.'

'We'll show you how to work the ship,' says Jakob, tapping a weevily biscuit on his knee and spreading stuff on it, quite thick.

'There's room for nine big fish,' says Walid. 'You cut their heads off, it's the law. But – with this sun, they'll putrefy.... The reds, the blues – alike in death. So, cap'n, what's your plan.'

'We'll try to find your mates,' says Fritz, flustered, spinning the steering wheel. 'Unless they find us first, and there's too many of them....'

'Relax!' says Jakob. 'We aren't *bringing* anyone, we're finding them. The law of the sea says – we don't know anything. If you find people – save them! We'll help you settle them below, but remember – there isn't enough food available....'

'Get comfortable,' Petronia tells the rescued pair. 'We hadn't yet decided who would pair off with who, among us four. But – we're prepared to wait.'

'I see you're the sentimental kind,' says Jakob. 'In a little while, there'll be hundreds here to organise. That will be Nadia's job. Petronia, your work awaits its definition. Maybe you can make a choice. Choose a partner who will help you choose. Time's limited, but you're straight it seems: so, there's Vinnie; or there's Fritz.'

'The cat!' Petronia exclaims, waving the alternatives aside. 'Of course. That's what we lack. A ship must have a cat....' and there it is. Grey, with dark hoops, could be black, or brown – the tail straight up, in pleasure, making for Petronia's hug.

'She's mine,' Petronia says. 'She died an age ago, but I can't let her leave. I call her, and she's with me. You see, you castaways,' and she turns to them, holding the dead cat close and stroking it. 'Life is not uncertain, not completely, not at all. It's complex, full of metaphors and cultural tropes you two won't recognise. First – complex, then, when that's worked out – uncertain. The new scene, the *Gestalt*, is shaky. Then, it gels. Uncertainty belongs to consequence, complexity to present days ... the present shimmers, but the past is stones....'

'What's your cat's name?' asks Jakob.

'I call her Halcyon,' Petronia says. 'After the days together.'

'That's not a cat's name,' says Walid. 'Especially not a dead one's. Now, let's be clear. If we find the others, there's hundreds of them, needing care. If they have drowned, the law says you must pick them up and label them. Let's say they are alive. They must be systemised.'

'Why are they coming?' Nadia asks. 'We're leaving. What do they want that we did not?'

'That's a huge question,' Jakob says. 'Here, there is no land, no referent. No shopping, no connection. How can you frame ambition when the view all round is just – identical? What is your aim? More freedom? More enslavement? Food? Drink?

'You are all seafarers, Nadia....' and she nods. It isn't so. 'You know why people leave....'

Once they all made jeans and pasta – now there's Chinese seamstresses who copy fashion togs – the moment is complex, the sailors come from Indonesia, and Nadia remembers those troupes of happy dogs. Round and round they went, the crowds were crazy with delight ... she sniffs, she wipes a tear. This is her one weak spot, like the immortals whose ankles let them down....

'It's the bombs,' says Walid. 'That's why they leave. They go to where they're made – it is safer there.'

'Old guys,' Jakob goes on. 'They sit for years, there is this button on their desk – they wonder: "does it work?" The urge to press it – grows. Who'd know? Who'd care? The fight goes on, it's sacred, it will last their lives, and yours, eternal stalemate, will the evil never be defeated?... The button! Hit it, you old guys.... Blow up the world! Blow up yourselves....' He pirouettes, does some business, vaudeville, with a stick, invisible.

'Oh come!' says Nadia, and she laughs. 'Who's got the button? Fritz has one of those. It starts the motor, that is all. It doesn't bring you food and drink – although, it's true, we do have clothes.'

'I'm sure the clothes would be a start,' says Jakob, anxious to placate.

The mood is getting edgy – 'Fish,' says Vinnie. 'They're food. Just drop a bucket down, and fill it up with them, all sizes and all shapes. It's free, abundance.'

'All the same,' Petronia says, 'it's not what I expected. Not at all.' She keens, pacing the deck, singing crazily. '"Far and few, far and few ... their hands are green and their heads are red ... the Jumblies ... they went to sea in a sieve".... Is that us?'

It's catchy, soon they're all humming along with her. 'I think it's been generated, not composed,' Petronia says. 'No royalties for robots! Or it might be folk. Traditional. One or other....'

'We're sailors,' Walid says, tiring of the folklore, 'but, you see – we never get wet. We never put a foot in it! We skim. Don't row, don't pole. We're waterboatmen.

'If you have ancestors, you shouldn't fall in love; that blights the tree. It spoils the symmetry. You bring in names that's quite incongruous, and on the apple tree – there's pears! But, if you have ancestors, respect the names: the branches grow and you are hanging on them – so, you never die. Apples, always apples.'

Jakob capers round, admiring: 'You'll see, you'll see,' he chants. 'When the people come, you'll see how they fit in, and wear those old clothes and make new ones – sparkling bright, birds on the sleeves – you'll see – they sing; the flowers – smell them! The sausage trees – plumped out with life.'

'The people rescued – they don't forget,' says Walid. 'They are yours. And Jakob's right – the animals you thought were dead – they breathe again and sing and roar, and not a needle ever touches them. They come on board, they're natural. The people carry them. They reproduce them, wear them on their backs. If you want, the creatures live for ever, make their noise. If you want others, beasts you have never seen – just put an order in, the people, they'll work all night and make them new, new as when you thought of them....'

'Do the sailors all eat fish?' asks Nadia. 'People you find at sea – they come from everywhere ... one never knows....'

'They eat exactly what you give them,' Walid says. 'They'll thank you, pay you if you want, show gratitude – all you could ever hope ... and more. Much more.'

'They're not sailors,' Jakob explains. 'They're passengers. They do what they're told. They owe you.'

'Then,' says Petronia, much impressed. 'There is no mystery. The boat takes in precisely what it finds, everything that's lost.'

'What I told you,' Walid says, 'Is what is. If that's a mystery – then it is.'

'Well,' says Fritz, 'it sounds like it will turn out right.'

'Yes,' Nadia says. 'The fish won't cost. And when we want, we'll dump the people, disembark's the word – another ship, a bit of land. We'll keep the clothes they make, with super-fashions that'll make your hairs stand up...'

*

Fritz sights the sieve at night. He sees the phosphorescent eyes – a cargo of alert, stressed lemurs – people from places you have never heard of, that you must look up, and find there's little info there about them....

'They're ghosts,' says Walid. 'And you can bring them back ...to life.'

Vinnie's awakened, tries to hook them with a pole that bursts the envelope, the overloaded rubber sack they're in. They flounder, and there's noise, and many go right down....

'You know,' says Jakob. 'Go far down and there are creatures there that glow ... it's not to light the dark. There's tests ... these guys,' he points. 'Have all been tested, like the bombs that no one ever sees.... They will not glow, because the light – it's all inside....'

They hear his words, survivors, everyone – you hear the cry, 'The Light! The Light! It's all inside....' and so they scramble up the ropes, all chanting, Petronia and Nadia joining in – the ship is pulled this way, that, it rolls and lists – but once on deck – they scatter down, down to the rolls of cloth, machines, the patterns, the naked plaster bodies, well-fed and well-proportioned, waiting to be fitted out, and in a moment there's a click, a clack, you hear the hum, 'fast fashion, faster, faster' ... and then 'stitch, stitch....'

'They're under contract,' Walid says. 'They'll follow you, just like I said. You gave them shelter and a job....'

'You're marvellous,' Petronia says, fearing and admiring him. 'You found us. Then they found us and you.'

'I do not bring joy, Petronia,' Walid says, solemnly. 'Look back on life. It was all predictable. As they say, it couldn't have happened otherwise, because it didn't. So, no one can be held responsible. I said before, what is, is. It's true, I have the faith, but that is quite irrelevant. Not having it, would not change, not have changed, what is; and what is, becomes – what was.

'Of course, they test the stuff, the doomsday, as they're called – that's why they have allies, and why almost all the sea belongs to no one. Maybe the people with the boxes on their heads – the super-brights – will lay a claim. It will not help – you know, you lower buckets from the ship, they fill with food. It's always so. The poor creatures can't escape. Always, it's open season on the gullible....'

'I'm not so sure,' Petronia says. 'We're many, and the catch is small, and getting – even scarce.'

'My!' says Nadia. 'You're a benefactor, Walid; don't scare us with this scientific stuff – it often seems to trend away from what we see....'

'Well,' says Petronia, finding a friend where it was unlikely, in Nadia – 'We're not sailors.'

'Nor am I,' says Walid. 'If I was, I'd not set foot on it, the sea. It has no friends.'

They laugh.

'The clothes,' Petronia says. 'They're wonderful. The ones we found first off, in the hold – they were drab. We thought they had been bought in stores, the labels cut away. But – I think another crew had made them from what they found, wore them, stripped off and swam, swam far away, to find the joyous shore. And now – the new ones you brought in, Walid, they make these wonderful outfits, that sing like nightingales, the aloes, green and blue, the baobabs sheltering the leopards and their cutsey cubs....'

'It's not the people sewing them,' says Jakob, who always follows every word. 'It's where the bolts of cloth were taken on, a port that's famous for invention....'

'Oh Jakob,' Walid laughs, 'You're a romantic, so naive. Invention isn't local. Everyone can copy everything. It's all on sale – the needles and the fingers; the bodies too – fat as toads, speckled with blebs like lentils or baked beans, or crusts like roasted currants ... scary skeletons, thin as kindling sticks.... It's work, that's all. We will decay, but work goes on, and Fritz will point us....'

He gestures. The sea's all round.

'Oh Walid,' says Petronia, pulling a bold face. 'You sound so confident, so sure. Poor me – I'm torn between a destiny with Fritz – who doesn't notice me; and Vinnie with his fingers, prying at me like ivy tendrils, sneaking in the masonry, entering the tower to bring it down, loosening the stones, cement, the lintels, creeping up the stair ... invading me....'

'Oh,' Walid says, 'it's certainly a mismatch, however it turns out. Emotion has no compass. Sentiments? Those are the only ones of interest to an audience ... but, they're of no significance!

'Remember, Petronia: your adventure, and the people you'll meet on the ship and afterwards – the open conspiracy – this is the world. This is the future-present, how it all turns out. You will experience every contradiction. Knowing me – you know how it all works ...'

*

'Fritz,' says Nadia, finding him alone, trying to work the wheel – 'Walid conceals it, but I'm sure he knows a lot about the ship and why it's here....'

'That's evident,' says Fritz. 'But what does that mean? If we don't know what he knows, and what there is to know – we're nowhere. We have suspicions, but it takes us – nowhere at all.

'Now, this wheel. I'm sure it's locked somehow: banal. Someone steered, got bored, they set the course, went off to bed – and there's a device that holds the course, that I can't change....'

'What's more,' Nadia goes on, 'intelligence. There's people think we'd need to wear a box of brains on top – like funeral toppers, full of extra stuff. It isn't so. Some people have brains that's mainly gloop. Others are already smart, with brains that's just as good as robots have. A pianist, for instance, has a brain with fingerings logged in.

'If you're an ordinary guy, you speak in tongues, inventing words and slithering over syllables. Nothing holds, because you have a bowl of cornflakes in your head instead of brains. Nothing's defined, all's fabulous, confused, you're terrified, euphoric, religious freak, iconoclast – whilst others are as ordered as an abacus. Those are the ones who're head to head with robots, can do mental arithmetic at the drop – the tables and the logarithms....'

'What's that to do with Walid?' Fritz asked, flustered. 'Or Jakob? There are no robots here, Nadia. I ask myself – you'd think we're in a fairy tale, but then – how do those end, what do they signify? Should I think of my last words – there is a radio here, but it receives, it doesn't send, plays *Flammen*, my favourite opera ... is it a portent? 'Flames', Don Juan – the judgement. It's impossible in my case….'

They laugh.

'Are you sure that's a radio, Fritz?' Nadia asks.

'No,' Fritz says, 'I'm not sure. You know, it's not my field. But two cap'ns with the same taste in opera? Me and my predecessor…'

'Proves nothing,' Nadia says. 'Coincidence is all it says: meaningless. A distraction.

'Look for land, Fritz,' she goes on. 'We'll run the ship up, on the shore. Then – everyone for themselves.'

*

'Smooth pathways in the brain,' Walid tells Jakob. 'No undergrowth. Concentrate on those.'

'One of the definitions of intelligence,' says Jakob, 'is swiftness.'

'*The* definition of intelligence,' Walid says, 'is that. Beauty is swiftness, clarity and accuracy.'

'You show it if you sew,' says Jakob. 'Real quick and straight.'

'You show it doing anything real quick and accurate,' says Walid. 'Just looking at the people here – there's Nadia – though she took to falling off the rope. Fritz? You can't tell, until he sinks the ship, runs it aground. Women and children first? No children here, except down in the factory. Women – first or last.... Eve or Avenging Angel: everything is always, anyway, up to chance. But look at Petronia – all the uncertainty about emotions: it comes from slackness, leading nowhere. Vinnie – he's had his shot. An old soldier, full of lies. That kind needs war for ever – more uncertainty. And if you never win a war – where's your intelligence?'

'There's vendetta, spite, and vindication,' says Jakob. 'Intelligence may come in, it's not the driver, though.'

'Exactly,' Walid says. 'Intelligence is the tool. The universal wrench. But – if you can't get through defences at first try – persistence is a luxury. You'll be impoverished, if you insist. That's why we'll dump this ship – already there are holes from rust.... You stand on deck and peep far down – and down there, they're working well. It will not last. Nothing, Jakob, nothing lasts. It takes intelligence to understand. It isn't good. Intelligence is not a guarantee of happy ends, ha ha!'

He laughs, Jakob joins in, but weakly.

*

'We can't deal with Walid, can't read him and Jakob,' Nadia complains to Fritz.

'When I can work the machinery,' Fritz says. 'And point the ship to somewhere like we hope, we'll understand them better, how they seem to be in charge. They aren't, of course. We are. But all these people they brought in, and down, snipping, sewing ... they're a weight on us, not on themselves. They're actors, and they act. We....'

'Don't have a script,' Nadia says, dismissing him, dismissing herself too. 'Petronia's a blob. Sex. Does she want it? Or not? What is it anyway? Is it a billow, or is there some context? A scene, a shape, beginning and end. Emotions are like hunger, Fritz – the jealousy, the itch, the thirst – you satisfy them easily enough, and then – they come again! It's belly-lust: you fill it up, it empties down the bog and then ... it comes again. What poetry!

'And Vinnie – he has a past – but, it's what he says. You can't ask questions of the past, not like 'Do you remember a younger guy, Vinnie. Looks like you....' Doing, being what? We've no way of knowing....'

'Knowing anything,' says Fritz, lightening up, and pinching her.

That's really not appropriate, thinks Nadia, but she doesn't say. 'All those people down below,' she says instead. 'They could overpower us.'

'But they won't,' says Fritz. 'They never do.'

'They won't,' says Walid, overhearing. 'What difference would it make, except it makes them criminals, ungrateful, disorderly. What gain? You give them work and food, a destination. Maybe you don't know exactly where we end, but you know more than them – how hard it is, to land, land on a shore, and disembark. Continue with the life....'

'When we let the animals go,' says Nadia. 'They were sad, infinitely sad. They were the entertainers – it was as if we said "We're tired of you. You haven't understood – our clapping and the cheers were not for you, your skills, your human traits, your being animal and limited, perhaps, but smart and quick, instinctive: no. You're prisoners under torture," we said; "now, we're freeing you. Enjoy your liberty ... away, away, get lost!"

'Poor things! As if unhappy animals could have made a show! It's left to us, unhappy guys, to take their place....'

*

'Do you like them, Jakob?' Walid asks, indicating the four, clustered in uncertainty, near the prow.

'We've been honest, Walid,' Jakob says. 'That's the important thing. We don't lie, and we depend on them to find the land ....'

'You must wish, like me,' Walid says, 'that we could feel ... the land ... a land, a home. A language. Friends – to see them, every day.'

'Of course,' says Jakob. 'You surprise me. Sentimentality. Everybody wants what you want, fewer and fewer can attain....'

'It's not that we have things in common with a bunch of guys, speaking alike, wearing the clothes, thinking the thoughts, the ambitions,' Walid says. 'We're not a clan. These voyages. The people to be saved – all sorts, from everywhere. *We* have a distance – they are them.'

'It's too bad,' Jakob agrees. 'Science gives us decades more to live – and near the end, death takes an arm, a leg, the brain, the tongue, the taste, the eyes, the colours, and you're down, down in a grovel like you were before you had long life, you fall apart, and nothing holds....'

'We must survive,' says Walid, sadly. 'The will, determination – making the pattern, seeing it through, though all will be scattered, like the sand....'

'Of a *mandala,*' Jakob finishes. 'At least, we're not the first, the only ones, to think that way. Enough that enough people think like us, though we don't know them, meet them....'

'We know they must be still back home. It's seeking out the people who must leave, who'll do anything for work, a voyage – then, land that we've yet to find,' Walid says. 'We must concentrate on that, it's our mission, I suppose.'

'We're very far from home,' says Jakob, and Walid briefly puts his arm around him.

'We have to find the people,' Walid says. 'They need work, hard work, that's why they're there, waiting to be found. Other people, all over, pretend they don't understand. We all need work, we go anywhere to find it.'

'It was luck to find this ship, all equipped,' says Jakob.

'Kismet, Jakob,' Walid says.

'I know', says Jakob. 'People, work, escaping, making things to wear and share. They're nearly all the same thing, but we need the right situation to begin.

'The four we found on board – the steersman; his shadow, Nadia; the psycho, security guy; the woman – Petronia: they don't feel good. They don't feel they're doing good.'

'Nor bad,' says Walid. 'It doesn't matter. They don't know how to spot a coincidence, and make evaluations, the next step, the meanings you put on. The shape of things – they do not see. All they want is getting away, they don't know where, don't care. Now, they're sick for land, to leave the ship.'

'For me,' Jakob says. 'Home was not so good.'

'You have bad memories,' Walid says. 'You can't cut them out and put good memories in their place.'

'I know,' Jakob says. 'It's the sea, I think. Being bottomless, you wonder ... where we'd all end up....'

'I know,' says Walid. 'You want a comforting response. There isn't one.'

*

'Do you suppose,' Fritz asks. 'They know where we are?'

'For sure,' says Nadia. 'Everybody does. But there's an end on it. There is no map, no referent. You know your place, your "where" you are – but where is that related, where – to anywhere...?'

'Jakob is sick,' says Walid. 'He always is – not sea-sick. He needs a recognition, something to lift his soul. It makes him savage ... the abandonment.'

'Oh,' says Nadia. 'No one's equipped for that. They won't send helicopters out to drop some plushy toy....' And she laughs, not sympathetically.

'The fact is,' Fritz joins in. 'You two seem quite ambiguous. You really don't serve anyone, not us above nor them below. Perhaps you'll want a cut, when we sell off the clothes they've made. No hope, my friend. We have expenses too – and shall have all our lives.... You don't come in, at all.'

'Suppose I fix the steering-wheel....' says Walid.

'We need much more,' says Fritz. 'Suppose the guys on land think we haven't rescued those below, but somehow we're exploiting them.'

'You disappoint me, Fritz,' says Walid. 'For us, what matters is creation – more than the maturation, transformation, afterwards. We make the barren teasel heads throw seed and grow new plants.

'I thought you'd copy us. You have no past, you recognise it. No destination. Everything we bring to you, to your resource, points to nurturing what is unformed, incipient ... the beauty of the cloth, the physical coordination required to make a covering to set off your poor scaly skins. Concealing them.

'What more is needed, what revelation beyond that? – sly talk, suspicion of some dirty plot?'

'We're open to a broad explanation,' Nadia says.

'Of what?' asks Walid.

'That's it,' says Fritz. 'We do not know.'

'When people didn't know who watched them,' Walid says. 'They said it was the eye of God. Now, the mystery's revealed. It's not the eye of God.'

'I'm sick for land,' says Jakob. 'That's all.'

'There's a procedure, Jakob,' Walid says. 'For finding land at peace.'

*

'Is there a mystery, Vinnie?' Petronia asks. 'Do you see anything inexplicable, without a solution, even a guess to work on? I can't.

'It seems to me, that we've found freedom – maybe only of a sort, here on the ship. We need to find shore, of course, and get rid of the people below, for their good, of course – let them take the clothes they've found, and all the ones they've made, or most, at least. Kind of – charge a fare, and nothing, nothing at all, to the ambiguous pair, Walid and Jakob, who know much more than they let on, without it being mystery, of course.

'What I mean is, in this temporary state – there's nothing much you and me can give or take from one another. We're the one and one who can't make two.'

It's neat, and Petronia's pleased that this word-joust gets her off a difficulty she can't deal with otherwise.... There's no liking, so what's left must be a chance of – love? Or something else, potentially, at least.

Too bad. This explanation – lets in water, everywhere.

Vinnie's formed like a hussar. Astride, his feet would touch the ground.

*

During the night – there's no lookout – the ship beaches on an earthy slope, unnamed and featureless. Walid and Jakob open the door, and lead the rescued people off, set off up the slope. They don't say 'farewell' – that would be for Fritz to say. Fritz stares. He doesn't know. Not anything.

'Where are they going to?' he asks Nadia. She doesn't know. Slaves or rebels, revolutionaries or clandestines. Forty thieves? Improbable. They don't know.

Petronia and Vinnie are glad to see them go, wearing the old dirty, shredded clothes that were in the hold when they arrived. The new bright billowy fashionable togs they worked on all these months – they're down below. Water comes in, and dirt of every kind – the clothes look sad, deserted: rags.

'Remnants,' Vinnie says. 'The column, stumbling up the shore. Bits of defeated armies. They pay to set up family camps. Never act, they wait: locally resented. An embarrassment to themselves.'

'However you see it,' says Petronia, 'they're refugees. Looking for peace, or stasis. Surviving. If they're revolutionaries – who knows what their timetable is? The more determined ones – they make analyses, and if it's not their time, they fester, die old and bitter. The imagination pushes you to make a truce, a deal. Set off again.'

'I think they're people who've escaped,' says Nadia. 'Look how quiet they were, how grateful for the work, and being left alone ... to work. Walid and Jakob – they could be generals, or traffickers – those people, the survivors – they don't seem ready for a fight. Walid did well to bring them far, so far, losing a few, but asking little of them. Work, not fighting. It's more precarious for us – we have no title to this ship, we don't know where we are. Fritz is quite useless as a navigator – and as a leader too. Besides, we wouldn't want a boss, even one who's capable.'

'You disappoint me, Nadia,' says Fritz, overhearing everything, each plot. 'You are my mate. You follow me, my course, and give advice – friendly, but informed. Because we're lost, you turn on me....

'At least, we owe no explanation for the people down below.'

'No,' says Vinnie. 'No explanation for them, nor anything to give to them. Most will die quite soon? Good riddance.'

*

'There's opportunities,' Petronia says. 'But – which exactly should we take?'

'They put this shore, the earth, to stop the flood, the tide. And then,' says Vinnie, craning to see how they couldn't take the fishing boats down to the sea. 'Here ... the obstacle!'

And there they lie, heavy and cracking in the sun, painted with eyes and teeth – but you can see they wouldn't float now, even if you pulled them up, over the bank....

'We might do something here,' says Nadia. 'Look – the boats lie crumbling there, like headless fish, or torpedoes, side by side – inedible, unloadable....'

'What should we do?' asks Fritz, 'Steal them, like we stole this ship, and couldn't use them – heavy as they are, and paddle-driven…? like we couldn't use the ship because the wheel was locked ... the rudder, that is, blocked.'

'It might be destiny,' Petronia says. 'We beached here, and nowhere else. The ship was following its nose....'

'It should have followed ours,' says Vinnie. 'Far off, there's shacks. But what work can they, the natives, or the migrants ... thieves, invaders ... do? I don't see trees, nor animals. We should gather up our eats and keep them hidden, if we trek on there.'

'Leave the clothes here, on the ship,' Petronia says. 'They're our resource. What else do we have? And what use are they – people here might dress quite different....'

'They may not like us,' Nadia says, reluctant.

'We're all so different,' says Petronia. 'They should like one, at least. It's true, we can't do anything, we couldn't get the ship to work. And there's Walid – maybe he lives here....'

'No,' says Fritz, 'at least that's out. We landed here by chance, he didn't steer or plan....'

'We need a place with two rooms,' Vinnie says. 'Fritz and Nadia, me and Petronia.'

'No,' Petronia says. 'I'd go with Fritz, but no one else.'

'I should be on my own, says Fritz. 'I am responsible, I brought you here. You three can bunk together, me on my own.'

'Or else,' says Vinnie, 'I'll go with Nadia. Any port; although it's true, there was no storm....' he laughs. It's a surprise – even a clue, that the weather's always hot and calm – as if the wind and rain have had their say, and don't join in.

'No, Vinnie,' Nadia says. 'My family all is dwarves, and I'm the oddity – and so I'd only go with little folk: they make me feel at home.'

It's unanswerable, it might be true. Vinnie's is the only personality strong enough that he's disliked by all. It's not the sign of a good soul, but nobody believes in those.

*

The settlement is shacks, and shops – except for heat, the village could be Arctic. There's a general store, fast food and betting – and a place for cops and legal and illegal stuff. Probably a lock-up – maybe underground. The villagers have suspicions – but is this after all, you'd ask, a village? Or a place where people pause, a hybrid place, with fishermen who're itinerant, and peasants who have lost their land, in passage; though they've no animals. Nothing but clothes.

Some guys start up the ship and back it out. The wheel is locked – so they're at risk of drift eternal. They jump off in the shallows, and the ship returns, is beached, when the light tide sets in.

'There's nothing to do here,' Petronia says. 'Though much that needs to do.'

'Don't meddle, don't interfere,' says Fritz. 'We've no title to opinions now.'

'How do they live?' asks Vinnie. 'No one passes, and they can't survive by stealing from each other.'

'There'll be an agency,' says Nadia. 'Hang around, you'll see a truck will come and give them eats to last until it comes again. It's an encampment, temporary. They'll hope these people take to nomadism, move on, and on, until they find a bigger camp and settle down.'

'That's no help to us,' says Vinnie. 'We know all about communities and genealogies, destinies and birth-rights, strangers, castaways and refugees. In fact, we know how a someone is a no-one, and a somewhere a nowhere. But all we are seems to be what we say, say to ourselves and each other. What we profess, could be what is believed. Yet ... clearly it isn't so. The people here fear and hate us for what we are – they know it, exactly, what and who we are. We don't, we play the part ... if we must, we improvise. They don't listen, don't join in, aren't interested....'

'We're not slavers,' says Petronia, 'or investors. Walid – was he? And Jakob? Together, but unequal, like us four?'

'We're too different, we four, too apart, for equality to come in,' says Nadia, decisively. 'And how much latitude do we have, in interpreting? Whose story is it – theirs or ours? Walid and Jakob – they could be preachers, leaders of a cult ... soldiers or benefactors....'

'All of those,' says Fritz/ 'Taxonomies work by consent. We don't know who they were. Nor, who are the people who sewed those dirty clothes they left behind....'

'We might have a story,' says Petronia. 'To give a romance its flight – you need a character, a protagonist, who struggles: but they're sympathetic. No one reads about a pig-head, or a militant.

'Strong opinions? – any romancer tells you to beware of them. In real life – beware of roots, especially if a tree is growing from them. In the fictive world, a protagonist must win the biggest audience, even sacrificing everything, and suffering – rightly or wrongly. The other characters – they can be real, but someone has to bear the weight, a structure that can make them plausible, even admired.

'It's not like that, the story we could make....'

'Why bring it up?' asks Fritz. 'We're in trouble here, not for what we are but because we are.'

'I wonder,' says Petronia. 'Should we have wanted to go with Walid? Should we envy them, his troupe? Why were we not among them? – was it because we decided, or because of who we are, individually, together ... or because we couldn't take the voyage? Enjoy the life? The trip? Drifting and being rescued? Escaping? Seeking a promised destination? – even if it was an illusion.'

'Or real, but not what any of us would want,' says Vinnie.

*

Petronia chums up with younger guys, the locals, tries to at least. They're predators, and she is willing, up to a point. One lad in particular has a trace of style, and makes her laugh. Vinnie explores the settlement, looking for a route that leads outside, if he could find a bike or truck, and Nadia mopes.

Fritz says, 'We had an adventure, with the ship. Each thought it was a way to open a new chapter – what has it brought? Was it adventure that we wanted or each of us – expecting quite different things. And now, what difference does it make? ... our difference.'

They barter with the foods they have, and try to teach some skills. Fritz is useless, but the villagers sort out the problems with the steering wheel. The rudder.

Vinnie could teach shooting, but it's not appropriate. Nadia tries tight-rope walking, and they take to it. She shows the way, they excel, inventing skills she'd never contemplated. They patronise her. But – they know they can't live like this. The villagers know they'll be moved on, so that poorer ones can take their place, or richer ones can settle and employ.

The four from the ship: they expect life will get better. They've always known it will. There's always been a mechanism, people to lubricate it, feed it. Things improve.

Here, they don't. It's not that kind of place – here, it's passage. Better and worse – they don't come in. You think 'worse' is for a small minority – perhaps.... But if you're in it, that big little band of the abandoned...?

'We must bear with them, the villagers,' says Fritz. 'But when they move off, we must take over. When new ones arrive, we must show them – how we're here and in command. Use every means – even Petronia. Play the culture card. We are the elders, we are few, but all the power is ours.'

*

'I'll call you Angelo,' Petronia tells the lad. 'Angels must start somewhere. It gives you something to aim for.'

He's not much interested. You'd say 'traumatised'.

'Where did you guys come from?' Petronia asks?

'Are you spying?' he asks. 'Or is this courtship?'

'Just tell me,' she says. 'Forget the categories.'

'In the mountains,' he says, tipping his head upwards, 'it was paradise. Then there was a problem and all we had left to sell and eat was animals, and then the others came and tried to steal them. So, we had to leave. They trashed all that was left and what couldn't be enslaved.'

'It doesn't sound like paradise,' Petronia says.

'When you can remember how it was, you have to leave,' he says. 'Memory stands in the way of pleasure ... of everything. Paradise is what you can enjoy but don't remember.'

'Well done!' says Petronia, much impressed. 'But – you seem to remember everything. You could probably have a try at remembering the future too....'

They laugh. It isn't humorous.

'We could be a bridge,' she goes on. 'If anybody wants to cross....'

'You don't impose yourself, Petronia,' Angelo says. 'That way, your life will be a load of regrets and nearly-weres.'

'Without me,' Petronia says, 'you'll be a parcel, trying to get yourself delivered.'

'With you,' he says, 'it's stories. You end one and cast around for opening lines: and off we go again. You're lucky – you don't find it difficult to hide emotions. No one told you there were any.'

'We're on a ridge,' she says. 'It's best to be there, up high, in case you make a bad decision, fall down, one side or another. There's too many things that might be happening, and we know none of them....'

'Yes,' he says. 'That's it, exactly. No one sets them up, the puzzles. No one cares if we don't solve them, or are swept away. Or, we solve them, and are swept away.'

'That's nothing,' Petronia says. 'We're on the wave, we're always travelling, there's always a destination. This feels different, as if there's nowhere to end up, no shore where we can be a castaway.'

'You're here,' says Angelo. 'This is your shore. It's us who's airborne. We could be in transit, on to nowhere, for a generation. A dynasty. A life.'

'If I were you,' Petronia says. 'I'd break away. Being abandoned, deserted, being nowhere – it's an opportunity. It's a misery.'

'You think being without order is a good,' he says. 'I know it is a bad. Order grows on order like an onion grows. It flavours and it nourishes – and it smells ... you smell when you ingest it, but you live.'

'It kills you too,' she says.

'It's true,' says Angelo. 'It shows how we can't both be right.'

'It shows we both *are* right,' she says. 'But – is there a way I can get out of here, and maybe you too ... me avoiding order, you trying to take it with you?'

'What are you, Petronia?' Angelo asks. 'If you are no one, or just special – you'll have to take your chance. The scratch-card – your heading, your sequence, luck – is "general humanity". If you are beautiful, know how to attract people, have followers – you'd have a better destiny. A bigger prize, if you had ever won.'

'Oh,' she says, 'yesterday, I spread my legs, prepared for 'cello practice – and wow! Out popped a khan of khans. That's quite unusual. Of course, we'll have to wait and see. I use as precedent Muezza. The Prophet's cat. No ordinary pussy. I bear miracles, Angelo: watch out!'

'You're right, Petronia,' he says, admiring. 'You try. You may not be a warrior, but you don't give up. Fritz and Vinnie – they don't see that being conquerors is not that great. Vinnie should know, that teaching guys like me to shoot – is counter-productive. Power is an onion – your ring grows round the rest, and then another binds around it. You empire-builders thought you were the first and best – you were the thirty-first who build an empire here, or thought of it. There's only shale, the soil is dead all round – but if you dig and dig, you think you'll find some precious stuff before you reach the hell-fire at the core....

'Then, you'll set us and our kids to go down in the hole, and tote the hods and pile the spoil.... Then? It's up to us, to throw you down the shaft, and if we don't – it's still our fault, and our initiative. The new occupiers, you ... you don't bring anything, except creative ignorance....'

He laughs.

'You have an inner life, Angelo?' she asks.

He doesn't answer – easy to say yes or no, but what's she getting at? She tells the other three everything about him, the affair. Almost everything. Except about how everywhere is dirty. You throw stuff in the street, the wind blows it back in, the shit flows down the street where there's a runnel dug, but it's not offensive, not at all, you don't stare at it, identify the ex-owners.

You aren't here for long and it's the least bad thing, not causing anxiety at all ... except there's constant struggle – with the dirt, the stuff you throw away and here it is, all round, all over, the water never is enough, and people steal the clothes – necessity, but having a whole ship that's full of clothes that smell of long dead fish – it's a richness.

Angelo is sure, that when they move, things will be much much better, though at first they'll surely all be much much worse, and Petronia will be left here, waiting for someone new to shake the dice and bless them, spit on them, shake them again....

Then – they're all gone. Violence has been the midwife – if they don't go quiet – they're beaten. In the very early morning – the night – the trucks park outside so you can leave with only what you carry. Then? A bigger empty place to live in.

The four seafarers – they're still there.

* * *

'And so,' Petronia tells Vanessa, 'It ended.'

'Tell me all, before we go down the slope,' says Vanessa, rolling cold snow into a ball, throwing it in someone's path.

'They took us off,' Petronia says. 'Our adventure – it went on. The rescuers were internationals of some kind. They giggled, jostled me and Nadia, laughed at Fritz, made banging noises at poor Vinnie, to make him jump.'

'Tell all,' Vanessa says. 'About your native pal....'

'Oh,' says Petronia, weaving her skis together, sketching a heart before, beneath, her: 'He went off. Resettlement. It saddens me, and makes me want to look for all of them – displaced, resettled. What does it mean, Vanessa? You might make any place a home – except the ship. The mystery remained. He had lived in paradise, poor Angelo. Something went wrong. He was unlearned, of course, but then ... School wounds, they say – I'm sure you went to school, Vanessa, graduated unhurt....'

They launch, down the soft slope they trundle, Vanessa falls, Petronia ploughs on, looks behind to see her friend, and falls.

*

The indoor snow is nearly slush: the air is warm. They drink, Vanessa asks, 'You know why this is called toddy, dear Petronia?...

'When they hunted foxes, those were known as Mister Tod. This drink's a reward, gifted after the death, sort of. Showing who was still alive.'

Petronia's not convinced. Vanessa goes on, 'You should have hunted Angelo, you know....'

'I feel for them,' Petronia says. 'For everyone, wherever they have ended up – except ... they move around. You have to watch them, they could take up arms, or bomb, or preach ... escape.

'And roam. Instead of watching them, you can just move them further off, of course, except nowhere is as far from where it was some years ago....

'I understand, although for us – it ended well. No charges for the ship are owed, the taking it, no money for the rescue.'

'Lovely to look for Angelo....' Vanessa says, quite dreamily.

No, absolutely not, Petronia thinks. She says, 'Of course, it's war against them all. The countries, not the people in the way. You can't move round, not on your own. They say one day there'll be a settling down – but now, there's people you can't talk to, even talk about. I forget why we always hate those people. Maybe it's because....' She pauses. The competitors, the South, the countries – they're quite unlike me, Petronia thinks, so it's not clear why we should need to hate them, or anyone ... or to like them, come to that. Angelo – years spent in a box, a container – tent ... under a blanket held up by sticks, waiting for what? for life, death – movement. Being moved.

And all those people, paid and busy, preparing war, preparing populations so they won't oppose those wars – the money scraped together. Our people, their people – people not to know, who patronise you, parrot all day the morning squawk.

'It seems a waste, if we should go and fight, just so's we can make a settlement,' she says.

'Oh, that's the way,' Vanessa says. 'We all survive, or most of us, and mostly things seem just the same. It all depends on where you want to travel, and who you want to come and do the modest jobs, so long as it's not you.

'Anyway, for you, Petronia, it was all exciting. You knew, the rescuers always seek out people like you, and Fritz.'

'No,' says Petronia, 'Crying and screaming while you wait – it would be natural, but unobserved, and useless. Living without context is the nearest to freedom and disorder you can get. Everything's familiar, but the meanings aren't revealed.

'You are a child, where the world is ready, laid out, and indecipherable. You have no bonds, no powers. You can do anything, but 'nothing' is what you do. You're free, and you can't control yourself. Freedom is emptiness, void, residuum. I thought it was my element, but it's like the bottom of the sea. Mouths ready to ingest you, always working, working like machines. Swim, swim – to nowhere.

Anything at all can happen to you, no one helps, no one laments for you. I hate it. I like the freedom where they tell you what you can do. Free fish? Free floaters? Does that make sense? Our ship floated freely ... lived in the sea ...

'There is no up or down. Good and bad – those disappear first, and we needn't rend our clothes, because we had a shipful of them, to take their place.

'Rescue spoils all that.'

Is it a kind of wasp, she wonders, that after intercourse, the penis, the stinger, breaks off, stays within the female. A nuisance! And is it a sting? A poison? After Angelo, although she had nothing to betray before or after, she feels she is a traitor, a sleeper, waiting till she might have something valuable to someone that she oughtn't to divulge.

There's nothing valuable, because we all know or guess the big things. They might ask 'how' we know, not 'what'. 'What' is for little things, for journalists.

And what Petronia has to betray is not secrets, not at all – it's loyalty. Being sympathetic, too sympathetic, where you should not, because you're ready to betray.

*

'The skiing went so well in Saudi,' says Vanessa, 'That they built them everywhere, all over, even when at times there's natural snow.'

'Yes,' says Petronia, impatiently. 'It all connects, the world is getting tiny, and we all struggle for a handhold and a hamburger ... but *how?* Drugs and guns, that was one link, and then religion, hallucigens, and then the little shooters, P38s and AK47s .... the nationals who couldn't live anywhere else in any other way, or keep their cows or do their trades and make their trips and holidays ... Yes, all that, it all fits together, and the hoods, the amateurs, the secret services – they give a hand to one another, and it all makes sense, and off to war we go ... instead of glaciers that move so slow, we're all on belts, conveyers, slide areas ... It all falls down and so we set to and build it up, breed bigger bees ... and now, of course, it isn't only flags and corporals' stripes we care about – it's lakes and mountains too....

'But, Vanessa, tell me this. Clothes. Where did the clothes fit in? And are you wearing one of ours, the perilous ones, sewn up like a mouth, a protest against destiny .... maybe some charity sold it to you, an artist painted shapes on it ... clothes!'

'Oh come, Petronia,' Vanessa laughs. 'You told it! Told it already! It all fits in, it all fits on! It's the unravelled sleeve that's knitted up. Silence that covers you – a cloak. All the depraved, the wealthy, the ambitious, great rhetoricians who tell us what is what, guardians of last days, they hold your hand while you go under, nine-ten-and out.... They must have made the plot that puzzles you – you, the complacent, complicit – you were the lamb that's saved!

'It is the chain, the sequence, Being! Your adventure. Us now sitting here, covered in those clothes!

'You came across the clothes, a ship, the fish – all had come loose and guys sailed up and took it over, made more clothes, led the tailors off ... and that is it: totality. There is the chain! A chain is made of links, and there's no links without the chain.'

'I guess, yes,' says Petronia, reluctantly. 'I thought we were anomalies, on a spooky trip, but probably you're right: when we speak of making sense, there's only one sense things can make.

'One thing follows another, and that is order. If ever there is one thing not following and followed – the universe is broken.

'It's the imperative, and up and up we go: – it is the history, the making, of the human mind, the mirror of creation, Universe – until....'

'We fall down on our arse, my dear,' Vanessa says, patting Petronia's.

'I resist,' Petronia says. 'A common-sense explanation of our mystery. The steering locked, the people fleeing – put to work, then disembarked. Us stepping in like pirates, salvaging the ship, no, no, it's all too pat. How could all that happen, seem mysterious?'

'Everything is complicated,' Vanessa says, 'to stop you poking in. You're much attached, I think, to mountain lakes – our patrimony. I see you in my head, with your bow, your arrow – defending them, the otters ... and the moss.

'But those big rockets? No defence exists, and they destroy the outlets and the sources – out the water spills, and that is that ... No lake! What does it prove? What benefit to anyone? What do *you* prove, my dear? By being here? What hole is it that you fill?'

'There's nothing simple,' says Petronia, as they hand in their skis, go out in the hot sun. 'You accept an explanation, but it avoids all your experience, your thinking ... the past, the future – it doesn't even let you live while things are going on. You are a lake – if you're not here, we'd miss you, only spite can take you off before your time and drain you out, before *we* do ...'

'You're a great person, Petronia,' Vanessa says, feeling sorry for her, her lame brain.

'No,' Petronia says. 'I think great things happen round me, but I don't understand them, not at all.'

*

'The meditation centre's closing,' says Mister Moon. 'I'll keep it open for you, Petronia, a few minutes. Tomorrow we shan't be here.'

'That's good,' she says. 'I dwell too much on all that happens – the threats, the messages, that ship, the series of attacks. They seem to be attracted....'

Moon doesn't comment on his clients, their mishaps. They dramatise, they try to find a link, a reason, purpose, some connection that would make them seem coherent, a hero or a target. Both.

There is no hope for them: – at least, they must abandon hope, and then they're on the path again.

Petronia thinks: What happens to me – it hasn't been a story, a philosophy, a science, it need have no rules, no boundaries, no probabilities. Any machine could have a life that's more connected, more directed. It's true we instruct them at the start, but they make context, they see the rooms, the spaces, how they join up; how you go from one to another.

Corridors. They seem to make a living space, except there's nothing live. Connecting, to make a meaning that we don't know, not for ourselves.... Sometimes – we desire, intuit, make a plan, but mostly – not. It isn't up to our intelligence – maybe machines aren't so smart, but our intelligence doesn't pilot us, not well.... The cleverest guy ends up in jail. Because she's clever, showed it, where she shouldn't have.

It's about the structure that we build – a bee constructs a comb, and uses the shape that comes most naturally, that resists, permits the life that's planned, the plan that we don't have. Resistance? When we were the four – did we think we could resist?

*

A dog. Caesar. 'Not a machine, a dog is what I need,' Petronia decides.

She tries one out, a Labrador. It's torment. It should be limited, easy to predict, to comfort and to trust. It's not. It's a life, unlike her own, in all respects – the intellect, the goals, emotions. Dogs pal with other dogs: they emote. They depend on humans: they comply. They could escape – some do.

'I took you on, Caesar,' she says. 'I do most of what you're built, evolved, to do yourself. What is the bargain, the contract that I've made?'

The dog might answer that what seems simple to him is the confusion, the complexity, that only humans face. Better, then, to be a dog, or have a dog's brain. Better? – than what? If there's the choice, we must know what the choice entails. We choose to be a dog, though it's unlikely that we can – but everything remains fixed, for ever: dog, or person. False simple; or intricate spaghettis?

'How did they catch the fish?' she asks herself. 'The people on the ship?'

'Follow your nose,' she says to Caesar. 'Freedom is the natural state....'

She lets him go, he doesn't seem to want. It's her who runs, leaving him there, puzzled, aimless. Freedom, like happiness, is constructed, like a garden. Does it resemble, follow, reason: or the wallow, like a pig's? Happiness, you can mock; what kind of goal is that, when others suffer...? Reason your way to freedom? Try that on the soldiers and the cops ...

*

'What's that on your arm?' Petronia asks Vanessa.

'It's a saying,' says Vanessa. '"Avoid disaster by doing what is right." It's at once pessimistic and optimistic.'

'And does it hurt?' Petronia asks. 'Getting it done? I only know some Arabic letters, not the words. Suppose they prick it: "Disaster comes from doing what you think is right..."? Those guys with the needles – they're full of frothy fun....'

'It's just a saying, Petronia,' Vanessa says, brushing her off. 'No one knows who said it first. And you'll be pleased – I hear we're going to have a war – the people responsible for Angelo ... your cause....'

'Oh yes,' Petronia says. 'Your general. I guess he's full of pillow-talk....'

'They're short of bullets, bombs and stuff. When we get ours – we're off,' she says. 'It's more an intervention than an all-out war. Minorities ... they always want a better deal. Never be one of those, Petronia, you'll call the big guys in and bigger ones will come and settle on the scales. Better a small injustice than a massacre....'

'You could put that on your other arm,' Petronia says. 'And if they get it back to front, "better a massacre..." it balances the other one.'

They laugh. Petronia goes on, 'I hope the ship, our trip – those people don't come in as bodies to be avenged ... poor Angelo....'

'Between us two ... are pieces of the earth – it's an escapade, that sounds like war,' Vanessa says. 'But really – it's for peace and justice. Both of those. Resettlement and reparation for the people driven off the mountains.... Find them somewhere decent, have them grow our food ... Breed the stinging insects who produce the fruit....'

'Knowing how people start off sticky, the more they move around, the stickier they are,' Petronia says. 'I remember how they identified – with the place, the height, the animals ... you'd have them become quite otherwise, settling them, undoing their experience.... They'll want to come in here, the city, they don't want poverty again, they'll seek a different place ... with apartments, selling their animals, stuff the animals have made – it seems it's turned right back, to start fresh history – but really it's a parody, a theatre....'

'Well,' Vanessa says, 'they're only part. And it's quite true – they get so used to being a resistance, they'll want to have their way, it won't be ours, for sure. Not even if they come in here.... They'll never get along, I'm sure....'

'We all forget,' Petronia agrees. 'There's so much to remember, we must forget, invent new things to cover up the patches where we scratched, where we were bare and vulnerable.... Forgetting's what we're good at. If animals do it, they'd be dead. We are the opposite ... onward and onward, you must invent, refine your mind and concentrate on being different. Forget. Others will remind you. Make a career, be obedient, be devout, be punk – be anything but what you were, and be exactly what you were, when now all the context is quite different. You can be "before and after" simultaneously.... Old you in the new: new you when your mind is blank.'

'You talked to them,' Vanessa recalls. 'Deep, teary stuff with Angelo. The languages, they are the same. We are their sisters, they – our cousins from the boondocks....'

They laugh some more, they feel each has perspectives that might put them into opposition, one against the other, disbelieving, misperceiving.... Then, Petronia thinks, there were the people saved from the sea to be accounted for, situated in your imagination, the tailors of the fashion clothes, who marched up the muddy shore and disappeared; the people who had dispossessed Angelo, those she had never seen, and didn't wish to, hoping rather they had moved on, disappeared, starved as a punishment, failed as herders and planters, distillers of bad hooch that kills you quick, within the night....

And the people who had caught the fish? Fixed the steering, jumped ship, and they too – disappeared. All bound, defined, by their habitats and skills and yet – Not. Not at all. On the move, the slide. Not bound to anything. Like Caesar, the dog: now free and bewildered, then tamed, complicit and obedient ... tossed like dice, winning, losing, confronting chance, cobbling up a history, ah yes – 'Traditions', a hugger-muggery of mafia and cops – bright sloppy clothes.... That's where the ship comes in, she thinks: The tailors, the fashion geeks, the cultural appropriations, the little bowler hats, the ostrich plumes, the lip rings, nose wires, ear-lobe stretchers....

'Petronia,' says Vanessa, adding a sharp edge to her voice. 'We have to sort this out. These displaced people – why, the tears come springing out, unsummoned, for their destiny; and it's not the degradation only, it's them going pious, coming here and killing us, and cutting off our heads, stealing our jobs ... the war, when won, will make a space where they can be sent back, under our tutelage, of course, in chop-chop time, when we have laid the mountain bare, and pacified the other side, and shipped off all the stuff they're hiding there, and make a peace ... *pax aeterna*, dear Petronia, written down and guaranteed. Growing food for us.'

'It isn't me, Vanessa,' says Petronia. 'I feel it isn't you. We may be for democracy – but democracy's no good when they can tell us what will happen if and when. It's better, sure, not to be murdered if our accent's wrong, but that is all ... the rest, the poverty, the wars, the keeping people in and out, it's been foretold, foreplanned and ordered ... sometimes, though, it might not happen, not at all ... all without us knowing anything....'

Vanessa laughs, 'Oh, Petronia! Don't be a goose. The plans, projections – they don't mean a thing! It's true they can't be changed, but they will never come to pass … it is enough you settle for a poor and scrabbling life, machines to talk to, scandals to raise nape hairs…. Accept! My dear, life is as it comes – you ought to know. Jump on the ship, jump off, sell castaways: remember, survivors can't pay you for being saved; sell on the glam ideas the lower decks sew in the clothes –

and then decide. What is your next part, Petronia my pet? What will you play in our Satyricon? An ostrich? Fans on your bum, a waggly walk?

'Consider time; the tendencies in history – those were a fraud they taught at school. Time passes, it can't move faster, not here – it can't move you where you want … we age, we consume ourselves – look at your fleshless arms, my sweet – soon, bones you thought were hidden till the end thrust out, and you will fracture them; your gut expands as if you're bringing forth a tiny hippo … but, relax. You won't...!'

Petronia laughs. 'Those feasts, Vanessa – always fascinating: orgies where everyone is impregnated, live beasts are harpooned on the dish, blind servants end up on the spit – and then … the books! All disappeared – the inside tales, the dirt … all lost! The hosts were credited with banqueting, with luxury beyond our hopes, and yet … and yet, they're sent by emperors to rule vast lands. They do it perfectly; so well they get up the boss's nose, and end garotted, eaten by pet lions, all that.'

'And is it true? Or plausible? The books they're said to write – the books of Satyrs, and of Satires – much read once, but now quite disappeared, without a trace, a quote. So, are we sure it isn't all a cod? Our leaders….'

'Hush!' Vanessa says. 'Cool down. Time doesn't move, and yet it does – it changes scenes, but not the script, the play. The first act's sci-fi, broiling sand, exploding stars, and red-hot mud. Then there's the dinos, quite a panto chorus line. Every shape – they stump around, maybe they gobble up the smaller cousins and in the end – it's Blue Bird time – they all hold paws and fly up, tiny, tinier – up in the trees and my! They sing. Then the last act – it's ours.

'Here we come, in ones and twos, thumbs on the ground to hold us up, blathering, farting like thunder – then…. It's Cuzco, Tenochtitlan, the empires, everybody clothed in saffron silk, Rome, China, Greece, the Scythians, the Brits, the Mongols, Françafrique, US marines – and all rampaging, inventing gods like mad and hoping to fuck goddesses … you see? It's all a satire, with the songs, the dances – heroes with wooden swords, the harridans – Turandot, Lady Macbeth, a satire, but you understand: the real's a satire of the real. This is the trick, the palindrome, the crystal balls, that squeaky cube, the Ouija and the resurrections, tea leaves and entrails – however it's imagined, however the tale's set up … this is the world, the universal play – the long-lost, ever-present *Satirae.* Satires. Or satyrs. Your namesake's missing manuscript, my dear: Petronius.

'It's a good script, a precious scenario. Convincing. Deadly. That's why we puzzle over it, its asks: "is the real real?" "is there a purpose, is there improvement, are there rules, or good or bad, supreme beings or a boiling hell?" Ha ha.... That's the response! Let yourself go! It's theatre, our sort struts on, the presidents, the shamans, prophets, emperors, good guys and bad.... Sway along, clap to our shaky shaggy two-leggèd prance!'

'I see all that,' Petronia says. 'And then? And then...?'

'And then ... it ends,' Vanessa says. 'As you'd expect. It all repeats: so, it must end: rises and falls, the plans, the thefts, the massacres, taxes for the orphans' homes ripped off. The last act – way too long. It ends, without denouement ... that's the joke. The end: – that is, The End. Don't think to change, my pet, to climb on the stage: stay in the audience, and applaud. The ticket costs you all your wealth, and more.

'There's no catharsis – or, at least: you're it! You die, and there's an end to it, to all.... Don't clap too hard, you might achieve a *bis*, an encore.... Another century of sitting there would petrify your bum. Long life is bad for you....'

'That's your General's take?' Petronia asks. 'It's much like Vinnie, talking in his sleep. Eternal return – which doesn't move a millimetre? Life ... is eternal Western Front?

'Now, it's the human play, like once it was the insect play. We're in the last act, the fairies, good and bad who sort things out – the curtain falls, and then we're off again, a new performance, and so, on, on and back. The trilogy of life on earth: the last, our feature, is quite short, but other acts dragged on and on – the dinosaurs, and before – creation, the ballet of the stars, the smoke, the distances. Emptiness and cold, heat.

'And you, Vanessa – you have an eye ... remarkable! You know the human age, what has been lost; the titles, clans and tribes ... divinities and shamans' scams....'

'Yes,' Vanessa laughs. 'I peeked into the testament. Too bad all the heirs and legatees are dead. The little that we've done – excluding damage, naturally – goes into the hopper. When the next lot, creep or flutter – brew their beer, they'll find our best achievements in a heap, a pile of hay, all chopped, and ready to ferment....'

'So sad, Vanessa, you're with that soldier,' says Petronia. 'You have the qualities I don't ... Nadia could spin a rope, Vinnie – he would start a shanty, knew the types of tree – the bushy-top, the pine ... and that was it. Fritz – so solemn.... Me – thistledown, I fear.'

'Fritz knew straight lines,' Vanessa says. 'He could be my adviser for finance … he doesn't steal or deviate, besides, the General doesn't give me any cash. Fritz is potential, I'll use him when he gets to steer a course. Economists – they're all like him.

'My military lover? If my general lives, I'll steal from him. I'll maybe copy missile blue-prints, try to sell those on….'

They laugh. 'But, seriously,' Vanessa says. 'The people where we'll wage our war – they're scattered safe. Some will survive – more camps, route marches. Someone always lives, lives on. New ones are born, neighbours you don't recognise, insulting you in languages you don't speak. Blowhards?

'We'll bring in half the world before we win or lose. Our war aims? No concessions. Everything just as it was when we were kids – or before it all went wrong. Everything like it ought to be, with us in charge but all the bad guys and the zealots gone, the bureaucrats dismissed, the planners ridiculed…. No "good guys", just the dependable…. And priests, and guys who go abroad and send us cash. No mission or – wait! The mission is me, him! "Me" everywhere, but like in chess – you need to cover everywhere, be everywhere. "Forget the queen, the knights – the king is me, but pieces matter, wherever you can put up a fight…."

'The king is lame, he limps like Timur-i Lang – but stands relaxed, and lets the others dodge and leap defending him…. Watch the bishops scamper down the blind arcades….'

'Everyone's like that,' Petronia says. 'It's rare that someone says they go to war to do some good. The fighting starts when all's gone bad. I bet we had a hand in everything I saw – the lines of people on the shore, the boats of fugitives … and it will go forward, on and on. Playing a hand, being around, being a force – not quite decipherable, but everywhere. Desperadoes. I hope those who so love their life survive, somehow…. The rest of us – will be something else, elsewhere.'

'Modesty; that's it, I do approve,' Vanessa says. 'Whatever comes about we'll mostly have it worse. God will not come, sit in His chair and judge us all, and I am much relieved.'

'I think you're wrong, however,' says Petronia, a little timidly. 'Of course, the king is not immortal, not in the game, not by descent. His only resource is childhood. Back: his life before. You can't go there, to when he was the knave. And nor can he: it's not in nature's gift. He tries, it's all there is for him: pathetic.

'As for me, the focus isn't on reality, realities: it's on my experience and the variety of what happens to me. A box of curiosities.'

'That's your story,' Vanessa says, irritated. 'I'm talking about what happens here, and why this is not the place to be, and why there's nowhere else and similar that we might choose to go.'

'I can agree,' Petronia says. 'These countries! With their interests, their soldiers and their budgets ... you play a hopscotch on the atlas – "here you can't do this, there you must declare what you believe and don't, or wear a hat or no you can't, must marry, mustn't marry – marry in your class, marry who your uncle says." It's all ridiculous, they know it is.... I escaped once – into confinement, it turned out, and now I'm stuck again....'

*

The other side. And if they win ... we shall not see them. We'll be reduced, that's all. Big countries lose their wars, there's no catastrophe to them – catastrophes still happen elsewhere, everywhere.... But – the big galleons sail on and on, replacing crews; some walk the plank, the captains grow demented, but the wind is strong, and on and on ... the pirate flags are kept in lockers out of sight....

'Maybe my General will do jail-time,' Vanessa says. 'I don't believe it. Win or lose. He's an expert: not with me, but in things that if you know them, you get paid, not jailed. It's not the enemy, it's his mates that's dangerous.

'He is my guarantee – although I hope his hands are washed when he's been fishing in the lab among the viruses.... Those are his squad, his active servicemen – slimy, miniscule. "March! Present arms!" How many arms they have! Or are they legs? What a business – and to think – we got together when he wanted ice-cream after his classes at the military school.

'I worked to scoop, to pick'n'mix those "walking cones".... If we lose our war, there'll be vendetta, for him and me. Meanwhile, he brews up vats of tiny bugs that kill their millions, possibly – a word, an order – that would be enough. His job – refining a weapon that climbs up your nose and multiplies ... a pick'n'mix of crude mortalities....

'My dear Petronia – I go to bed with that!'

She keens, her eyes are full of ... marching mites? Of orders unconfessable, then denied. A lover teeming like a termite hill....

'It's true,' Petronia says. 'You do smell of formaldehyde....'

They laugh. Vanessa's ten years more than her, looks thirty extra with the stress. 'Suppose they win,' Vanessa says. 'The mountain folk. They're fierce. Already they dispossessed the other clans – suppose they capture our poor guys, break every bone and send them back in sacks, or roll the heads down on to us.... And we'll be forced to drop our bugs on them ... and will we catch the plague as well...? The aim's to make something with no cure, of course....'

'Tell me, won't you,' says Petronia, quite alarmed. 'If there's alert, and we must block our mouth and nose....'

'I'm not quite sure,' Vanessa says. 'He might get into trouble – even telling me....'

'But he's a General,' Petronia says. 'They move in crooked lines, they're never hit ... they're knights, they're warriors.'

'Oh,' Vanessa says. 'That's just our joke. He's a major, they all are, the lowest rank. He's a real sweetie, it's just ... the job ... you break secrets and they throw you in the pit. In it, there's scorpions and spiders, so they say,' and she shudders. 'Your own side is vindictive – they know where you work and cower.... It's right, of course ... you only hurt your own, yourself, by speaking out of turn....'

'It all goes on!' Petronia says. 'The same. Here or there, friends, enemies and allies.... This is our forest, we're the animals who live here. What can we do – occupy another forest, pal with some other animals, or drive them out? We two have some substance – people who don't, they're moved on and away. We stay here because we've gravity. You have a soldier. I try to sell my story. We don't want to end like Angelo. We don't want to lose the war. Win or lose, we'll end much poorer. All we can trust is – there will be an end. Something different....'

'No, Petronia,' Vanessa says, losing patience. 'It will be the same. I hope it will – except, there won't be war. There won't be war; just waiting for another one. Instead, there will be poverty. Poverty lasts for ever, but wars don't. They won't take us for soldiers ... but heads down, Petronia....'

'If we'd the choice, Vanessa, would we go on? The world? More children? We're so destructive....' Petronia says.

'No,' Vanessa says. 'I'm not! I don't destroy. I suffer and I wait. Survive. There's no quick answer, no solution, except to wait. We don't know what's wrong and if it could be right, or even different.'

Silence.

Petronia thinks: You're born with nothing, but quite soon – you have attributes you didn't want, but they are permanent. Living in a war where all you can feel is fear. Living on the plain, fearing the mountain people, the strangers praying prone instead of on their knees. Not praying. Blaspheming. Your family wanting to move but being poor and stuck. Being kept in a place although you're not valued there. Being fired for your opinions. Going to jail for them. Fearing people who go to jail for their opinions. Despising them. Ignoring them. Wondering if the world will end … or if humans will die out. Not wanting to die. Not liking animals, not caring about them, liking flowers but being indifferent to trees.… Not liking snow. Suffering from heat.…

How banal it all is, Petronia thinks on. You can think anything at all, best not to say, and anyway who cares, it's all been said by people better qualified, but there's the need to get away, to find somewhere where everything signifies, where happenstance is on your side....

Being attached to Vanessa is banal too: though she's superficial; and I envy her.

*

They love the cake shop. Petronia doesn't earn a cent, so Vanessa pays for her – they share a *bigné*, Vanessa pays, then takes a whole cream horn, eats it herself.

'That box,' Petronia says. 'I'll swear it hopped. Is it for me?'

Some hope…!

'It's quite embarrassing,' Vanessa says, cautiously, she opens it and shows.

'Why,' Petronia exclaims. 'A lovely squidgy toad! We trod on them when I was young, to see their souls ooze out – maybe they'll go extinct, and we shall feel remorse.…'

'I fear,' Vanessa says, closing the box so hard it crumples. 'That is my lover.'

Petronia laughs. 'So anyone can kiss it, see if it is a prince – and would it be naked or wear uniform?'

'Oh, uniform for sure,' Vanessa says. 'There's been an accident. The whole laboratory – you can't tell one from tother toad – they all have jewels on their heads, a greeny-yellow skin and warts. I think this one could be mine.… I haven't kissed it – if you want, Petronia, do try. I hope this change is not for all of us.… If they're all princes – coronations will be commonplace, wars of succession infinite.… I don't know what they eat – I think it fancies *tartufi*, the most expensive kind.... And does it mean we're all princesses? Fur slippers, or glass? Rat coachmen or the strapping kind?'

'My dear,' Petronia says. 'There is some luck in this. It's magic – shut up in a box, when we had too much space for spells and omens – the ship, the sea, the settlement. You can keep him in your reticule – and when he wants to mate, just drop him in the fountain in the park....'

'The ethics prof says there's a puzzle here,' Vanessa says. 'If he is one of us, we can't dispose of him the easy way – crossing the highway for curiosity, lunchtime in that cage of cranes ... the city zoo is always short of crawling snacks. No, he'd even be promoted for his conduct, if we can tell it's good.... As for due honours, I believe a colonel should have silver facings and some epaulettes....'

It's a mass of awkward judgements, staring up at them: it essays a croak.

'I think he suffers, being what he is,' Vanessa says.

We all do that, Petronia thinks, and says, 'All animals must feel like that – being below us in the chain, fair game for anything evolved to have an appetite....' She thinks: the kissing game's for frogs, not toads – Vanessa need not fear she could be called on for more intimacy....

'There's pets and science, those have special rules,' Vanessa says. 'Science – imposing more experiments on what was natural, conserving, isolating, patching here and there in tiny spots ... it's shaky ground. If he was in the wild – we must assume they're eaten from necessity, picked clean; and prudence tells the predator to aim at moderation so's there's always a supply of fresh young ones.... Necessity: "freedom is the recognition of necessity". That is the quote: it should placate my toad. He would be free. I think if he's a pet, our duty and his rights might chime, and I could buy a cage, moss on the floor, maybe a turtle for some company....'

'I see you have dilemmas,' says Petronia. 'I'm still amazed that life could take this turn. It seems quite alien....'

'No, no,' Vanessa says. 'It's gotten in the magazines, the generalist reviews – they raise the question for ecologists. Is nature cruel, and if it's not, could predation be justified as necessary, and so condoned....? Will they come after us because of that? They do already, naturally....

'It's only... Petronia, I'm destroyed.... Was this my soulmate just a day ago?'

'Maybe,' Petronia muses. 'You're a widow now. You'd need to dress as such, and make an application for a pension too....'

'Things turn around,' says Vanessa, brisk and feisty. 'You start the war fighting Germany and the fascists – you end it starting to fight Russians. You get a formula the wrong way round – and see what can happen to your elite warriors... But – he's cute, our toad. He's much more beautiful now than when he wore a mask and rubber gloves.'

'If it changes all of us,' Petronia says. 'The error, if that is what it was.... It might mean the world won't end. Toads aren't attached to life, not like humans are – but they don't make deserts and big bombs....'

'You're used to mysteries, my dear,' Vanessa says. 'I see you're right to leave them inexplicable. The explanations of what you experienced seem quite incredible: – the ship, people who come and go, some forced and some adventuring, and in the end – who disappear ... they disappear, and then they reappear as someone else.... We shouldn't be surprised. Metamorphosis. Think of the coca bush that ends up processed in your nose ... the revolutionaries trading drugs, the smugglers, the states, their fortunes, soldiers, stories tall and muted ... until at last you don't need grow anything, be anywhere – just make a drug lab in a shed....'

'I don't follow you, Vanessa,' says Petronia. 'I don't understand how money works, and how it drives the states ... the fights .... I know, it's my weak point. It's like with war, and why they need to fight to make a peace....'

'Let's try to understand my toad,' Vanessa says, irritated. 'See what he wants, if he is satisfied, and if he'll change to something else.'

*

'I know I can trust a man who loves cream cakes as much as you do, Takis,' says Petronia. Vanessa is absent, cosseting her toad, letting him hop around, dodging the Samoyeds in the park.

'You can trust me,' Takis says. 'I'm a human being, I live within the rules the species gives....' They laugh.

'My friend has had a catastrophe,' says Petronia. 'The chemi-warfare lab went critical....'

'I know,' says Takis, 'I was in the corridor – there's croaking often, man and beast, this time it came right down from the top. They were all over, climbing up the walls, mating in the gents.... Their nature – it came flooding out.... Are they still military, and trained, hierarchical? Or will there be emergency recruitment.... Can toads desert? And be cashiered?'

'What exactly do you do, Takis?' she asks: she thinks that maybe she could sell his tales to foreigners, make the cash she needs and which her fictions and her facts don't generate.

He has the stock potato-face – sarn't majors, adjutants, 'bad cops': – that one. He has a natural smell, it must be powerful, he hides it from you – wow! Smell the after-shave.

'We have in mind,' he starts, quite pompously, 'to use the war to make, to liberate, an agricultural zone. We'll have them grow the food we can't, and sell it on to poorer folk, who'll be our friends, for always.

'They're our brothers, sisters, who have strayed, changed sides, forgot the culture they were raised on – our land, our soil, organic to us, a danger if it changes owners, security for all when we win the war, and win against all those dragged in and hostile, trying to make a front to cripple us, and in the end – expunge us from the history.... A quick, hygienic war. That way, the natives will be doubled up – over the strawberries and beets. The weeding will keep them occupied, and we shall sell them tractors, all that noisy stuff.... Our chiefs think the ecological crowd here is more a danger to them than the fascists are – and they're right. This way, winning the war and planting artichokes – the social temperature comes right down, and we shall prosper.... Things will go on, the bosses too....' he too goes on, and on. Petronia grows bored.

'My social temperature's gone right up,' she says. 'It must be the tunes they pipe through in the shop....' Indeed, it's rowdy oldies. Takis says,

'Ah yes. The Stones. They hit the F sharp minor mystery. It strums upon the sexual chord – that's why the women – and the men for sure – went crazy for their shouts and twangs....'

'I can imagine that is true,' Petronia says. 'I'm pleased you understand the mystery – when you're a castaway, the thought of sex is less pronounced than needs for drink and food. It seems an age since I last had a powerful man....'

'Oh,' Takis says, trying a leer, 'I'm sure I can find a remedy. I always carry at least one powerful man around with me....' They laugh.

'That is your secret, Takis, not an easy one to keep,' Petronia says, quite fascinated. 'You're like the toads – you need to sow your seed around. And the politics ... the war aims? Are those secret too?'

'Not at all,' he says. 'You all can guess exactly what's our plan we haven't advertised. What is the *clou* for you is who I am. The source, authority. The blacksmith, the inventor. That gives your treachery its price – should you decide to try it in the market-place.'

'You guys seem afraid of protestations,' says Petronia, '… those eco-warriors, bare hands and feet…. And yet you have an army and the bombs….'

'Oh,' Takis says, off-hand, 'it's not the threat of wounds and death – it's our legitimacy that's at risk…. We have the right to use our violence, and define what violence is. That's philosophy, and ethics too. You could say, our violence we call law, consensus: what you call democracy. If we are soft on violence other than our own, you break the contract and at least will surely end in jail. It means you mustn't cross the line, and we can set it where we want. If you think to shift the line – it all falls down.'

'But,' Petronia says. 'I'm sure we have democracy, and yet – I hear you guys – you often talk of nation's good, of values like the nation and the family…. It's not just that we must keep quiet, or risk a beating. No – we must be good in many many other ways … not just the way we say we want….'

'The state must have monopolies,' says Takis, 'or it's not a state. We can use violence and say what violence is and why. Why it's ours, the definition: and not yours. Why we do what we want, and say alternatives are extreme.'

'Oh, Takis,' says Petronia, 'I'm not one of those, not a dissenter, not at all. You rescued us when we were on a distant shore…. I'm sure you're for the best, and keep the explanations to yourself….'

'Work it out, work it out,' says Takis, laughing. 'If you can't, that's all the best for you. Befriend the strongest. If you don't, it will cost and damage you. When things degenerate, befriend anyone who'll pal with you.'

'It seems to me,' Petronia says. 'You hit on something, when you cite a key. The universe may be tuned to F-sharp. That's known, but it was the Stones discovered it, and their faces were carved into Mount RockWell as a reward. That tonality is fertile, like me, like Vanessa too. It reproduces, procreates itself – it's logical the Stones should hit on that, the key to everything, except … it's useless if you strut on stage and turn on partners – thousands – you can't satisfy …. Even if you're omnisex, attractive like ripe mangoes….'

'That's not our case, my dear,' says Takis. 'Soldiers take their time. We've gone fairly close to what's the centre of existence – the universe, the sex, and politics…. To ride, you need two stirrups – one foot in each, like mine. I know there's sides, I'm in both at least – as many of them as I can.'

'All tuned to F-sharp?' Petronia asks, provocatively. 'Two sides, the head, the tail....' and Takis slides his pigskin gloves beneath his epaulette – the silvery kind that doesn't tarnish – and they leave the shop, abandoning their cakes, but greedy. For each other, and themselves. Mmmmm. Each other is the other's hit!

*

'An adventure, Petronia,' Vanessa exclaims. She's still carrying the little box with the 'mistake' inside. She's written her address on it, in case it gets forgotten.

'Takis? He has a stock of vinyls,' says Petronia. 'In most keys, especially the minor. The sex? It really wasn't anything, not special, but then – it never is. He turned the sound up loud to hide our squeals – it wasn't necessary, I promise you.'

They giggle together.

'And is he loyal?' Vanessa asks.

'He's very safe,' Petronia says. 'But then – on the ship and after, there was no protest, dissent, still less an opposition. It's just – mistakes occur. If you're a boss, you boss: – you don't peer in the labs, or wonder where the water's gone, or if there's cucumbers for lunch. These are like the numbers on the dice – you never know which one is coming up and stops you moving on … or maybe two black jacks are next to one another, and you lose the count and then your stash.... He insists. Loyalty is due to him, without a limit – but there's no return, and no reward. You can't be loyal sufficiently, not ever – you don't know what he'll do. I'm sceptical, and so – disloyal. I'm on a list – he's put me on one, and another "list of lists". He says that if you're loyal, you can't go wrong. Be loyal to who's the boss.'

'He's dull all round, in other words,' Vanessa says. 'A lover's better dull, of course, than totally transmogrified like mine.'

'He's in Intelligence,' Petronia says. 'That means he doesn't need to ask for cash … nor work for it. He has his patrons, and they too are loyal … and further up you go, and the loyalest of them all is the top guy, and he is only loyal to one – himself, the source of power, legitimacy. So, in the long run, there's no guarantee. You need to always be intelligent, and know when not to show – you're not....'

'Oh, dull, dull,' Vanessa says. 'Intelligence means you find out stuff your side doesn't know – but other guys – the other side – they know it all, they're paid to know, defend the secrets – so, where's the luster, dear Petronia? The Romans....'

'Oh, I know,' Petronia says. 'There's always friends of bosses, bosses too – in a conspiracy, they gave out dogs and even slaves to younger guys, and horses too, spread out the banquets, promised orgies till the dawn – and then the soldiers, waiting in the wings.... Those stubby swords – between your ribs ... they conquer, massacre – or run....'

'And you and I went on all right,' Vanessa says. 'We were Assyrians, then the Greeks, the Romans and the Celts – and here we are, eating éclairs, while our lovers....' And the situation strikes her, and she weeps, thinks of disposing of her toad. 'Destroyed by their technology, their foolishness.... Your Takis, a big snoop, no more; teller of tales on innocents, a cup, an ear, against the wall to listen in.... And did you think, my dear, you'll be on film, and bartered round the mess-room for a peep...?'

It's a horror, Petronia thinks, and there's a mystery. Another one. The toad.... A metaphor?

'How do you know about the chemi-lab? And who was turned, and who ran out in time?' she asks.

Vanessa stares at her. 'I'm the last person, Petronia, whose word you ought to doubt. A toad's a toad; a lover – often those are toads....'

'I don't believe in prejudice,' Petronia says. 'In thinking some plants less worthy than the flowering kind, or animals less cute than those who're put in films.... To me, a toad is wonderful....'

'Oh, to me as well,' Vanessa says, closing the topic and her lover's box.

Another mystery, or just an inexplicable? Something with no cause, but with effects and images etched into reality and your experience, but make a part of the significance which you're not party to, or ... you don't know where you are. It's like the girl who ate the cake – not knowing if it made her huge or tiny as a speck, nor why it's there and where it comes from... That's life, Petronia thinks. We'll never get to quiz it close....

And yet, and yet.... Who told Vanessa how her officer became a toad? *He* could not – so, who?

Is she a sneak, a snoop – a go-between, who spooned in Takis to me, source of cash and retribution, vendetta … mediocre lover, master of all knowledge that is sensitive…?

I've heard about the universe being in tune, F sharp, she thinks. And the Stones, with all that dope, their spiritual awareness must have been the tops … and yet, and yet … I have my doubts … one ought not, the sacred books tell you not to doubt, there are no proofs, no certainty. Accept, enjoy, and trust! Trust. Prudence. Much the same.

*

'Vanessa and I have sex,' she tells Takis, to have him see that sex with him is a cold soup. Nothing against cold soup. She doesn't much like soup in any state, it's like there was once something good and what was left is soup. 'It's cakes,' she says. 'Yumyum!'

It isn't funny, not at all, and sounds as if it's true, fitting the category 'truth' like little else has done.

'Look,' she tells Vanessa, 'Everyone likes cakes – there's Russians come here, exiles and visitors, people from the embassy, and Chinese too. We could overturn the order, the orders. We could overturn the world, here in this shop, just moulding, sounding, what comes in and ponders by the counter. The whites – they're mad for cream – if we had different coloured foods … soften them up … there's reds: and blacks … cherries and blackcurrants?'

'We might,' Vanessa says, 'change everything. Transform. But what would be the difference? The States goes fascist, militarist … mutinous generals, the putsch, betrayals, plots…. China has factions, popular movements, does all our work; is created as much by us as them … lies and heroes, avoid those millions of the dead in uprisings, Russia is clumsy, brutal, melancholic and incompetent, unconvinced of everything … drink and cash, the women angry and ethereal … prison-house and dormitory of all the nations. You'd think, "let's change everything, utterly". The world. We do it here in this shop, using the all-sorts people who come in.

'It'll be everything, turned upside-down; and yet it will be exactly what there is now, and will be exactly so when everything is upside-down again. And all will be our work, ours and the baker's…. *Cannoli* for shooting missiles through, sweet shells full of viruses tasting like confectioner's cream…. We'll win no credit for it, and it's just. It will be radical, terrible, we two shall die and rise again in grubby white grave-clothes. It will be the *same*, Petronia. Orgies, conspiracies, massacres and crowning. Things are as they are, the people … everything is set up like a violin – the strings, the notes, are there, you're set with them. The tunes, the trills, glissandi, all yours *a volontà* – but in the end: there is the violin, only that, a wooden emptiness, the strings tuned to your civilisation, your time, your climate and your history, the hierarchies, your evolution. It waits, the instrument; silent and inert.

'We'll strive to make "what is" entirely different from what is, and it will turn out once again to be what is. What was is folded into what will be, like sugar in a chocolate cake. You must understand how "what is" imprints into yourself, in all of us. What is, becomes; what would be different, is the same.'

'If only we were intellectuals,' says Petronia. 'We could make what you're saying cleaner and more glib. You mean, we've broken something. Knocked everything out of shape? It was a globe we discovered, and we ran all over, and we stayed as we were, big ones still big, white ones white, and so … all was discovered, but the greed was magnified, all set to carry on the exploiting and the taking more, more – whole countries, deserts, forests – the discoveries made armies to hold down the slaves – those people in bright fraying clothes.'

'No, Petronia,' Vanessa says. 'Forget the clothes.'

'Tell me, then, Vanessa,' says Petronia. 'The countries that we're forced to live in – they modify themselves so as to make a bigger load of bucks? That's what they think?'

'Be very careful what you say, Petronia,' Vanessa says.

*

'With all that's happened, Petronia,' Vanessa goes on. 'We have a case for protest. For upsetting.'

'Restoring?' asks Petronia. 'Order?'

'Of course not,' says Vanessa. 'There wasn't order before. Maybe there was adaptation to a flow of time, but not to every flow and tributary, and in the name of no one, no one in particular, or else on behalf of powerful guys of no account. No, it must be protest first, then when we have attention, we reveal what is to be done.'

'The idea is great,' says Petronia, thinking of the fish, the ship, the castaways. 'But I am skint, and if I give the time to your campaign….'

'I don't ask anything,' Vanessa says. 'I have my evidence in here,' and she holds up the little box, the creature inside shifting round, making it bulge out here and there. 'If it catches on – we'll see. If not – we'll see as well. The point is – what we know already. You – the people coming, disappearing, disappeared. For me – transmogrification. Things familiar becoming other things.

Our case is waterproof.'

*

Vanessa isn't up to it. Not to her plan. She crumbles and disperses. Singing lessons! A big debit on a poker site.... The cakes – give her fissures, furuncles on the face, and she spends much on skins – artificial, doctors, packs of slime. All does no good, the system holds fast, nay – it strengthens. Her rebellion – turns on her and excavates her so she slumps.

'This isn't what I thought....' Petronia says. 'Orgies and banquets – those, could be fun. Exclude the import and the slaughter of the animals – we're on a roll, with fans, and charming people loving us ... but yours, my dear Vanessa, cream and chocolate – is self-indulgence. You're a symptom, not a cure....'

'What's to be cured is civilisation, Petronia,' Vanessa says. 'We have to figure out how that can be done, especially when the people ... they run around, from country to the desert, to the sea, to water-hole and food handouts, waiting in line for years.... Faced with the dislocation and the misery, I could forget my own despair, my tragedy....' and she lifts, waves, and shakes, the box....

'No, Vanessa,' says Petronia. 'You're not even fun, and more – you're shortly out of funds.... We have at least to make the pastry shop a hub of innovation, discontent.'

'Mine is a protest,' says Vanessa, 'of the body. That is my fortress. Not soldiering, not football – I shall multiply and bring forth ... smart foetuses. Just ask them, test them: "All the American supreme justices since the flood?" ... "Every production in the world of the opera *Flammen?*" – Fritz's favourite, a marvel: "with performers too!"

'I have a vision, dear Petronia. I am the mother of the magic new.... I lift them, one by one, show to the crowd, my unconceived offspring, each a genius: five-octave voices, wizards on the *oud*; the Yankee Stadium filled with their waving arms – a million of the tendrilly limbs attached to five hundred individuals. Freaks, Petronia. Super humans. Short-lived and ready-formed. Tinies and squeakies. No infancy and no maturity – just BANG – and here we are. Us as we ought to be – to have tried to be, going beyond, innovating. Accelerated evolution, made to last….

'Those are the harbingers of new civilisations, the messengers, playing mah jong with what exists, doing better, better than better – building the walls against the past, re-cycling the detritus that the monsters built with such slog, such carnage and such pride…. Bone walls. And my two fingers gesturing as witness to my sacrilege.

'They'll face us down, Petronia, the new; show starfish can wave an arm better than the supreme leaderships…. And all from me, all virgin births….'

'I feel for you, Vanessa, for your health,' Petronia says. 'Although … you're right, of course. The human summit – reached by Assyrians, and by others we don't recognise and haven't yet dug up … is in the end quite trivial. A hummock. Your brood, Vanessa – will win every prize … I don't say "every honour", there's nothing honourable in doing simple things. If a tortoise jumped two metres high – yes, that would be remarkable…. But not when you or I take to the track. We leap untrammeled, without shells. A hatch of merely human geniuses – is rare, but unremarkable. We two are examples of the best … the swiftest….'

'Enough, Petronia,' Vanessa snaps. 'You see the point, at once you break it off. A point is not a manual, or instructions.'

'I am ashamed,' Petronia says. 'My triviality…. Of course! That Bishop and his cow … the field God made. The mind moves on – cows don't.'

I'd sell the story to my publisher, Petronia thinks, but she would ask: 'And should I laugh? What emotions do you seek to play upon, elicit? None? Cold turkeys, everyone; as usual rushing to the abattoir, and then the baste. You have a talent for the odd, Petronia, but that is it! How should we respond? Like Vanessa has? Psychosis?

'Concentrate on orgies, dear: and banqueting. And then rehab, and being a fine administrator – stepping into someone's shoes and tramp around the world, collecting anecdotes, amassing allies and the plaudits of the powers…. Be sympathetic ... lose weight, tell how…. Be ghosted. If you're a genius….'

'But I'm not,' Petronia ends for her, the publisher. 'I want to make sense where there is none. What happens to me are things with significance, episodes, situations – but without sense…. Happenings, like mouflons rolling down a mountain-side, and yet you see – not only mouflons, but a raptor, a mongoose, a cobra, and so, and so, in crazy sequence – history: all falling in the tarpit where I watch, and instantly they're fossilised, the old, the living, the living dead – and this we call civilisation, that we've made. It isn't time and climate and evolution's hit and miss, mostly miss.... We live in it, this charnel-mine we dig. We count ourselves as a success after a few centuries, and the graceless and resentful dead are useless gobs of meat inedible for millions.... We stand in line with them, we Jacks and Jills, a-tumbling down, our iron crowns hammered through our papery skulls....'

*

'It's what she wants, Vanessa's satisfied,' says Takis. 'You fear, but when it happens, there's no fear, and so – what you fear, you want.'

'That's nonsense,' says Petronia. 'She didn't fear it, the change. It's not her becoming soulmate to a toad – she's become entirely something else. If you can't become an emperor or a boss of bosses, you become another thing. You speed up everything, and get it over with. You win at everything, but qualify as nothing that resembles "human". She's something never seen before, not made by nature, but by herself, her will.'

'It's true,' says Takis. 'She has no lookalike. She's an original, an installation with a motor that beats and whisks and moulds incessantly.'

'And if she stops?' Petronia asks.

'She can't,' says Takis. 'She has no twig to throw the switch. She'll be a pizza with fish-mouths that tell a murky story: then it's on and on, she'll be a haggis spawned by the living flesh, an inexhaustible growth on growths ... a tree with buboes, mangoes made of snot, the baby alligators minced in pumpkin pies....'

'And what will be the end?' Petronia asks.

'There's no one who can call a stop, decree an end-state, a conclusion that resolves,' he says. 'She's a kaleidoscope of entrails, of hidden forms that make the shape – eternal burning bush, the nest that flies, the eagles that take root, shrubs bearing quinces....'

'She's my nightmare,' Petronia says. 'The familiar, the determined, the predictable without a sense ... turned into a monster of no species, no stable shape....'

'Exactly,' Takis says. 'We're in the mixing bowl where everything ends up and everything's produced. We can be anything – but have no will, no purpose – not even a development from small to large – we start off smart and end up foolish ... beware the metaphors: you'll become them – while you sleep or while you try to grow your pearl in chilly oyster-beds up north ...'

'It isn't what I want,' Petronia says. 'Though the profusion, mobility, is such, it's hard to refuse all swarming fantasy.... Conspirators must feel this....'

'Yes,' Takis says. 'And you won't feel a thing. You're in the book, Petronia, right from the start. Imagined, not imaginary.'

'I don't feel anything now,' Petronia says. 'At all. I thought the fault was yours, Takis. You, as Intelligence, must be familiar with beings unknown to common sense and common folk.... I see the benefits of 'no sensibility' may stem from you.

'An orgy? Your speciality: it doesn't do to feel too much, while you are splaying out, or you'd not want a repetition the next day ... and on and on, decades of it ... centuries....'

'Intelligence – it's the name,' says Takis, 'like on a door. It's doing a crossword puzzle and taking in the garbage, everybody's, all down the street.'

'I don't believe you, Takis,' says Petronia. 'I've been on a cruise with chancers like you, who couldn't steer, didn't know where they were. I'd set you free, only you don't know what it means.

My theory is – you can't waste time – but you can waste yourself. You have to go much faster, all of you, all the boys and girls you are....

'Don't get caught pants-down in the bushes: go very fast, don't touch the sides.

'Am I Shiva? Eternal happiness? Yes, that too. But there's not much of me, and I won't have that wasted....'

'It's stunts?' Takis asks, put out. 'Jousts? Your wall of death – lose gravity, you skitter down the sides, end up down, among the trash, the lolly-sticks and sticky wrappers....'

'You have to know the design,' Petronia says. 'Or you can't win, you can't play. It's not a game, no one wins, the prize is one second of my time. There! You won – the prize has disappeared, become the past. I learned that on the ship, but never knew where we were going. I still don't. It wasn't going here, that I *do* know.'

*

Free. I set you free, Takis, she thinks: and you should be more than grateful. No one ever did that for me, nor, I'd bet, for you. There's nothing more than that you could expect, and almost no one gets there.

Too bad, you're free, and I am not, or – I am nothing yet. I'm toparch of a void. It's good. Knowing where the substance is – immaterial, that's for sure, but waiting round the corner.

Solitary confinement. Solitary freedom. Takis is my phantom Bunkie, the guy I think is shut up with me, within me – a hallucination, a paint splurge on the wall. Quite predictable, if you are into previsioning. You adjust to what there is, being alone. That's what you are, what everybody is.

Vanessa frets. That's a mistake.

What do I dignify? Love. I've been loving, tried to give love, or say what's not available. That's all I had for Vinnie – my love was telling him I'd never love him. Maybe – I should have said – 'leave love out', it's wind in a bottle, once uncorked it flies around the room, a bad smell to everyone but you.... I have no talent. Nadia, now. She could do anything at all with ropes. You can be a dwarf and walk the hi-rope. Or do it blind. Better so! We never saw if she had a face – she was always so high up. But – you're not often called upon to do what she did every afternoon – the wire, trapeze, being fired from cannons, having water poured inside your knickers from a pail....

It's true, the circus is a trope for me: where you do brilliant but useless things. It may be where philosophy had ended up, transformed. Changed, a changeling like Vanessa's soldier – when you are clever, you don't fight – you send others out to do it.

You could say – that's the best definition of a cleverness. It works for soldiers, but – poor Fritz! Not for navigators. Great helmsmen – they must pretend, stand at the fixed wheel and make a show of knowing where they and all the passengers are going.

The cake shop – everyone drops in, many in uniform. If you can't pay, when it's busy you can wait on table, and if you just can't pay, you can wait outside. But – the cake shop isn't everything, though it may be civilisation. You can't protest against a pâtisserie.

In olden times, there were human sacrifices to keep things moving on. Now – it doesn't do to think, besides, everybody thinks and it's banal; and if everybody ordered éclairs, and had them delivered, there'd be nothing special any more, and the bakers, the pâtissiers – they couldn't keep up with you, your appetite.

It's just that ... you don't know what you're caught up in. It's like the ship – you jump on, and you know it's full of souls, and where you land – there's silent souls all round, although some mouth words, like Angelo, who talked too much, Walid and Jakob, like a double act, a straight guy and a joker. Two straight guys, two jokers? Pile on more jokers – they won't make you laugh.

*

We want moments of drama. Not this.

*

'We, not you, have a difficulty,' says the official. He's Takis's boss or deputy – maybe he is Takis too. Takis would not change a word, nor would a different setting matter. Takis speaks as if he is the boss – behind him, behind each boss, there is another – sometimes another bigger, an enormous boss, sometimes the gardener, a concubine, an old school friend.... Anyone can make it to the top, the bottom too.... It's them that says – 'Your country – save it! come what may.' 'Use the weapon – or we shall be crushed.' 'Sink the liner, it must be carrying arms.' And so, and so. He says:

'You, Petronia, have not been made one of us. You were absent for many years, we rescued you, and others who had been away too long, people whose present was unclear. You were all in danger, but everybody always is, and most people who're in danger – they end bad, start bad or are bad, or else they slip away. Some slip away in trucks with all the other people ... no one knows how they end up, they don't give names, the names won't stick.... I don't know, so I suspect the badness of what you did, or wanted to do. Tell me, together we can stop you ending real bad, and not even knowing how bad....

'You're independent, you're a writer of some sort, as we all are, but you insist. Your pen – brims with unseen life. You haven't registered, you're pleased you haven't and no one ever registered that you were even here.'

'It's Takis!' says Petronia. 'He wants revenge....'

'His work is sensitive,' the guy says. 'We just run checks on people very very close to him.... He is a visionary: that's not an easy goal, and not an easy place at all to be – Europe? The world? Bring Russia in. It's always been in – in Europe. In Asia too. Then, other continents. Bring China too. Or maybe – they are "in" already, waiting, waiting till we all are one. The initiative's to take, by someone: then we all stand as one. Have done with countries – on with continents. New Rome, New

Mongolia, if you prefer. That is the plan. More power, and more equality, more rights, more laws....

'You're sceptical, Petronia, don't like countries, nor their states. Is China – Russia – are they countries? Maybe you don't like nations, nationalities, and nationalism. You must decide, be clear. The choice is country, or empire. That's it. There's no "neither", not in anything. Life or death. No "in between".

'Or, you don't like Monsters? – they come out of eggs – the individuals. Some buried in the sand for centuries. Monster collectivities? Your civilisations, modernities, parties and programmes....

'Takis himself – Russian, Ukrainian? A Pole? Rusyn? Or all of those: American? You see – it doesn't matter, in the scheme of things – everybody wins, and everybody – to compensate – must feel they lose. But really – let's forget the win and lose: just think of where you stand and if you're sure you're stable there – wherever you might think you are. Stability, assurance – are you sure...? You know exactly where you stand? On what? We know, Petronia, you're never satisfied. You have an argument for any stance you choose to take – and you betray! We know!'

'Vanessa!' says Petronia. 'Her toad! Spy in a box! My uncertain past.... Telling my tales....'

'They cluster round you, don't you see?' the guy insists, 'You are presumed an innocent, but there's a web, a carpet, a texture of the unexplained.... You can't be trusted, you're perfidious.'

'Yes,' says Petronia. 'I don't grasp the people, the situations as they happen to me, without a purpose, seemingly, but portending, portending tales, a tale, I cannot understand, and where the context – seems quite catastrophic.'

'And yet,' he says, 'the rest of us might apprehend that this is so, but it is what we call our life. The people close to? – mostly frauds, seducers: but our task is "sieve them out". What is left is good, it's yours: you must enjoy it, or you'll feel abandoned, deserted, all your life....'

'Yes,' says Petronia. 'That's true. And even so, I am discriminated. My ideas, my aims, my vision....'

'Speech,' the guy adds on. 'Your flowery turn of phrase. Ethnicity – if you understand the term at all. You have no origin ... no source....'

'Save me,' says Petronia. 'If that's your job, then save me. I don't know if it's salvation that I want....'

'Deportation in extreme cases, or incarceration, that's the offer,' he says. 'Where to deport someone who has left already, or has never been? Incarceration – maybe you think you're there now, that it's a metaphor. Like salvation. Let you go? How, when you know the offers, and that if you refuse them, your case is finished? There's no alternative. "Off you go"! I don't think so – nowhere in the world would you be let go ... You're ours, believe or disbelieve it. You've been caught, and thrown back in: still hooked.'

'Your mistake is calling me, although I'm dross,' Petronia says.

'No,' he says. 'But as we call you, we shall call multitudes.'

'You beat them terribly and let them go,' she says. 'Or torture them, humiliate....'

'Cells,' he says. 'We're all made of them. Often what they call cells is really drainage. Or acne. The Emir of Bukhara – he had what they call a cell: really it was a system: the spiders ate the flies and the scorpions ate the spiders. No human was involved. No one likes a dirty cell. Or universe.'

'It's good if you can sit down,' Petronia says. 'Voyages are inconclusive, but you feel they're taking you somewhere you might want to go. Or away from somewhere that you don't. Then there's our ship, that didn't fit the category.'

'I'd feel happier if I could see you all together, all the shapes. Fritz, Vinnie,' he says. 'You must remember – there were many things in your adventure you didn't recognise, you didn't see. And yet ... there they were. You may be hiding – not the whole, a part....

'Fit all the pieces, all unknowns – and together, it should make a circle. You, Petronia, are the only one who's out of cash, and complaining. Looking for something dicey, or have already found ... a bargain with me? Revealing something that you didn't understand?'

True – that would be risky, very bold, she thinks.

*

There's come and go, and traffic: operatives. There's interest in Petronia, they mention Fritz and Vinnie, think they're curious ... but – there's Nadia too, who relies on, exploits, the symmetries – balancing, thrust, gravity and elementary mechanics. Finding the centre point. Swinging, like the monkey on a rope: – risking, even a fall – of infinite length. You calculate the speed. It's cautionary. Mechanics doesn't show the hit, but you can guess.

They don't probe with Nadia, but in a way, 'not fitting in', 'complaining' – these too are ropes of infinite length. If you let go, do you go down faster than the monkey? It's a better spectacle for certain – monkeys falling from the roof would be a tragedy – skimming down ropes is artistry. You can beat the record, possibly.

Petronia has an other option, that Takis takes her, her case, as his responsibility. Investigating what she says she hasn't seen. Being his.

Most countries know how to make you suffer. Most people know how, too.

You can change opinions, faith, loyalties, dress: but if you don't have a document – that's it. Tough. At least you need a 'nullaosta', a confession, self-incrimination, self-description, a denunciation. And Petronia's journey, from ship to muddy shore, to the cake shop – inexplicable to her, is a plan, a plot, to any normal observer.

As for the dead ... they're to forget. Who's there to tell?

*

'I went to the wrong country,' Petronia tells Vanessa. 'The wrong place – it all seems the same, all seems like this: scrabbling, hot, people in crowds waiting to leave and to arrive, hunger and exotic fruits – going for export, just like we hope....'

'The first time, it's just threats,' Vanessa says, humouring. 'Or promises. It doesn't hurt. It's normal. There's civilisation everywhere, so why the fuss? I thought we'd changed our names and could have gone or stayed.... We could start a charity, that's often the safest thing, you might get some cash as well....'

'I don't mean places are the same,' Petronia says. 'Or that you don't know the difference – but parts are the same. Similar. The minds, those *are* the same.'

'You're a great humanist, Petronia,' Vanessa says. 'It's your greatest fault.'

'The dirty rivers, the dirty sea, the dark air, the cheats, the frauds – always the same,' Petronia says. 'Procedures. Ceremonies. The laws, the breaking of the laws, the tortures and the deportations. The deep cells, infections, rare deformities....'

'The wars, that we are all part of,' Vanessa joins in. 'We fight everywhere, we recruit, we make the guns, we take them in, they take us in, someone's children tortured, torturing – they, we, are theirs, everyone belongs to something ... and so and so ... all over. Invade, and hope to find out what. It's like a play where all the actors speak different languages, but we grasp there's action, and the play, in its development quite incomprehensible ... winds through to its denouement and we realise we've understood each word and gesture.... Right now, the Americans are at war everywhere, in their name or others', part of a series, they're the default setting for human beings, and everybody suffers except some of their favoured sons, and when they'll have gone down, if there is anybody left, there'll be war by someone else, all over, maybe more than several contenders all at once – not trivial and nasty like now, like ours, but all against all, until it settles down perhaps ... and I call myself out of this, it's not my world, my interest, not people I can feel affection for ... I pass!'

'Vanessa!' says Petronia. 'That's a kind of humanism as well.'

There's a long silence: then Vanessa lifts the cloth she wears over her ravaged face. 'Put me down, Petronia. Put me down. No more, no more words and explanations, no more 'young genius, old experience', no more rot and slime, no hopes, no programmes full of promises. Put me down.

'Dispose of me, or leave me; don't compose me, and don't close my eyes – let me stare and gape and sprawl....'

'Of course I can't,' Petronia says. She's thought it through. She will be caught in endless troubles, bigger than her friend imagines or could have caused, alive. 'It isn't me, I'm wispy-whimsy, ingenuous, betrayed and condescended to – I cannot take the lead. Escape, mature, Vanessa.'

'Do it,' says Vanessa. 'Like they say: just do it.'

'I can't,' Petronia says. 'I don't know how.'

It isn't true, of course, we all know how, and if you don't – you ask.

Vanessa's become a rare, a unique, animal, and now she seeks extinction. It's quite natural. You could put her head, a trophy, on the wall, like Vinnie said about the fish.

*

'It's the wrong question,' Takis says. 'Will things – my life – improve? Can they? Start asking that – and you're in the water, dirty water. Not your question to ask, you're tiny, without stature. You don't rate an answer, not to anything. You wouldn't grasp it, if it came. A nonsense, asking when there's no one who can answer. Answers are for medium term – people are short term, their purpose, if they have one, is smaller, shorter, still.'

'It's better if I'm on my own,' Petronia says. 'You have the war to think about. Perhaps I should enrol myself....'

'Absolutely not,' says Takis. 'That way you'll attract attention. Suspicion too. Volunteers are all put on a list. Be sure you won't get off. You won't know you've been put on – except.'

'Except? Even more disconnected things?' Petronia asks. 'Being given things to do, and then told what....'

'Or not,' Takis agrees.

'You soldiers have good times,' she says. 'Exercises. Planning invasions, genocides, and then the exercises when you get to shoot your guns at trees....'

'It's true,' he says. 'There's war and peace. I offer you.... But – it's not the real thing. Peace and war? – better – inclusion. You'll feel pepped up, secure. Being inside – it makes frustration grow. If you're that way inclined you want to set the streets on fire and do some mayhem, loot some stuff and catch some louts who set the streets on fire ... beat them, lock them up....'

'I don't want other people doing it with me,' Petronia says. 'There's no taste for that – I'd want to tear the buildings down and turn the streets to bogs, ravines, hollow it all out and make a wilderness.... Without a purpose and without an end. It's what the foxes feel for chickens, wolves for sheep and lambs – a frolic that shows that you are top, there's no one tells you when to stop....

But I want more – I want there to be no one. To be in a dead place. Not to hurt people or steal stuff or offend the uniforms and flags ... to be in a place that's lived and now has died, no one at all is left, and I can peer in everywhere and figure out who they were and why, and see the place, now uninhabitable, is silent, split down to rocks and shale, walls of flint blocks that hang in space, the streets like threads of dust that lizards make.... Like I was seeing entrails and veins and marrow bones, but all is quiet and finished, has moved and now does not.'

'Loot,' says Takis, ruminating. 'For soldiers – it's the root, the source. Our motive, our reward. Except – you never find the right size. Socks and shirts. White goods? What you want's too heavy to carry off.

'It drives you – the incongruity of what's to hand – to lift and shift, more and more. Grand theft – the empires; the pilfering – those statues with the penises smashed off – sheer envy, dear Petronia, the icons, forests of true crosses – churches, museums, stuffed with it – our loot! ... Ah – the unending campaigns, the endless baggage trains ... the women stolen, more than you could ever need. The men enslaved....'

'And yet,' Petronia says. 'You soldiers are afraid of the civilians. In the northern lands – you fear the nature-lovers. In your south – it's adolescents, the young useless boys, the lads: no hope, scorned and unemployable ... trashing the cities, burning cars – quite superficial, and unavailing.

'It will take much more.... We came out of Africa, and now – will Africa return...?'

'You mean,' asks Takis. 'The Africans? Rioting? Dodging the draft? The Europeans are obsessed with fighting over their exhausted soils, the poisoned rivers – as if regeneration was a possibility: conquest a triumph. True everywhere. And Africa – still tributary, for ever....'

'No, no,' says Petronia, aware she's letting out her secret faith, but in full spate. 'The Africans will come, and cast it down, make an end to it, to us, our works, even, perhaps, start it afresh, a new design – out of the torrid deserts, into the northern tropics.... A refuge for them; for us – the verdict. Oh the destruction! A mercy, a release, to see it all cast down, dispersed. I am close, close as possible to being African – they have faith, they're merciful. Not me!

'How I long.... How I hope.... They hate the ugliness we've made, our mean spirits, our spitefulness, the smallness in our hearts. Our viciousness and our contempt.... The junk that we call treasure and invention ... how they despise us ... our heaps of money we call art!'

'They'll take us over, all of us,' says Takis, bristling.

'Oh how I hope so....' Petronia says.

'Petronia,' Takis says, quietly alarmed.

'Yes,' she says, 'today I know it isn't so. It's something I say, before I think. It will grow inside me, the conviction. I'm sure, like ironwood, it will be with me, growing all my life, until it's a certainty, a pillar, an ebony tree.... Me, transformed!'

'You're not for me, Petronia,' Takis says. 'Why have we drifted close, why do we nudge together? Just tell me – who is so dangerous they must be killed and be anonymous? If you don't know, just guess, and free yourself. Nothing, all dead and unproclaimed – just tell! It can't make any difference.... That ship ... the voyage and the landing – who were all those dead?'

'Oh,' says Petronia. 'It's curiosity. Why? Who? It fascinates you, keeps us together, now – I want as much as you to know the secret. I can't leave you. It's attraction between enemies, boxers who embrace, praise the opponent....'

'I know exactly why everything has happened and will go on happening,' he says. 'To you – it's all mystery. "Why does nothing *mean?*" you ask. The answer is, it does to me. Who cares it doesn't mean to you? This is the solution to the philosopher's quiz: there is no ordinary language, no ordinary anything, no common meaning. It's quite simple. Religion, science – they pretend we're all equal when it comes to comprehend or be bound by them. It isn't so in any other way. What you see as common life is only life in common lived on your little telephone ... that isn't anywhere at all.'

'I set you free, Takis,' says Petronia, 'and you responded by rattling my chains. Your Inquisition – knew I was an apostate.... I don't know anything else, don't understand the questions. You're pushing me – there's nothing there, nowhere down to fall....'

'It works that way,' says Takis. 'And – you'd be happier elsewhere. You're subversive – but of what, and in what's name? What do you know, what did you see, suspect you saw? What is it, what you don't know, didn't see – people? Ideas? Things?

'You want things to be different, no more than that: and no one, no one at all, likes it. "Difference" is the very least to wish for.... You knew nothing of a plot, but entered into it, and stayed in it, unknowing and unseeing. Is it possible – you ask the questions, don't know the answers? It would make you negligible. A small fish – too small to eat, too big to throw back in.'

*

Vinnie was a lover, Petronia thinks: a lover feels and you are felt. Then he stops loving; you are still felt. It doesn't seem symmetrical. Fritz – a fine commander, giving orders. Most things are made now so that they don't respond to orders – nor even to obscenities. Command's an empty box. Despair – it starts this way. If there are children – they take up your time, but they're the mark of failure: you haven't made it – here comes another generation, a new bunch of people you must instruct in everything; absolutely everything...

'"You're free,"' Takis quotes. 'Is that a pair of handcuffs: an isolation cell? Freedom is losing everything, except – your freedom. That is yours, unique. Life in the void – your freedom's very like unfreedom ... you fall, you hit the shale. That's not being free. It's gravity, for gravity there is no cure. You're attracted to the freedom four walls gives, Petronia. Confinement – and away you ride, just you, astride yourself. You wanted to ride the Chinese way – but they don't have an animal you can climb on to – you are the runner, the steed, the rider. Dragons – belong to nature and to heaven – nothing to do with you. My realm – is pain, uncertainty. The good thing about pain and prison is that usually – often – they stop, they relent. Uncertainty – nothing is uncertain for long, reality insists on focus. But you, Petronia – the booze, the orgy – do they stop? You don't know. You flicker in and out, maybe it's not happening to you, if you're masked you could be anyone. But, if you're free, you can't get out of that, you're free and there's no one else in there with you, your skin is made for one, no room for other adults.... Your unique freedom excludes the freedom of the others, of any other in the universe. Maybe it's so: you don't know anything, you've nothing useful you can say. Your being makes you ignorant. How can I be sure?

'Sure of you, or anyone, of how you speak and reason?

'You give me permanent uncertainty: you may not know what I suspect you know. You don't know what I don't know.'

'Within those walls, I needn't be certain about anything,' she says. 'Much is up to other people, to play along. I wanted to be free, I followed people who told me how we all could be. Indeed, when we all are free we're all confined, confined by what we need to do and are, so that when every single one of us is free, it's all to do, and it goes all round the world, and that's the Chinese steed....'

'I don't believe it, not for a second,' Takis says. 'If you want, you could be locked up, and see how free you are, you feel.'

'I'm not ready for that yet,' she says, and they both laugh, not much.

*

The cake shop changes, radically. In a small space, a bucket with an octopus, pails with large snails, small snails. Covers to stop escapes. Tripes in long troughs, like the headless fish were in. Udders and lungs. Things from deeper down, lighting up the water, heavy lids to keep them in....

No one, no one at all comes for days. Then most of the old crew – soldiers, juniors, craftsmen and shopkeepers – they come back, and there are tourists, students, singles who bring magazines.

There are connections – all the world has a thin voice that comes in here, and orders.

I can't suppose my four walls have the fourth wall, Petronia thinks: an audience. Could I turn, and there's a void, full of normal paying spectators: an open wall? They clap, perhaps, but do not speak, engage. They watch me in my cell. Whatever I feel like doing – they applaud, a little – and then leave.

Sex would be violent and perverse – unwanted, that is, so I don't imagine it, here in the midday profusion of hearts and brains: livers and tongues.

*

'No, no,' Vanessa protests: 'No food! It comes horribly ... they look underneath the leaves for crawly-wrigglies. The sinless lambs – they throw the poor beasts down from the rock, scoop up the bits. How could you think of working there, Petronia?

'When it was clear we'd never have the revolution, certainly not a better one than they had had in Paris, and Moscow, and Beijing – it was clear we'd have the Monster. And for sure – it came, it's here for ever. So now – I love the prophets who foretold it – all of them. They pretend one day there'll be no monster, not any more! Prophets: yum-yum. They taste good, but they don't fill you up.

'The donkey-riders, the fall-guys and the bearded ones, and all the Americans, with their gadgets and equations, their slogans done in poker-work, prayers to small guitars, acoustic of course – sure, they all have trains of monsters, but just little ones.... Their big one – is really big! Over everything, like ketchup. We, instead of revolution – we have our Monster too ... instead of little pests ... there's what we've got. One Monstrous Monster, or several? You can't tell: they're brothers, twins. You smell them, they're unclean – and you must have a picture of each one beside you bed. Those too – they smell.'

'It's normal,' says Petronia. 'But where there's a big monster, you'll find little ones.

'But, Vanessa – the revolution, you didn't push for it, you didn't devote your cunning and your wisdom to see how it made landfall, if the rudder was fixed, if they ran out of fuel and stokers, if they saved the vast territory, saved my Angelo's host of grandfathers....'

'Oh,' Vanessa says, 'I must confess. I see monsters everywhere – I have been prudent, not to call it pessimism ... déjà vu....'

'The subject's closed, then,' says Petronia. 'It's incorrigible. Like I think – everything is.'

'If that were so,' Vanessa says, screwing up what was once her face. 'There wouldn't be my toad. He was invented to be good, the scientist who banishes the bad. "Experiments". The exercises, then the fresh lists black as black, the exhortations. "Enemies". Good allies and the bad, and "we're the best there'll ever be". The counter-revolution – my! it's strong and well-prepared. It must know something that we don't.... Invade the invaders! My toad – he was in the service of someone who thinks rebellion's on the cards, when everybody knows it's past, long dead, unborn....'

'Oh Vanessa,' Petronia laughs. 'People love preparing where there's no resistance. When all is frozen, any change is revolutionary, a rebellion: for or against a stretching of the legs? Invade with armies or with dope or with songs. My Takis now – he's not a warrior. He likes an easy victory that sets him free for early evening drinks.'

'It's all about what we eat,' Vanessa says, picking at a red patch on her nose, staring vaguely. 'Or almost all. How you are educated, brought up, socialised.'

'They're thinking of making a little dancing space downstairs,' Petronia says: 'A kind of *déjeuner-dansant.*'

When we speak, Petronia wonders, does it come natural to everyone to speak the truth? Really, truth? Somewhere in between true and something else, or do people choose: – true or false?

What she tells Vanessa, what she told the guy in the prefecture, the prison – her loving another place, more, totally, than where you should adore; more than where they issue you your documents, conscript you; even a place that hasn't been, or was and now has gone.... She loves that place that is not, that she can't describe, that doesn't fit a true, a false. True love? Nonsense?

Freedom is knowing what you don't know: knowing nothing: knowing what you know and don't tell.

*

The casualties are starting, here they come – and lovers prepare to sleep forever with their dead lovers, have their dead children who in turn ... more dead children. The soldiers – everyone of us – they flock to the offal restaurant. We've seen it all, over the green land spread the human parts – break the taboo, cannibalise, go downstairs and have a dance and wave your arms, if you still have two of them....

'This is ridiculous,' Petronia says. 'I must go somewhere else. Desire is fickle, but it pricks. You've sabotaged yourself, Vanessa – congratulations ... you're not presentable. Farewell, my dear – some time quite soon.'

*

The Ship: the movie. That would be a project, thinks Petronia.

'Nadia,' she begs. 'Teach me to do tricks.'

'You're too tall, Petronia,' Nadia says, skimming the menu and rejecting everything. 'You waver. And when you're on the rope, you need steady, fixed horizons. That's the first thing – anchors. You hold firm against them....'

'That could be difficult for me,' says Petronia. 'And there's my fear of falling ...'

'You fall to learn,' says Nadia. 'And so you learn to fall. Within reason. You may not understand why balancing is the point....'

'No,' says Petronia. 'It isn't me. But if we do the movie, I could have stand-ins....'

'There's no such thing,' says Nadia. 'If that's done, whoever does it is the star. And if it's faked, why bother?'

'That isn't how art is done,' says Petronia.

'This stuff is horrible,' says Nadia, seeing 'udders and lungs, Tuesday special – wings' on the menu, which she tosses on the floor; and exits in a storm.

*

'You looked for significance, but jumped on to the ship. Give your life to fortune – and fortune will tell you what it's all about: distorting mirrors ... the image always is of you. Being deprived, a minority, or persecuted – what I say is true, even if someone fights your corner, gives recognition to your strength. Individuals adrift in chance? Expect nothing – you'll be gratified. People come out bad and sad, whatever benefits they have. Equality doesn't mean this,' Nadia says. 'You two, you and Vanessa, are a mess.'

'"Equal" means different,' says Petronia. 'We don't need everybody to agree....'

*

'Don't mix with Fritz,' says Vinnie. 'He'll turn you in. I might too, of course, but it isn't worth the fuss. The risk,' he adds, 'is me, my image, my imagination. My colour sense.'

Vinnie's bearded – could be after Clemenceau, the painter's friend, the workers' foe ... but he wears a pair of light pants, feminine, with sunflowers sliced by ill-judged seams, and two large blooms, one on each buttock – a spirited fabric, but where indeed to place the emphasis? Sunflowers – a story of the world. They're big as peonies – one on each knee is naff, but on the bum – is frolicsome. He's too startling to be a deserter. He's an old gun but – must be quite noisily – discharged. Flash! In the pan. What a flame!

'I'll tell you what you want, Petronia,' he says. 'Much more than you divulged to me of what you are, and what I'm not.'

What I want, Petronia thinks, is how to sabotage, small scale, and not be caught. It wouldn't help in any case, to denounce my source – what Vinnie has become: – a warrior retired, haphazard, unconvincing.

And, surely, direct action was never on his mind.

Small scale, secret, untraceable, Petronia thinks. That's me, my mark, my sabotage. That way – I don't need classify who's on my side, or who's the biggest enemy. I don't need classify the empires into big states or multinational ones, divided partners in a world system or a contest with many sides and allies – I don't need look for friends, opinions, movements and trends.... I don't need contact minorities or groups who're plainly marked-out, carrying on an open opposition, struggle in the light to spread enlightenment, no classes rising to fall and revolt, everyone in the same hand-basket, same destination: me and my mind, a mind without difficulties, subtleties, no hidden unhappy families, no lost loves. Me: not interesting, you'd think; that's all.

Not needing to deny what I don't know and didn't see, to avoid the punishment that's coming anyway. It comes to me, and I shall bear it everywhere – the graffito: 'The big change! No escape, no preparation, and no description!'

'It's the kind of game we carry on in barrack-rooms,' says Vinnie. 'In the dark, anonymously. How to screw the system, not to be caught, never to admit, not to aim at damaging in special ways, but just – slowing it all down. Fucking it up. Mysteriously. And in puzzling ways. Acting like fortune, with fortune's long and feathery wand ... that sets the fire, frightens the horse, turns off the light, defuses bombs, retracts the orders of the day, strikes down the newly voted in, dishonours the statesman just retired ... giving a significance to the destruction....'

'Destructions – those all come, irrespective,' says Petronia. '*There* is the flaw.'

'Just knowing how it works, and doesn't,' Vinnie says. 'Costs you your life, your livelihood, your freedom and your health.'

'I'll do it anyway,' says Petronia. 'I question, I don't feel. I arrange and paint, I don't observe. I'm a bone: finger? Toe? Both.'

'You're rubbish, Petronia,' Vinnie says. 'I like rubbish.'

'There are worse places than this,' Petronia says, ignoring him, not wanting to judge herself, or him. 'I won't call them countries, because countries are always there, but bad and worse – they change places. If countries can't be abolished – and they can't – at least I hope none disappear. They won't. Save them, even the losers – no place must disappear, think of the people! Countries, without them, what do we do? Roam? Stay put? There'd be no jails, but we'd all be stressed out, like now. Living like bears.'

'You bring in gangs and infections, Petronia,' Vinnie says. 'You're a bad thing, and I hope you and only you are responsible for being bad, and it's not down to anything else that you can blame, like other people.'

'That's a kind thing, Vinnie, the first I heard you say,' Petronia says. 'I don't know where my bad and good come from, I've no idea. Like all the other things I've been telling you. No idea, except fault and blame, but that's no good for you, or Fritz and Nadia. And fault and blame – they stay with me alone.'

*

'If you don't like what happens to you,' Fritz says, 'often it's other people – they come and change things. My grandfather – he loved the purple sausage they had when he was young. Then they left out the beetroot and it turned grey, like it had always been.'

'I remember purple sausages,' Petronia says. 'I was very small, they were quite long, longer than me. We were in Lvov, and maybe we spoke Polish ... Lwow. Was Lemberg – long ago....'

'In Lviv, and spoke Ukrainian,' says Fritz, 'or maybe none of that and you spoke Russian. Unless it was Armenian or Ruthenian.'

'We didn't speak much,' Petronia says, 'in anything at all. We had no parents, and the grandparents didn't speak to each other.'

'You see?' says Fritz. 'The colours change, grandparents die. We all came from marcher lands. Let things happen, you'll find they change, all by themselves....'

'That's not the point,' Petronia says. 'I don't know why things happen to me, and I don't like what does. Besides, everything's changed utterly, but there's no agreement about what has, still less "why?". Of course, no "why", no reason for anything at all....'

'I give orders,' Fritz says, 'and take care they're ones that will be carried out. Any idiot can give orders that'll be disobeyed.'

'It isn't orders,' Petronia says. 'It's unsticking what must be unstuck. That's the job, the job that's never done.'

'That's stuff for engineers or masons,' Fritz says. 'Middle-order guys.'

'It could be anywhere,' Petronia says.... 'Past becoming more past, unreason into reason into unreason. Transforming – Pakistan from India: disappearing – German East Africa; miniaturising – Mongolia. Purple sausage into grey. Parents into grandparents. Past – the revolving drum, ever older, ever scrubbed up to shine. Some of it is politics, some is where you are, your family, the hut that falls into the sea, your early life in callipers, in bare feet, in carts drawn by Shetland ponies....

'Being lost on the heath for years, driven from the forest by hornets.... Deported, sent to a camp, bombed, dosed secretly with acid....'

'I don't think that's the point,' says Fritz. 'It's all civilisation, variations and selections. The civilisations that have died – we think the people in them were all, well, 'civilised'. Maybe the kings and shamans set the tone and didn't stick to it. Too many sacrifices? Then the fall, oblivion.

'Civilisation. That's your beef, Petronia. Or – is it happenstance? Don't tell me it's the same.'

*

'You suck that up,' says Takis. 'And if any of it was true, it would be irrelevant. Petronia's a southerner: she lives and dies the same, nothing outside changes. She doesn't know what change is, unless it's in her body. She's moody and frenetic.

'You think you lead, that you're unbroken, Fritz: and so you think the people led are born with bridles. It isn't so.

'Vinnie's a soldier, but first of all – a melancholic. If he was less afflicted with melancholia, he'd be a suicide. Or a hero, a warrior – over the top! Bang! A medal for his smithereens!'

'I never thought Vinnie could be led anywhere at all,' says Fritz.

'I'm biddable,' says Takis. 'If it helps – but, Fritz, don't try to lead me anywhere at all, or I'll denounce you. All societies run by denunciations – those trump laws and pacts. Blacklists formal and just neighbourly – that's the most basic democracy....'

'You seem to have a fine, a subtle, mind, Takis,' says Fritz, assuming a thoughtful mien. 'But you have the fault – the light touch. You throw it all away for a glib conclusion. "What is anything about?" I'd ask. From you, there is no answer: it's all in your parting shot – when you think of it. Those Parthians – they go on and on. You don't stay around to see if I fall off my horse....'

'It's true,' says Takis. 'I make up stories, so the emotion and the truth – they dribble out. Profit is loss, you gain so you can lose. But – patience! The pretence and the lies – they seep away as well. A story – no one believes in it – but what's belief? It lasts until there is a contradiction – and contradiction is the nub of all reality.... Things change into other things, that they were not – quite different.'

'Oh nonsense!' Fritz shouts out. 'We must believe that all is for the best, and we can check it, all the time.... Or else – it's anarchy and questioning the boss who does the best he – I – can....'

'I make the crime and I can then establish guilt,' says Takis. 'I am the judge. Without the law, there is no crime, nothing to be guilty of, so making laws ensures the guilt of all who come before me. I must be merciful and realistic. Everyone hides something, even if they don't know what it is, or how it might be seen.... It's the old soldiers, Vinnie for sure, who do the massacres and then feign justification, or if that fails – it's "orders", or a mistake, or "much exaggerated".'

For once – Vinnie assents in silence, doesn't add his small change to the argument. He isn't present, either.

'We know all that,' says Fritz. 'Massacres – they happen. Some planned but mostly – the mistakes, the tiredness, "let's get it over with – and try out our equipment on these folk"....'

*

'I hear all this,' Petronia says. 'I have a consideration you should know. I don't convince myself.

'It's true – I'm bits of everything, convictions make me even more a patchwork, and should have made me worthy of a hearing. I'm victim, which is good, I guess, but I'm a perpetrator too. Historically, that is, by descent. I've ancestors. I should be credible....'

'You're not,' says Vinnie. 'I always said – you are a fake. Self-pitier. You, Petronia, and each one of us, can't make a little change. And the big one ... it's poised like the great wave, above our heads. I must know why it's there. I'm making one exactly like – and I don't know how. What do we do...?'

'We hold our breath,' Petronia says. 'And yet – we climbed aboard the ship, we four. We lost our nationality, our class. It's true, around us there were crowds of people infinitely worse equipped than us. But still – a glimpse of what awaited all of us – we had.'

'Trust me,' says Fritz. 'For doom is quite like all other gloom – it hits selectively. Gain wealth, invest in good doctoring – ponies and peacocks ... a boon to every paddock ... splash out and give to charity, and never fear. You'll last much longer than the rest, give orders, propose remedies, enforce the policies – you'll be a matriarch, a boss, until you tire of it, and then – you'll have a pass to paradise, for sure....'

'You can go easy on Petronia, Fritz,' says Takis. 'She's on a list. All lists are black, in black ink, of course, but hers has emphasis. You and Vinnie – there is a question about you. Those people drowned when you were riding on the ship – did you take stock? Ask? Even mourn?

'And on the shore – you guys, you four – you held on to your privilege, and even created more of them – thought of writing it all up and selling it, even a poem, or a picture too....'

'Oh come, Takis, go easy on them,' says Vinnie. 'You can't be hard and humanist together. You have a fascist mindset, Takis. Accept it. You are reactionary. Inherited advantage comes from the roots, it thinks there is a substance lasting from way back. We four castaways – we thought we were the tops. You can't expect us to be generous. The humanistic litany – that is for the opposite – the victims, the disinherited, the sons of nobody, the beaten, the enslaved....'

'You might be right,' says Takis, 'But you aren't. Those two bands, groups of the predestined, that you mention – are allied. If one's defective, there's the other one that works. Change and change about – sweet, sour, some honey in your tar. They're complementary. The tough and the accommodating; the privileged, and those seeking the big privilege, biggest of all: equality. We have the mandate for the soft, the hard: we have two voices – that's success. Left and right – that's all societies. We set the fires and put them out – it's governance.... Don't illude yourself, society's a cart: it needs a "Stop", a "Go".'

They fall silent, and ponder. It's undeniably so. Confusing, too.

'I feel I should know more,' Petronia says. 'Study, feel. Climb the tall mountain of the mind....

'Where should I start?' And she turns to Vinnie.

'Oh, call on me,' he says, 'I've no credentials – only stupidity; to risk my life, to raise my flag, to show I am expendable and, for the nonce at least – you can take shots at me, like I was cruising in a row of ducks – a prize for each you hit....'

'Well?' asks Petronia: 'I think my first concern – it ought to be ... Time. Understand that; and any chrism it might confer – to rocks and oldsters, even life. And trees. Ruminate on duration, our fleeting flight from nought through ought to nought. And then philosophy ... except....'

'Yes,' says Fritz, 'Old Hegel did for that. There is no end to it – you reach poor reason's summit, and then you see a panorama, a vast plain, like Waterloo ... ruins like Stalingrad ... you can do anything, defeat, be defeated – all flows past, away, but all will leave its mark ... it's all a picture by an artist who wasn't there who took it from a picture by an artist who wasn't there, who.... Nothing was explained, except an everything was built, wider and taller than the everything there was before, was still. So then, Philosophy must be divided up – language, ethics, metaphysics, and how to dump your lover thoughtfully ... but that's no good. We need a statement, at once, all tied together with good spelling, answering in a phrase: "What's to be done, what's left"?

'The point is – you'd give orders when there is no plan, no policy, no principle, Petronia. What you don't have, what isn't there – can signify anything, or nothing. Be bold. Make the gesture of contempt! Declaim! Exploit the blanks, the voids ...'

'Yes,' she says. 'I see the prospects. I must dump Vanessa – she has made her own catastrophe, and let her dwell on it, in it too. I must find another ship. With other comrades. And try to understand, instead of panicking. Help the weak and overpower the strong. Be strong myself. Accept the contradictions, acknowledge them, proceed as though they were not there.

'But first – explain the ship!'

*

It's not a ship, it is a bus. A coach? – but, surely, coaches are powered by horses. It goes fast, but so do ships, though you don't perceive it so. This one has a driver – what does he know? Everything – there's only one road you can take. A destination? Where to stop? – and pee or ask the way or buy some Tupperware or take a pic?

'Do not distract the driver' it says – he's lucky, he's distracted already, spaced out in this deserted space ... maybe it reflects Nadia's circus ring, with dogs and ostriches. Tarrara! goes the band, classical: and round and round the animals trek, and if one drops they feed another in – you start with Pomeranians, end with Labradors. Alsatians too.

A troop of 'boks goes skittering across the road in front – kicking up their hooves and showing off their scuts.

'There's something smart about a tail,' the man sat next to Petronia says.

The bus is very cold. The men, mostly with full beards, are grey with hoar frost, their hands and heads. They don't speak, don't read. They could be Georgians. Outside, it must be raging hot.

'Is that a come-on?' Petronia asks her seat-mate.

'No,' he says. 'It's a regret. We lose our tails before they can be admired. No – the come-on is in here. I do short trades....'

He lets her peep inside a scuffed brown case. 'Imperial railroads', she sees: 'Petrograd to Rostov', 'Yellow River Ferries preference stock'. Share certificates.

'Everything in time's redeemed,' he says. 'Even the sacred books say so – we have to wait until we're dead, though in death, I'm told, we don't perceive the length of passing time.'

'I don't have cash,' Petronia says. 'I mean – I carry none.'

'I know exactly what you mean,' the guy says. 'Cash. Now present, now invisible. Do not lie, but do not tell the truth. I know poverty when it sits down next to me. It often has, and wears my pants and shoes, and shares my stomach and my throat.'

'I hope we reach the end quite soon,' Petronia says.

'Indeed,' he says. 'Or you'll forget why you're on the trip.'

'Things happen to me,' says Petronia. 'There are suggestions why, and why you shouldn't ask. You lose your country, and your family. You are defrauded and seduced. Is there a pattern you could understand and break? We're instructed that we have important rules, and many many laws; and values too, and faiths and sensibilities, and yet, and yet.... The things that happen and transform – they're always exceptions to the norm. The Mayas, Incas – the Shakas – they write identities with such confidence, you see their art and science – quite unmistakable. And yet – poof! Like the gazelles – a cloud of dust, and they are gone. They leave a trace – quite unmistakable, and yet, and yet – how are they changed, and are they still...? Where shall *we* go? When? What trace is left? Yours, mine? – and are they both the same?

'And me?' She sags.

'I'd take you in my arms,' the guy says, 'but it would be misunderstood, my dear. You realise – conviction, revelation or conversion – those are *trompe l'oeil.* Wood painted like Carrara marble. You have to deal with fakes as well. All spoofs. Better – they are real, but like infections that you pick up as you run your race, or pebbles in your shoe are real – but pointless. You didn't ask for them, and there they are. You know you're mortal, and an animal, and undefended. Why rub it in with fever, spots?

'You'll think I am an Uzbek, from my name. Mirkat. My mother loved one such – but my father – he was different, a German settler from Lemberg, a place you won't have heard of, I am sure....'

Petronia keeps schtum. Here is a scam, proclaimed. And who could care about paternity? Who fathers who? With what consequence? Most of us, we come from Lwow: so what?

She wants that the bus should stop, the driver say, 'We're here. We have arrived.' A purpose, a motivation.

'You must be very very old,' she says to the guy sat beside. 'Names remembered, hidden – all change, even if the Lemberg Germans didn't change, just left....'

'All fathers too,' says Mirkat, laughing noisily. 'There's just the two kinds there have always been: too close, too distant. That is it!'

'That's just a part of it,' Petronia says. 'The family. All those years – "women in common", or at least, a currency. The emperor's head – on the block and on the sovereign: the ladies? "Half sovereigns". That's only part of it of course....'

'Where we are going now,' says Mirkat, 'is different. The real south....'

'It's full of what I call my civilisation,' Petronia interrupts. 'The origins, the lost splendours. Now, the shaky reprise. And lots else too. And – shall I drown in it? Will I be noticed, and will it all make sense? Why do I expect the worst?'

'All of us,' says Mirkat, shaking his beard till the icicles tinkle. 'Are wondering that. All on this bus, that is. The South – our hope, our mother, found at last.'

'You're just a would-be capitalist, Mirkat,' says Petronia. 'Too old to soldier, and full of ancient tricks.'

'Yes,' he says. 'Living by my wits – they're addled now. Necessity has run its course, my last dinar bought my ticket here.... I feel I'm coming home. Home's not where I want to be....'

'I'm interesting,' Petronia says: 'But you don't recognise it.'

'I'm on a trip,' says Mirkat: 'I'm sure you're fascinating, but I am interested in themes, not people. It's how people intend to live their life – not by wisdom, probably. That's for academics. It's where the pursuit of wisdom takes us, you and I, we take it as a rule, a guide – amid other people maybe having lost it, or been mistaken ... The pursuit of consistency, post-reason, in a universe of dusty emptiness ... pursuit without prey, without our fox. Wisdom – why, that's in the fox! The hunt! Never the kill ...'

'But you and I – we want wisdom at the start, not all along,' Petronia says.

What then?

The bus slows, there are people ahead waving their arms, but not to any music you can hear: she says, 'I want to see if changing habitat, changing all the people, the politics, the clothes, the faiths – what difference it may make to me....'

'Put like that,' says Mirkat, 'it's all in vain. You want to see how deeply you've been socialised – who cares? Only you is interested in how you change or don't.

'The ship has brought you puzzlement, and incoherence. Do you just want destruction now? Can you change anything, when everything has changed, is changing; and does it promise anything ...? I understand, you want to see the mechanism of life, dismantle it like an old clock, and hope you'll discover what time is. People tell it like it was a story: life. The bad mother, the orphanage, the rape, conscription, palace guardsman, nurse to the sultan – everything is burnt, you're killed and raped and have to escape on foot across the desert.... In the end, you find release, or peace – sat in your hut ... discovered by a film-maker, feted in LA, crowned story-queen, married to the vice-president, making peace in the Sahel, father of a nest of marmosets.... Yes, yes – I'm phony too, Petronia. Stick to the banquets and the orgies – forget the wars of liberation and being pilot of a fighter plane....'

*

The bus slows, a bunch of people get down, peering at the checkpoint, some wave documents, others try to conceal themselves behind their comrades....

'You should have met my friends,' says Mirkat. 'There's a scientist, called Kaufmann, who thinks he faces his extinction. And Asia, she's an actress who's lost her personality, and doesn't know whose character she's taken on. They're looking for a place – Kaufmann wants to start again just as an animal, in a species with a future. No expectations, no literacy, probably no clothes. And Asia – seeks a place where character is given to you for all your life ... Stasis. Frozen identity. The boondocks. Weeding.'

He stumbles down the steps, the sun instantly melts his icy beard, his hair: for a moment he has lost a generation, forty years at least, his face is smooth, his hair dark, wavy.... 'I'm afraid they'll think I am a rebel,' Mirkat says. 'Even a revolutionary.... I never trust the soldiers, they have no belief, they don't believe your papers or your books, your pleas, denials – nothing, nothing at all.'

The coach is driven off. They never see it, never again, it's gone and anything of theirs they left inside. There's nothing, nothing at all around – except the barrier on the road, the road that rolls on and on, quite featureless. The sun is very hot.

The soldiers separate the passengers into small groups, then divide them again, over, and over, on some other basis. They single Mirkat out, rough him a little, take him off, 'We'll never see Mirkat again,' Petronia says – but no! Here he is once more, stressed out with heat and thirst. Anxious.

'Kaufmann!' he says, to a tall gaunt guy, 'I feared I was a step away from my extinction. It's true – we all go there – extinction. There's never more than one of us. Too bad. Rabbits and bats – they're just the same. Individuals, despite appearances. It's lookalikes you mean: they dwindle out. Examples thin out, the last one, you recognise. It's like they all once were – remember: species, a *specchio* – a mirror, looking-glass. A likeness. One looks in the glass, and it looks back – and there's another figure, you – identical, instantly. That's all – people who look and sound and reproduce like you. That's the best that we can do. We die, the image won't. We'll never know. We hope – in the mirror, there is always us, when we are not. Does that satisfy?'

'Casuistry,' Kaufmann says. 'There is a classifying error. They say a bird's extinct in Canada, but not in Greece – it cannot be – that's

Schrodinger's cat again. No humans will be unanimous in being like me.... I'll be disowned, hurrah! Me, just me – alone!'

'No, no – just one or two will be like you!' says Asia. 'Stand-ins – I know. And – in any case, why the regret? You fear you'll disappear? It's rather grand to be, then not to be. To have lived, unique – then not. There may be imitations – but you, Kaufmann, you alone are genuine. The true amber room, the ur-text, collected works of Sappho, forgotten at the manicurist.... Lost and found, and lost again and still unique. Rejoice!'

'No,' says Kaufmann. 'The chain is broken and the link is lost, the balance cannot be restored, a piece is missing so the puzzle never can be solved. Something's eliminated – why? In the name of what?'

'That's my position,' says Petronia. 'Asia and Kaufmann – both seem right – just like the dinosaurs, extinct but taken flight, into the trees: delicious bulbuls, delicate ospreys.... The original, but radically changed.'

The other three turn on her, start to dissent, and Mirkat says – 'Evolution, Petronia? Really? Is that what you mean by "change"? Trial and error, always lagging behind the challenge, climate, habitat, always at catch-up – not to mention meteors, volcanoes, and starvation....'

*

'None of us is right,' says Asia. 'And none of us quite wrong. Mirkat risked the most – but now it seems – they'll put us in a camp. And hope we shall be sorted out ... According to what documents we have or don't.... Punishment or resettlement, most likely both.'

'The bus!' Petronia wails. 'Started so well....'

'An illusion, alas,' says Kaufmann, as a big truck shows up, the tailboard's dropped....

'Help me!' Petronia begs, 'I fear I can't climb up, and might be left behind.'

'Yes,' Asia says. 'That is the snag, the trick. No one wants the truck to leave without them.'

*

The four continue – arguing, exchanging, making alliances, making points – not acknowledging the others, their comrades on the truck. At last –

'Ah,' says Mirkat. 'Maybe ... what luck.' He points – a grassless field: with mushrooms? Puff-balls? No.

'A tented camp. We might stay huddled close together – if it doesn't rain, it's healthier than barracks any day....'

'Lectures...' says Kaufmann: 'To organise.'

Asia ventures – 'Shows!'

'Clients,' says Mirkat, returned fully to his patriarchal look. 'Nothing up-front, but all on promissory notes....'

'We must be protected here,' says Kaufmann. 'A kind of reservation. If they make us work, it means we're favoured, and in luck. If we're idle – it's a punishment.'

'If only we knew why,' Petronia begins. 'It seems much better organised, but otherwise – it's like the ship, except ... we do not move. And there's no fish.'

'Let's ask – "why do they want to keep us here?"' Mirkat says. 'To learn? Surely, they should want to know what we're discussing – unless we're stupid. But they don't ask. Nothing, not a word.'

'If they're separatists....' Asia has a guess.

'But there was nothing there, or here. Nothing to desire, nor claim nor to divide from,' Kaufmann says: 'And we can't be ransomed: – we are looking for certainties, because we're dissatisfied with what we have. ...so, we've no value. Nor bargained for, as we've reached no conclusions: we're not a subject .... no valuation is yet possible, no price ...' He's much puzzled.

Curiosity? Human trafficking? Trespassing? Nothing seems to fit, and the work they have to do is hard, and work and not working are both boring. Work – is both real and metaphorical: breaking, carrying, the stones.

'Just walking out,' says Asia. 'It would seem an insult to those who can't. And where would we go?'

'We'd go to where we stopped,' Petronia says. 'That's what you do, after a banquet or an orgy. If you do nothing, you can't be guilty: that's what you think. It's not so – you can't count on innocence. Just sitting in your hut – you could be thinking of a career, as a rebel of some kind, a fellow traveller at least. But us – we feel we have escaped, and so, we resume the journey, the stop is the start, you'd say. That's what the Romans did, and ended up all over ....'

'Yes,' says Kaufmann. '"Ended up". Like the Byzantines ended up as Turks. And Mirkat's father from Bokhara .... a phantom sperm ... and

here he is, Mirkat: beside us now.... Not German and not Uzbek – what's left?'

'My father was not what he had wanted: Uzbek,' says Mirkat. 'But, morally, of course ... he ended up as what he wanted. Morality – it has no passport. My heart, like his, is always there; what more is there, if you're not there?'

While they are arguing, they have reached the road. Morally, of course, they deserted their comrades. Practically – the four new friends did not acknowledge their situation. In this unique case, the wire, the guard dogs – did not operate.

Don't think you can try the same trick yourself.

There's no bus, no ticket, but you can walk.

Someone will stop for sure, give them a ride.

Prison farms have signs that say 'Do not stop for hitchhikers – correctional facility' or suchlike. No one stops for hitchhikers anyway. If it's not icy, snow up to your nose, it's hot, and there are black-flies. No one escapes and those who do don't expect a ride. They've escaped but it wasn't from farm, nor prison. It was from life.

Yes, Petronia thinks. This is not civilisation, not as I knew it and rejected it. I'm on the way to the unknown for sure....

That's a hypothesis, though not cast in classic form. The black-flies kill you if you escape – that's not uncertain, not at all. Cheaper than warders. You might even substitute the warders with black-flies. Mirkat would say it wasn't capitalism: 'You need some fall guys you can cod,' he'd say – it isn't warders keep you in, it's flies.

'They think if you escape, you'll die in the hot sand,' says Kaufmann.

'So,' says Petronia, 'they're in control. There is a hand ... a mind. Someone's. I never thought it might all be planned, but why? What motivations...? People dispose of their own bodies, of themselves, their thoughts – they spin them up like swathes of silk ... or spinning plates on sticks.... Surely no one's behind all that?'

THE SHIP?

'Yes,' Asia says. 'I know those tricks. On stage, you can do almost anything – but don't. There's nothing in the script that says you oughtn't improvise: make it all up, or play a mute ... but even in free fall, you recognise the beat.... You're a machine, but one that purrs, drinks red gin from a cup and wakes at noon. There's things we know about – the sun, the distances, the bugs ... the weapons and the punishments. Who gets hurt, and who lives from hurt to hurt. But on the stage – you're loaded, primed, you recognise your cue ... you can't avoid it. You emote, it's normal, there's no other way, you're born – tailless, nude – you end like that, and you'll have followed faithfully – the beat.'

'I remember,' says Petronia. 'Someone who did not.'

Poor Vanessa. Rotting, determined to be unappetising, inedible. After the stage of mush, what's left, becoming hard, takes shape unstoppably – like you can see a goblin face, some squirrelly features.... 'As though, even chance,' Petronia says. 'And decay, take on a human shape....'

'We were the lords,' says Kaufmann. 'Not for long, but quite decisively. We shift from camp to *bidonville*, to *banlieue*, and then we're on the move again – yes, there is control, but no – there's not. Control – that if it doesn't work, and surely won't – it's an illusion. Grasp that, Petronia, and you'll understand what we are useful for and why we're not....'

They tramp on, beside the road. There are patrols, but they don't seem to see the four ... 'Look!' says Mirkat: 'Our faces!...' And it's true – they're dark. The sun? They're black – deeper than you'd find in Lviv, Bokhara; or lovely Asia's Islamabad.

'We're labour power in surplus,' Kaufmann says. 'In waiting. We worked real hard when we were in the camp – now we're outside we are competitors of stone-breakers ... poorer than slaves, but hopeful. We're idle, 'nothing doing, doing nothing' – so's the guys inside will strive ... we're their potential replacements. They bust themselves because of us....'

'They say there's poor so that the rich are rich,' says Mirkat. 'It seems that there are poor so that the poor stay poor....'

They laugh. Poor Mirkat – always says the obvious. A dumkopf, though quite lovable – his brown bag like a bookie's, holding masses of $2 bets....

'My friend Vanessa knew how big stuff worked,' Petronia puts in – the others ignore her, she doesn't see – they're walking in, or over, the big stuff now! Under the dust and sand – there's riches that will save the world, for sure: dig it, the Mine! It's Yours! ... just dig!

'Nothing happens,' Kaufmann complains. 'That's to say – too much happens to make sense. You need "not much" to happen, then you can

guess how and why it does. We all had lives we can't explain before we got here, and now they seem inexplicable once more....'

'Try to be simple, Kaufmann,' Mirkat says, irritated by being called stupid. 'Some things we know are too big to be reversed, and we accept that responsibility for acting big is offset, pardoned, by our ignorance and interests. By being small.

'The end of the world ... too big to be assigned, blamed on. But all these inexplicable curiosities that fall on us – everybody claims they're inspired, everything must be, by respect for humanity; humanity – can put things right. And yet ... where does the universal inhumanity come from?'

'If we can't stop it, or anything at all, does it matter?' Asia asks. 'Like – where does all the money go? Come from?'

The others feel she hasn't understood.

Did *they?*

'It used to be colonialism....' Kaufmann begins, and Asia says, 'Like when we got to see Vautier's movie on the Côte d'Ivoire, slaughter in the colony – and now there's war eternal and its preparation everywhere. Apocalypse – comes in small bits, free samples too. Was it always so? It was? No lesson learnt, an infinity are given.... Defence and attack – they seem to be the same.'

'Maybe we always got things wrong,' Petronia says. 'That's what I think....'

These three, she thinks, are worse than on the ship. Asia – worried for her career, that she calls 'art' – Kaufmann obsessed with death – how, when it calls, you can be out? And Mirkat? What is left for him? Bets, held in a bookie's brown scuffed bag.

... and even worse, Petronia thinks, we're Africans. But not African ministers or fashion queens:

Just common folk ... As Asia says – the trauma will not end – the powers imperial live on, a yoke around our neck so that we must toil and haul like beasts ... those liberation wars, why did they stall?

Although – Mirkat has a plan, that in his bag there is a resolution for us all, even the most modest punter gets to win ... the cash; what Asia wonders where it went. He says 'redemption', available to all. Salvation, or crime and punishment? Both: resolved by graft.

They trudge on, in angry silence.

On the ship, Petronia thinks: Every one of us was striving to move, to master, to make sense. Here and now – we don't know if what happens will be worse. It seems quite barren here – though we don't know if the shale beneath our feet is worth a fortune, and worth fighting for....

'If only,' Asia pants, lolling out her tongue. 'There's another camp.'

'I miss....' Petronia begins – she can't say 'chocolate éclairs' though that is it ... it smacks of pathos ... preciousness.

She misses Angelo too – but he is, was, dangerous, he'd take her 'to the other side', where she seems, anyway, to be landed on.

*

They eat the grey spiky things that run around the bottom of the ditch beside the road. They're plentiful. Kaufmann eats them too, without regrets or apprehension.

In the morning, Asia's gone. Escaped or stolen, sequestered.

'This is not in the plot,' Petronia says.

'If you make our lives run according to your plan,' says Kaufmann, 'And Asia comes into it – we'll punish you.' He means it. He's a long, wiry type, built like a big hyena. Mirkat and Petronia are scared of him: she wouldn't want him in her plot.

'Actors fade away,' says Mirkat, trying to console. 'They have a shred of immortality – a smile, a lisp, a frown. Those live on. Divinities have always been uncomfortable – with those shreds of colour it is hard to trap – actors seem a challenge ... afloat; not here, not there.... Gods can't punish or redeem them....'

'Maybe we should tell somebody about Asia....' Petronia says.

'That would be unwise,' says Kaufmann. 'Round here, at least.'

'Induct me,' Asia says to the kidnappers. 'To your mysteries. I am the lost goddess, so, my compliments – you found me, rescued me from my abandonment. Tell me how you propose to honour me and fear me. Set me up, and I shall teach you how to pray to me....'

The guys laugh a little, and the head one says, 'My compliments to you. Your quip has saved you from the twists accompanying the bargaining in all our thefts of personalities, celebrities....'

'Alas,' says Asia. 'Divinity has no price. It's as good as worthless when the next immortal, the bigger one, pops up. Maybe an attribute is handed on ... in the end, into the spiders' space below the stairs we go.... Syncretism, our downfall, like cannibalism....'

'Don't be too mouthy, Asia,' says the sergeant. 'As deserters, we need a regular source of pay. You were more appetising than the others

– the creamy lady, "orgies and banquets". No use. An old guy trading short, and that guy who only thinks of death – you were the best, my dear.'

'Oh,' Asia says. 'I'll bring you tears, emotions, when you set the price for me. I'll start with 'A doll's house' – you lads could build me one....'

'Forget it,' says the head guy. 'Asia is not divine. Europa – she might be. Asia is thrown into the boiling-pot: each against all, and every string is pulled elsewhere – from across the world, until it's late, and each is arming against all....'

'Well,' Asia says. 'Settle it quick. Cash me in and let me run. If I'm a blasphemer, forget that too. Take what you can, strike while I'm hot, I'll get hotter that's for sure, and fuse into a useless lump... Don't reflect. To think? It's late....'

No use, of course. They've no idea who Asia is, or who will pay for her, just as she's quite ignorant of who they are. They're stuck, all stuck, in uncertainty. Look at her career – she's been worth a lot – but now, right now ... nothing at all. It's a pain, but ... nothing to be done.

'I fear,' Petronia says, 'We must move on. We'll have no news of Asia, not for years. Never, perhaps.'

Asia swelters. It's very hot and dull, like the earth before the dinosaurs. She gets by because she makes them laugh, the deserters – the visionaries. Perhaps she should have made them cry.

'You know, Petronia,' Mirkat says. 'Asia is a tragedy, but for the moment – we can't do anything for her. Who are we, anyway? I'm an old peddler, I don't matter. You are spoilt, Petronia – maybe it's good you don't like banquets and orgies. You can't find any substitute.

'I'm too old to try it on with you.

'Kaufmann matters, but he's insupportable, and is quite impotent.

'People love me because I offer them a flutter, and when it doesn't work, they hate me, but then – they forget. All that really matters is, if we can keep the show going, even if we fight each other like porcupines in a sack....'

'I want something else,' says Petronia.

'You won't get it unless you bring it,' Mirkat says. 'And you can't. Think instead what you can put up with, without threatening people stronger than you are....'

'Oh,' Petronia says. 'You might be right. But that's so bleak. Of course – Vanessa is bleak too, but I don't want to end like her.'

'Then we must keep going along this desolate road,' says Mirkat. 'See how right Kaufmann is – there's nothing left, no animals, no trees. He's right – and now?'

'Soldiers,' says Petronia. 'They don't decide a thing, even though they're everywhere.'

'That's what we hope,' says Mirkat. 'They've no power to decide anything except which way to point their guns.'

'It's so hot,' Petronia says. 'I miss the coach's air conditioning....'

'For me,' says Mirkat, 'That was a catacomb. I miss cream cakes, but they're not good for me.'

*

'Don't provoke,' Petronia says. 'People you can't beat. You'll be at war for life. That's what they say – people who find they cannot win the battle they have started. Accept them, let Mirkat do his deals with them. It may seem trivial, but it works.

'And yet,' she adds wistfully, 'there's still the ship, and our adventure to explain....'

'Ah!' says Mirkat. 'Yes, that *is* interesting. Why things happen, and when you can't explain them. That's worth study, even if, in the end, we may not know. That's our limit, but it's also a satisfying place to reach. It shows we tried.'

They laugh.

Kaufmann was passionate for Asia – but she ignored him, and he was timid – she came from a different sphere: confident, exposed, a public face. They scarcely spoke. Kaufmann saw himself as the only consciousness alive – and she could play almost everything and everyone, if contracted to; and so.... When she was captured – her voice, her face and body were all already independent. Continents away. Available to contract. They went on being used, while Asia herself slumped and dried out like a fig: in the shadow of a rock.

'I could even stay here,' Kaufmann says. 'And look for her, or guide – who knows ... someone who comes and seeks....'

'She could be anywhere,' Petronia says. 'There's silence. She could have gone extinct....'

'We lived with her,' says Mirkat. 'With all her faces. It was demanding, it was good. We never spoke to her – it was her job to speak to us, it didn't matter what, it was all written down by someone else, she didn't mean it anyway: – what counted was the conviction that she brought to it. It swept us all along, and now....'

And so, not much is explained.

Petronia and Mirkat carry on, limping and stopping frequently.

*

It's not a settlement, because you can't settle here. It's a circle of patched-up buildings.

'They're lucky,' Mirkat says. 'You see how they lived, up on the top floors. That means they'd only militias scouting round, who won't go up the stairs. Missiles and artillery – you live down, down in the cellar, or you dig one out....'

'We might have reached peace,' Petronia says. 'Often, places of exile or emergency – those are the safest.'

'Here's not Lvov, for sure,' Mirkat says. 'Nor Love.'

'There's no humans,' says Petronia. 'And no dogs. They'll have left, all of them, animals as well.'

'Silence meant solitude,' Mirkat says, 'Now it means fear. I know every surface, every rustle of a lonely life, and it knows me, we cuddle down together every night, but fear – you can't curl up and sleep with it.'

'How sentimental you are, Mikat,' Petronia says, and laughs. 'I'd no suspicion....'

The place seems deserted. The buildings – maybe thrown up for guys who come to cut down trees, to dig a mine, to make the road. She runs up the stairs of one. At the top, she opens the door – a room full of young children, propped against the walls: they stare at her in silence.

She runs back down, not a word to Mirkat about the kids – 'This place is spooked,' she says. 'Onward! On we go.'

She thinks – if I was responsible for the plot, I'd not have thought of bringing in those kids.

*

'Mirkat,' Petronia shouts, 'Keep up! No slowing down.' He's stalled, he sways.

He straddles a shallow trench, legs braced to keep him up. 'This is the line,' he says. 'Where they froze the war. On my left there are the poor, and on the right – the rich. I turn around – and it becomes the opposite. They suffer in their different ways – the poor, they kill themselves because they live in huts, and have to march in celebratory parades. The rich – must work like oxen, to stay in their race: they kill themselves from lack of inspiration. All are tired – like me.

'Democracy's a wonderful invention, Petronia – it lets you have suspicions, criticise the boss sometimes – but it can't fill in this trench.'

'So – what's your point, Mirkat?' she asks. 'You're frozen here, immovable, and I plod on, under this huge sun....'

'This line's a symbol, so am I,' he says. 'Though no one sees it so. A frozen pause. You must trudge on, find something we don't know, away from commonplace – maybe you'll become a symbol too....'

*

'Sign this,' says the lady, 'If you want to be repatriated.'

Yes and no, Petronia thinks: The internationals. These working people, the stateless ladies, have no country, they have nothing to do but send the lost, the abandoned, the uncertain – to a country. And it starts all over....

'Send me back where I came from,' she says. And that the lady does. There are soldiers and others, taking the lady's orders, it's a marvel, they have done a deal. While you've been away and much restricted, you will have missed a turn or many; stung by a snake and died of hunger, but they have come to throw a six for you and start you off again. The soldiers – they all look like Angelo might, if he had not met his sticky ends and finished up wherever he has gone. Petronia does not do the rounds and ask each one, soldier and similar, if 'Angelo', the name, means anything to them, although no doubt like Kaufmann and Mirkat they all know what they're doing here and how they have arrived and what the sides are; which ones to avoid. Nothing needs to be explained, they know why you and they are here and for how long, and as work goes, this is seemingly quite privileged, although they have to keep a distance from the clients, have a third eye in their back....

So, Petronia starts again, from where she climbed aboard the coach. It's a re-wind, that leaves Mirkat, Kaufmann and Asia where they are, also the bearded guys from the coach, the maybe-Georgians, deserted, in the camp – but for her, it's a Hellzapoppin sequence, where the projectionist sets the hero-character on the reel, the celluloid, right back at the beginning with a different script, a different setting and a zany impetus. And you don't see how it's done, the projectionist is a phantom, a creative semi-mortal ... but thanks to the magic of the cinema, it lets you too, newly enrolled as a protagonist in the movie, unpaid, playing yourself, make quite different errors, undergo new malevolences, not those already experienced in your life, but at least ... you're in the movie, at the start, the new start. And the movie unwinds, without a memory or past. The movie's like that – always different, always new – but always the old one re-made, same characters with different brains ... same celluloid....

This time you see you're in it. Have always been. Who directs? Another character? Probably – the writer producer, director, they're all beside you on the stage, one or all – will end up on the cutting-floor ... or in the projection booth.

*

'Get on the truck – quick, quick – leave everything behind....'

Your benefactors, the good fairies, the internationals who now you see and now you don't – they are the lucky ones, the specials, who have access to all countries, but not one of their own.

And they, of course, can't pass this blessed statelessness along to you and certainly it's not as fantastic as it ought to seem, because you just go back, where you once might have been, without a cent, and you in no way are invited to join them, an organisation that saves people, up to a point, and naturally not everyone, not many either. But – don't ask.

Once, the internationalists were comrades, and knowing them was a risk, and being one was even riskier. It's all different, mostly, now. Someone sent this lady to me. You are trucked back where you escaped or were driven out, in the nicest way, and there it ends. And starts.

*

Vanessa is dead, they say. The only person Petronia can find is Nadia and the rest have disappeared ... and all those that you knew are bankrupt, or quite sick and not communicating, or they're at the front in tanks....

'Teach me, Nadia,' Petronia says. 'To make my body a fine instrument. I'm on a winning streak – they took me out of danger, here I am, and maybe civilisation has its good side, they sent me where I said I'd been ... not Lviv, of course....'

‘Yes,’ Nadia says. ‘They would. That is your privilege. They save their own. Underneath, you’re one of them. Potentially rich: and, actually, coloured right and speaking smarmy.

‘And someone must have spoken up for you ... a state. A service; a secret one, if you had spun a tale in order to be shipped out.... You’ll find you’re always on a list, even dead, even useless, someone will read up on you, the file, not your inventions, tales, but what you might be – a danger. Then that’s why they reel you in, poor fish.... Run from home, get into more trouble – they’ll get you back, and ask you questions....’

*

‘Takis!’ says Petronia. ‘He hooked me, and it’s for ever. Poor Mirkat. He had no one to intercede for him....’

‘He was a symbol, dear,’ says Nadia. ‘And you are too, but in a different way. You need to check in, see what is required for saving you. It’s much too soon for me to put you on the hi-wire, or the trapeze.... It’s your pay-back time. Nothing anywhere is for free, that’s why you need to carry obols with you, for the boatman, in case you fall downstairs or eat a poisoned bun while you are spending leisure time....’

She hums ‘The daring young man on the flying trapeze....’ ‘You can fly in so many ways, now ... without a tent and clowns,’ she says. ‘You, Petronia, you’ve not yet begun to live. You even thought you didn’t want to – but your trek has cured that nonsense! You want to wander, and then to settle on a person you might want to be. You’re different, you think. You’ve been doing everything, but it never shows. At least I know about myself: I’ll always be the tallest of my family.

‘Orgies and banquets – those are taken lying down – stand up, Petronia! Make your own civilisation and run it.’

*

‘You leave me in this ruin,’ Vanessa says, whining. ‘My monument. My cenotaph. MY BODY! – and off you go with Nadia....’

‘What, Nadia?’ Petronia exclaims. ‘She’s a tumbler, a monkey on a stick. I never really left you, Vanessa.’

‘You thought I’d died,’ Vanessa says.

‘That’s what I heard,’ Petronia says. ‘But the noise of your complainings made me doubt it....’

They laugh. 'Takis saved me,' Petronia goes on. 'Now I'll have to pay him, when I see what price he set on me. You did nothing, Vanessa. You didn't help me. We were eating-buddies, but it meant nothing. No bond.'

'I was not myself,' Vanessa says, haughtily. 'You're so pretentious, Petronia – slippery, voracious. A puff adder.'

'Smooth, Vanessa,' Petronia says. 'Smooth, not slippery. Plumped up, not puffed. But beware – people round me – they end real bad. They disappear, and I come through....'

'It's illusion, Petronia,' Vanessa says. 'Being in your own skin – it gives the impression that you're more alive than others, more complete, more assailed, more travelled, more authoritative....

'Central; charmed and personable. You'll find – you lose your chrisms as you plod along ... your skin as well.... New ones grow, but ... there comes an end.'

*

'Vanessa – her mind swings,' Petronia tells Takis: 'A loose shutter.'

'I'm not interested,' Takis says. 'She's depleted goods. You're the sneaky one. A nihilist who goes off with the separatists....'

'I went with no one,' says Petronia. 'It wasn't that sort of trip – no leisure, and everyone deserting. And into it came, somehow, like the emblematic story of everywhere, of civilisations at least – the awful history of Lviv.'

'A fine city,' Takis says. 'Full of culture. History, too. And you've no title to belong there, Petronia. Besides, no one stays in Lvov for long. Everywhere and everyone is on the move – faster and faster – today on an iceberg, tomorrow – in sandstorms. There is nowhere you can call your place – it's all like Dresden; people melt, it all falls down....

'They say your people came from Lwow....'

'It wasn't me,' says Petronia. 'No one I know has ever tried to live there, then to be blown away like thistledown. Remember, I've never been attached to anything.'

'My compliments,' says Takis. 'You've become more interesting. No longer victim, but after your adventures – a resource. No longer wondering why things happen, but how you can scheme yourself to somewhere where they don't.'

'Oh,' says Petronia. 'I'd done nothing, to be a victim. And the ship – those people, hither and thither – what had they done...?'

'It was clear,' Takis says. 'You were an enemy. In those days we could say the enemies were on the other side. Now – everything is sides, a polyhedron. You need to ask, in a multi-sided figure, which is the most resistant side? A hexagon – is that stronger than a dodecahedron? How does each resist implosion and explosion...?

'We claimed the most – to be the lawful, most tolerant and flexible of systems, and we were top at boasting that. And so, having the most to lose, we needed to be clear about the enemy. What they could do, and think, what made them dangerous, all that. But now....

'Someone like you, Petronia, who has as yet done nothing, but has met all the representatives, clung to all sides, speaks the languages, knows themes and discourses, is fluent in the idiom of yesterday, tomorrow – of justice and bewilderment ... you probably would say....'

'Oh no,' Petronia says. 'Say nothing. In the family, they used to say "orgies and banquets those trip you up. And after trying those, they send you to the heights, responsibilities, and then there comes the punishment, for being too efficient, honest, seeing both sides .... one path leads to cirrhosis, syphilis, the other to the garrotte, to exile, to poison in your g and t...."'

'Yes,' says Takis, with enthusiasm. 'Beware the white spirit. Better stick to the *mistrà* – starting transparent: then, with a drop of water – clouds. Thick and permanent.'

'I don't speak languages,' Petronia says, 'I won't fuck men more powerful than me – I seek nothing from another person.... I only give the favour that a masturbation gives. I can't give you your fantasy. Some people lack the imaginary entirely ... though no one will admit it. Their vision is a postcard, a frozen scene, a panorama lightly photo-shopped to stop the movement, to freeze the taxis and the shoppers on the Champs Elysées....'

'I'm sure those languages come back,' he says. 'You heard them all when you were in the street....' He presses his knee against Petronia's thigh – she takes it as a threat, since she's been clear; she doesn't need, believe in, promises.

'Now, you should have less to lose,' she says. 'Before, you had a sabre, and an opponent. Now, in a team, you've mates who cover for you....'

'It's not at all like that,' he says. 'Each member of a team can boast a price. A fencer, though – the show is theirs, but their opponent is just one. A good fencer wins against a better one – but also, most often, against a worse. It's natural. The fencer with her foil is like the diamond on a drill. A bright-star.

'A crowd, a team, is different entirely: it can beat another whole team, reserves and coaches, backers of all kinds, and fans. The team – is God.

'The fencer – just a guy with a fake sword? The quarter-back – is the starring deity who wins the city's wars. I'd be she.

'And I retract: we're not exactly like I said.... Clinging on; not the tops. Regime? We're rank and file. Precarious. Spavined. And so, we seek out pompous ones like you, jail you, don't let you out, and some – they croak.' And he makes frog-noises, to make the point.

'You need to keep your place,' Petronia says. 'And win. You could just as well seek mass transfer to the other side.... But to me, it sounds as if you have a different plan: that owning to it – is a treason. You don't confess, to anything. You're the guy who coats the foil tip with the venom. You mark the cards, deflate the ball....'

'That's why we need to see,' he says. 'How strong your legs are. Can you run? Wave your arms and shout? I ask myself the same, many times a day.'

'It's not my thing,' Petronia says. 'Tactics, that is.'

'Exactly so,' says Takis. 'That is exactly what I said. You're a born enemy.'

'I oppose everything that threatens me. Duff choices that endanger my existence,' she says. 'That's why you think I am an enemy.'

'The cake shop, the offal point,' he says. 'That crowd. They ate together, then they danced together. Everything could be passed across and shared, everything most intimate – the guts, the brains, the eyes, the heart.

'We could put someone you know on trial – for passing. Trading and excreting. Hiding the deaths.'

'That would scare everyone,' she says. 'A smart ploy, yes.'

*

'I know what you want,' Petronia says. 'I know no one, I have no information. In general, the result of my observation is – everybody is like Fritz and Vinnie. A few are like Nadia, who has more control.'

Sport? she thinks. How I hate sport, refinement, being good and getting better and, worst of all – being best. The body, and its trickery. What idiocy, and how I hate what everybody likes, the little tripping songs, the movies with a quirk, the noise, the silence ... the hairless skinny bodies....

'I'd take lessons from Nadia,' Takis says. 'Except I'd need to buy insurance. And, Petronia, you mistake the nature of this industry. Information – is not something you know or don't, and get it from a source. It's what we all have, and bargain with. Or else – it's poetry that no one wants to publish.'

'That's mine,' Petronia says. 'Poetry. It's obscene and apocalyptic. Everyone has that inside, it's mystery where it starts, and no one wants to share the source....'

Takis laughs, and nods. Petronia goes on. 'And don't insist with Nadia. If you had read the book at school ... those dwarves, her family – they are compressed and miniaturised. Voyaging afar, even in worm-holes, makes you desiccated, curled and squashed, like ox-tongue in a can, diminished and compacted in your physical size, while it expands your brain – and so you need a larger, more elastic head. If they are called to reach their real, their authentic size – they're thirty metres tall, Takis – like the angels, who, when they hear the trumpet call, must leave their dwellings, stand in the garden with their swords and wheeee! Up they spring, like magic beans that take you up their stalk, into the castle where they are the shock troops, the Potsdam Grenadiers of the Immortal Lord .... except – they are at once the sturdy stalk and full of beans; like Serbians partying on dodgem cars – they are their ladder and the climbers too – they swarm, multiplying in the service of God, like huge rats raised on pituitary glands ... a gigantism you will find in peas grown by Lysenko in his garden of delights....'

They laugh: 'Yes, yes,' says Takis. 'That's the trick! You know your literature and science, Petronia; the poems written inside aubergines ... all that. Ah yes – you don't imagine how often I've sat here and heard the same tale from my clients, my visitors! The detail changes, obviously – accept it, don't travail. There's lots of you, Petronia, but only one of Nadia....'

'That's why you waste your life,' she says. 'Sat in that banal chair, trying to control the waves, the light and dark ... and all of me. And fantasising about a world where people don't fear you and despise you.'

'Oh, that song!' says Takis. 'I hear it every day, it never palls. The things you think should make me sad – are what drives me, on and on....'

*

'They think I'm dangerous,' Petronia tells Vanessa. 'I don't. I'd like to be ... awkward. Autonomous. But, I can't think of anything I'd do that can't be stopped before it starts, or when all concerned along with me will not be caught and punished.

'If they run out of cops and soldiers – it doesn't matter. They can get some robot stuff sent through the mail....

'Can you think how we could think, as we want to, dear Vanessa?'

Vanessa nods. She usually nods, but sometimes shakes her head, and sometimes shakes.

'Why do I want, why bother – to wonder why it's all as it is?' Petronia asks. 'As if I'd say – it's all – everything – a miracle. Say it must be as it is, it will change, of course, but never as you want, and by your effort.'

She has no answer: receives none. 'I want to know,' she tells herself. 'The ship – where did everybody go, and come from? Was it a war? A trade? A flight, escape, an opportunity? A vision, since we were shipwrecked, castaways on a ship, cast off among the cast-offs ... a paradox, but then – the body doesn't recognise a paradox, a metaphor, *aporia*: it marches on until it can't. It doesn't pick up signals that will do it harm, that poke a finger in its brain and shell out info, like you shuck your pearl out of your oyster....

'It seems there's no way you can know, not for sure ... what you can't do, what is fore-known, what's interdicted, what has penalties foretold – as sure, at least, as once you thought you were.

'There's something you are free to think in, a space – the past. A no-man's land, it's hard to occupy, to flatten, to depopulate. Like almost all the present, it doesn't quite exist – or, NO! It doesn't exist at all, although it's left its traces all around. It doesn't bother anyone because–'

'It's past,' Vanessa says. 'Now, Petronia, wheel me to another place, although....'

Petronia knows – Vanessa on her couch, with wheels, is set up for a banquet or an orgy, but – the body isn't up to it.

That should make Petronia reflect – a jog? A working-out? Some polish to bring out muscle-tone? The mind, the brain – a wrestling mat, a place for free-for-all, and grand theft – and now, the body too? Vulnerable, crumbling fast, needing a perpetual fine tune – an instrument so wonderful you can't rely on it: how tough it is to prise it off its bed and out the door ... thronged round, there is the sun, the cops, the insects and the bugs ... bugs of all degrees of toxic penetration, alas

– the leg that yields, the tendon snapping like a stay-wire holding the big top, as you prance and twirl....

'No time,' Petronia tells her friend, 'for indulgence of *luxuria*. It's time for an austere regime – counting the body's beats and once a day – a riff. You get to do a solo. An orgasm, quaff a jeroboam of blue Bols, execute a hundred press-ups. Remember you are watched and measured. Think very carefully – or, better, not at all....'

'I'm with you there,' Vanessa says. 'The body. It's never done me any good....'

*

I make a magnificent mistress, Petronia thinks. The first night, I'd make him a fine last supper. I never cooked for anyone but me, and not so much for me. But Takis, he deserves a special touch ... What should I put in? Why, of course I'd ask at the offal point. Everyone who deals in food will know what kills the humans off – a gland you find in snails, an ape's brain braised in butter that will rot your own – stuff for the gourmet.... A sauce that shrinks; shrinks your guts so nothing ever passes ... ouch!

That's what the banquets do for you, while you were waiting for the orgies. Everybody has to praise the chef – he's done for all your friends and enemies, a little praise may save you.... It won't save Takis, not from me....

JUST A HYPOTHESIS

'Regret,' says Takis, 'For what we missed out on, or did clumsily – that's probably universal. But part of being human is regret for what we know we did that's wrong. Not just a vague sense of blame, culpability, guilt for history or what society or people have made us, made us do – but knowing we've done wrong.... that we, all, are capable of being bad – it's explosive. It leads us on – to forgive the unforgivable, stimulates us to being good – or more often, going on to be more bad.

'There's no one blameless – and for most, it's a long-term situation, long-term blame – living with people we treat bad, exploit them; or we have clients that we need and string along, but who don't need us, who'd do better never to have known us. Not to mention the betrayals mental or physical – of partners, friends, or countries ... philosophies, standards, values.... Blame and guilt – produce forgiveness. To forgive is justice – it's the nearest you will come ... should come.'

'No, Takis,' says Petronia. 'That's not me. I feel no guilt or blame, I never betrayed, did nothing I regretted at the time or since. Don't try this line with me.

'I told you – I understand why people run, escape, are persecuted and restrained. What I ask is – what do I do, and why am I there? Why do things happen to me when I have no response, and no responsibility?'

'Is there chance? Happenstance?' asks Takis, puzzled. 'That's a hard question with an easy answer.'

'No,' says Petronia. 'I know all that. Why am I there, why are they there? Why do things, situations, happen to me, and what do they mean?'

'Why do I do what I do, and what does it mean?' asks Takis, still more puzzled.

'No,' says Petronia. 'That's easy. You're weak, a sadist in a mild way, a bureaucrat without imagination, but with fantasies of survival and not being held to account for what you've done. Like all bosses, you're a spy. That's not me, not at all. I can explain *you* totally, but not....'

'You. The ship. The fish,' says Takis. 'It doesn't matter.'

'It matters to me,' she says. '*Les mains d'Orlac* ... the innocent who lost his hands, they grafted on a murderer's pair, and he became a murderer.... I ask myself, do you need to lose your arms and legs...?'

'It's a movie, appears in a book,' says Takis. 'Why do good people do bad, out of character, it asks. It's an invention. A fraud. Someone else's hands.'

'Yes,' says Petronia. 'We are characters; where are we going, why are the scenes set up as they are and what's behind it all? Why is reality – like that: real. What decides, between what is real, what not, what is being, what non-being. We know how our problems can be – could be – solved. So – what is left is ... "is there ... a mind – yours or another's, a determinacy, over-determination, accident ... that reveals what matters, why...."'

'Nothing,' says Takis. 'There's nothing. No Mind. We don't believe that any more. You're right – it doesn't matter because that's the way it is. You don't have a puzzle, because we solve the puzzles, and if we don't – they solve us: dissolve us. All that's left – *is*. But, you're wrong, confused, because it's not like that – although I don't know what *is* like that, nor what is not.'

We all think, all the time – is this info we want let out, and will it harm us, will we go to jail? Better to be Takis than in front of him ... what does he want to know, to have us confess, invent?

'I told you, Takis,' says Petronia. 'Behind you is you.'

*

'I feel it's time for another trip,' Petronia tells Vinnie. 'You'd be welcome to come along – no contact, naturally....'

'I'm flattered,' Vinnie says: 'A long trip's what you need, but – have you heard the phrase "*un bacio della morte*"*?* Your comrades may describe you as that, when they holiday with you ... a kiss of death.'

'I don't even know the language,' says Petronia.

'We're waiting, Fritz and I, for an invite from Nadia,' Vinnie says. 'She's about to win a castle – the highest one, who climbs up and up and does their turn, without a fall, inherits the castle from the one before who climbed and climbed and....'

'Now, that's a sport that makes some sense,' Petronia says. 'But castles are no fun to stay in....'

'Well,' Vinnie says. 'That's settled then. I'll stay and wait. It's remarkable there is a prize so big. And Fritz agrees. When you return, tell us what was inexplicable, Petronia – and if you liberated camps and stopped some wars.'

They laugh: 'I'm wary of the banqueting,' Petronia says, 'but orgies are on my list of things to do.'

'Advice,' says Fritz: 'Don't start your metaphysical conversation when you're on the bus....'

'No,' she says. 'No bus. It might be camels this time. Yaks or donkeys.'

'Keep it simple, Petronia,' Vinnie says. 'No questions, only answers.'

'You needn't tell me, Petronia,' Fritz says. 'But are you on one side, or all of them? There isn't room or time to sound out everyone, so they just classify you as 'suspicious' ... sometimes 'auspicious'. No one does well, but that is good, we're poor, and so the country's running costs are low ... You're like us all, except – the link to Takis. A bond or bondage...?'

'Of course, I write it all,' she says. 'All that I see and feel.'

'Maybe the emperor's your fan,' says Fritz. 'There's a study for you – the emperor of an empire that's invisible but real, and has a budget and badged personnel.'

TRISTES TROPIQUES

It's hard to fall off a camel – harder than off a horse, they say. The motion, they also say, is like a ship's. Petronia laments in silence – you can't speak to anyone face to face: – you shout into the back of someone in the line in front. The camel takes you, like Petronia's ship – to nowhere in particular. But with determination, purpose, it would seem....

'*Malaise,*' she says aloud. 'Is that what I have? Discomfort with everything and no tools to help me dig a way – out of my cell, on to the overhanging cliff where this grand jail is built.'

The guide shouts back: 'There's nothing here. Before we get to something, there are ten days, where nothing is, but everything is always changing – the dunes.... You'd assume there's something underneath that gives a rudimentary shape. It isn't so. Or, rather – we don't know. Each day the landscape is entirely different and, to our senses – it's the same. Similar. There is no measure – nothing of substance – maybe the wind. Nothing of time – maybe from the last time I led some curious and sceptical guys around, some memory remains.

'Be patient....'

No, Petronia thinks. I have my answer if there's invites to an orgy, maybe I'd join in and find a different soul inside myself – the banquets too – you can always spit things out or throw them up. But – 'nothing'. How do I confront it? Patience is a con.

Experience, she thinks. Experience is real; it's what I'm having, and for some, it is the only test of what is real. And yet – they say experience is experience *of* the real, but it's incommunicable itself, untestable except by people who agree with what can't be tested or agreed – by saying 'yes', or even 'possibly'. Who trusts them anyway, the guys who say their 'yes' and 'no'? Think of Lviv – what sense does 'territorial integrity' have? Same country, different people? It's true you can't move continents around, or even provinces – so what is changed is real but it's not location – it's authority and maps and trucking people in and out and making claims ... But after all, that's all we have, I guess – like climbing up and down these dunes that tomorrow – will have gone. Or trekked to somewhere else, lain down on other dunes....

And take me, take Vanessa – even Vinnie. What are our distinguishing marks, our features? Parents and beliefs? What shifting landscape made them, then us together, and ... now...? They change, like these enormous fucking dunes that take all day to climb and next day they are gone and there is flatness all around.... I bought the books and saw how states begin in toil and blood and they are improvised and angry, I shall be mobilised, and Vinnie now's so old there's no more hope for him than linger in his hut and brave it out and famished, eat the cat and curse his god or gods and hope.... Hope? That's slender, thinks Petronia, if you think of Lwow.

'Experience....' she shouts to the back of the guy some distances in front....

'Wonderful!' maybe she hears the shout come back. 'A mirage,' she shouts out, 'the real' ... a hot wind takes it back – 'Ignore it,' comes the shout, and then the sand comes whirling round, there is no forward and no back.

Hold on the rope, she thinks, if only there was one. Hope and rope – a classic rhyme – those camel trains years back – they sang the same song over, hundreds of times, to keep them all together, all in line, but this time – we are citizens from everywhere, we don't all know the words of anything at all....

It's dark. The guide says, 'Each one tells a story, so we can go to sleep.' They come round to Petronia.

'I don't know stories,' Petronia says. She's the only lady philosopher vacationing on a camel. 'And I won't sing.'

'Your name,' says the guide, 'Make up something about that.'

'My family thinks we – the family – can go back to the Romans,' she says. 'There's been a poet, a gourmet and a lecher among the ancestors.... Just the one person.'

'We all have those,' the guide says. He's weary. 'We all go back to one person ... there might be two, but we only know of one ... an Eve who created Adam and regretted it, had to give him something to do, and stuck a penis on ... a folly for us all....'

'The Romans found a paradise here,' says a guy. 'They ruined it and made this desert. Here, we were all Arabs then, but dabbled in theology – and what a mess we made.... Invasion, occupation – it denatures you and makes you wild....'

'I'll witness to it,' says Petronia, but they start to shout her down, and pinch her.... 'Where's the lechery, then,' they shout, and someone says, 'give us a line of Roman poetry, to see that you don't lie....'

Of course, not one true line comes to her mind: 'dulce et decorum est....' Is that a poem? It's the last quote needed at this time.... 'pro patria mori....'

'It's just a name,' Petronia says. 'They give you one that shows you are in favour of the winning side. We didn't prosper from the strategy ... banquets and orgies, responsibilities, betrayal – then the garrotte ... that was our parabola of fame, and I could say I follow, in a modest way, the path of their excesses, their intellect, their gluttony....'

But the other travellers won't be appeased.

'You made this ghastly landscape,' says the guide. 'Atonement now, Petronia. This is the spot where you can make apology, and we can take resentment out....'

They gather round.

Maybe, Petronia thinks, humiliation is included in the price. I never read the details of a tour because I know I'm ignorant of what I'll see, and that is why I want to go....

The difference between rape and an orgy, in its outlines, is you pay to take part in an orgy, but not for being raped. 'Hey,' Petronia shouts. 'Remember! I haven't paid. Only when I get back safe.'

The guide remembers. 'Stop!' he shouts. 'We all want to take it out on Romans, dead or alive. They're like the Russians, probably also like the Chinese ... for sure, like Americans and all their worldwide friends – and stop! A list's invidious. Everyone wants to make friends, however dodgy, to join with them to beat their enemies. That is the world. Make friends from those you've bullied and defeated. At last – someone has read history and drawn the lesson. Friends! Go forth and muster them! See if you find – just one.

'But there's exceptions, possibly. There are individuals – like Petronia here, who renounce their antecedents and repent – in the name of dead and living; and are eager to rewrite the past .... Not gang up on the rest.'

'Yes, oh yes,' she says. 'I suspend my search for what is real and not – and whether it matters all that much. I am not I – not the creature with a past, with ancestors. Not an "I" with precedents, a future too....'

And on she rambles, gaining time – and wonders, did she pack her snicker-snee, a lady's shooter, or a viral spray ... defence and lying is permitted, if it saves your skin ...

'Tomorrow,' shouts the guide. 'Discovery begins. We pass the shifting sands, and all is clear....' And so they sleep and dream. The camels too, pretend to sleep – they share one dream:

Flat, flat, as far as you can see. No rope, no rider, and no merchandise. No burden on our back. No silly roundelay, no need to have a guide. On, on, for days, pass them exactly, they are identical – a diet light and knowledge long accumulated, that ripens into wisdom. 'The present is the mirror of the past' – that's a wise, even the wisest, observation 'they' can make. Every seven days there is a hole and you fill up with water, and then – it's flat, flat for another seven days. And that is wisdom, all you need to know, and it fits perfectly with what you need to live your years allotted and your kids maturing and your muscles going slack, and there's no destination, and it's good and what to do besides, if there were *destinations? ... and you fill up with water and you walk on for seven days, it's flat, and there's a water-hole*

But you know, that camels will go on and on, so long as it is flat; and if there's dunes and wind and storms – in the end, it will be flat ...

Wisdom, Petronia thinks, not daring to sleep or dream – is, that in the end, it's flat.

*

'Don't be afraid, Petronia,' the guide Hashim tells her next day. 'Fear makes no difference, and being paranoid would make no difference at all.'

'I'm thwarted,' says Petronia. 'That is true. But I'm free ... just, things don't seem to come to port.'

'You lose jobs?' Hashim asks. 'That's a good sign, tells you how you won't find rest.'

'Oh,' she says, 'I never worked for pay. I prize my wits, but in the end....'

'They don't put your wits on the menu in the offal joint,' he says. They laugh.

'Yes,' she says, 'there's that. Not managing. Meeting Takis all the time. But there's my enterprise. I need to know: to seek discovery? Or invention? Which do you aim for – discovery? What's there. Or invention: what isn't there. If your real is solid and extensive – either way, it wouldn't bother you. There's enough all round for everyone....'

'No,' he says. 'No aims and no ideas. I took a course. I come from far away. It's you the problem, not your method. You're vulnerable because everybody sees and knows you are the enemy. I guide, but partly – I'm an enemy too. Your enemy. I recognise the normal ones, the law-and-order types: tourists, spectators, investors – come to see what 'nothing' might be like.

'Are enemies to fear or to expect? They are far and few. You expect an enemy to have some friends, to balance out – with you, it isn't so.

'You aren't my personal enemy, Petronia, only because you've not yet paid.'

She confesses – 'I don't know if I can. Takis would pay for me – but no man I've ever known has been grown up: – they're like a grandad's suits, hung up and mothy, inherited from the dead and worn and worn because the cloth is good, when they should pass, pass out of style ... into the bin. Men are cheap. So, if they pay, they want return, that costs much more. Much.

'I want to miss nothing, but not be bought, not by anybody.'

'I don't believe it's money,' Hashim says. 'That's clean. For you, it's not having a destination; being sat up on a camel that would walk on for ever.... You think someone must know where you are heading ... but you can't ask the camel that....'

'Oh, destinations,' Petronia says off-handed. 'It's knowing I have on the right shoes at the start. So I could run well, real fast....'

'Well,' says Hashim, 'quite evidently, Petronia, you can't.'

*

When the trip is long since past and ever after, Petronia thinks of Hashim as 'that shit'. She'd had no expectation that he'd be from 'another side' she might be looking for.... He sees her as one of those who ride out in the nothingness, say nothing worth reporting. You can't spy on her. The experience of being lost and guided, roped in to strangers, and insulted – some people seek it out ... Petronia does.

There's bombs to blow us all up and away in half an hour – and yet they pay Takis to quiz and niggle with Petronia ... because you never know who's the real enemy... or if everybody is.

*

Hashim says, 'We have arrived.'

There's high walls with crumbling tops, the colour's sand, they're made of it. It is a wonder. Until the colonisers came, it served as a defence and garrison. Palace and holy place. Afterwards – a wonder all the same.

Cash. It's everywhere, but not here, not visibly. You scrabble for it, like for water, spilt on the sand.

Hashim insists – 'look what the whites have done to Africa', and all agree. Before the white guys came – there was an empire, armies, trade and even slaves, but it all went fairly well, kept to its path. There were the poor who worked, the rich who said they did as well, but didn't sweat. And now, it's all been stolen, carried off. Slaves by the ton. People have no resources, Hashim says, none at all, not even risking going down a mine. Nothing grows. It's hot – like everywhere is hot. The tourists nod and don't enquire, and there's delay. They blame Petronia....

Hashim says he'll keep Petronia here until she pays. The others, the travellers – they agree: it's malice, but – so what? The camels – they've been rented, now they leave the scene. The tourists, without Petronia, take the bus.

'I can't pay unless I go back where I left and send it to you,' Petronia tells Hashim.

'Go back, and I'll never see a cent,' he says.

The others go down south, Petronia stays, confined, the locals say they can't decide who's right: Hashim and Petronia aren't ones of them, not known nor trusted, and no one understands the arguments. They say: avoiding being sucked in. The mediators say Petronia should have paid up-front – 'the world is made that way – you want to see the wonders, so you invest in your desires ... and pay for them, before you leave.'

*

'Don't you want to touch me?' Petronia asks Hashim. 'Not that I want it. Rather, I want to be the object of desire. Touching makes desire diminish, if it should flare. Touching the object – produces something, not desire but – like holding a vase. Or, with the eyes: a picture. A dog, a horse – a journey, a danger outstripped. Touch them, you take their magic charge, they're neutralised, digested. A void filled up in you.'

'If I touched you,' Hashim says, 'it might not be desire at all.'

'That's what I said,' she says. 'It never is. Not stable. You, Hashim, think desire is bargaining. No: – I'm a lute: how's your touch? You don't look musical – but the instrument's indifferent anyway. It's in and for itself – it doesn't care who strums. It doesn't negotiate.'

'I'm big in Darband,' Hashim says, disconcerted. 'It might be the most wonderful place anywhere in the world.'

'I met some Georgians – they too were big in Darband and everywhere, but they fell foul of someone,' says Petronia.

'Other Georgians, for sure,' says Hashim.

It's not so, Petronia thinks – they went into a camp, and couldn't explain where they were from. Besides, Hashim – a course in tourism, in guiding? – real big guys don't do that.... There's trucks, that leave at night. They take the hopeful ones, the desperate – up north, to prison, to enslavement, and a drowning of what's left ... then, paradise.

Maybe, she thinks, I'll hitch a ride and pay the traffickers later when I'm safe.

It doesn't seem a likely scheme. She waits and waits – more tourists come, she mixes in with them – some go south, to gawp at miners, gawp at anything – and some have seen it all, and go up north. Home. The counting isn't good, and she fits in ... bus, plane. She waves to the trucks when she's in the bus – she's the only one who does.

Hashim might telephone and have her dumped, in nowhere; but it wouldn't serve.

Her idea's stupid, and it works. She's just an anomaly in the count.

*

'It was hard,' Petronia tells Vinnie. 'And there was nothing problematic, still less inexplicable. Lots to puzzle out, but no puzzle overall. I'm back at the beginning....'

'Nadia,' says Vinnie. 'She didn't win the castle. She's in an iron basket, and can't work the television without help. Can't work anything at all. A tragedy.'

*

'No, Petronia,' says Vanessa: 'I don't sympathise. You've become an ambiguous figure. You knew what you risked, everywhere and here – and you draw back. Now Nadia has fallen and....'

'There's nothing left for you, Vanessa,' says Petronia, much irritated at not having a good audience, 'Except to take yourself in hand.'

'Your trouble, Petronia,' Vanessa says, 'You pose false questions and if there's answers – there's nothing you can do with them. You're an animal on the forest floor – not the wise owl who sees and parses.... You must react to chance – the falling branch, the sink-hole, and the fox.'

CHANCE

Petronia follows the ad. 'Have a child the easy way: adorable new-borns – OR skip the tedious stages. Post-adolescents available, no incestuous tendencies....'

'It might be something I could try,' she tells the guy. 'I'm not too keen on continuity – families, the pledges, and the law. Divorce and burial, all that. And wills. Mine – is not so strong ... I thought there might be orgies, something might crop up – but no! Buses without air-conditioning – that's the nearest I have come to feeling pregnant. It deters you....'

The guy gives her a leaflet. Vanessa says, 'Yes! What an idea. A son – to keep you and me interested, and all the lady heteros as well. I might consider cleaning up my face....'

'I'd like to try a son,' Petronia tells the guy: 'About twenty and post-Marxist, a pseudo-virgin, no outside ties, and no beliefs – though open to adopt all mine.'

'Everyone wants that,' the guy says. 'Don't you have some special needs? Some people look way back to Roman times, they want some guy to follow them and rule the world, command the legions and the bombing planes.... Kill their family and friends, their associates: they want a challenge – even when they're parenting from choice....'

They laugh.

'No, no,' Petronia says. 'I need a person who will share my questioning and straighten out my path.'

'And how'll you pay?' the guy asks her: 'And go on paying? It's more a rental than a sale, you see.'

*

'There's three levels,' Petronia tells Vanessa: 'of mother. "Normal", "mediocre" and "demanding". I'm "demanding".'

'He'd need a room, or space at least, Petronia,' Vanessa says, repairing her features, smacking her lips to flush them red and fleshy.

'I don't think of that,' Petronia says: 'It isn't up to me.'

*

'"Helio",' says Petronia. 'Sounds Spanish. Colombia perhaps. Don't tell me – keep your secrets ... your traffic, the cartel.... Find a place to doss, and if you and your friends are the dancing kind – best go outside, I wouldn't trust these floors....'

Helio meditates, takes special stuff to concentrate. He's a champion at electronic games, and has a special friend who sings hillbilly songs....

'It doesn't work,' Petronia tells Vanessa. 'I had a plan – I shouldn't have. I'd go with Helio's flow, but it's erratic. He doesn't share his pills – and these games! He makes out on the net how he's some politico in Africa. It seems to me – he is inveigling....'

'Oh, throw him back in, Petronia,' Vanessa says. 'You've nothing to bequeath, and he is not discrete. There's no familial link. It's a mismatch. No profit. He's a stereotype and a security disaster – there's nothing to be done with those.'

'You know,' Petronia says, 'I'm much too young to be his mother.'

'You make things up, Petronia,' says Vanessa. 'I know – it's your uncertainty. It's you that's the self-centred one. A son! But, if you reflect, to live without continuity – what's left?'

'Another question I can't answer properly,' says Petronia. 'However – I sent Helio back....'

'First the dog, and now the son,' says Vanessa, smirking, hiding a robust laugh. 'Beware, my love, your brakes have failed.'

'And I owe them – the traffickers: the tourist crowd, and now the adoption racket,' says Petronia, desperate and near to tears.

'Forget it,' says Vanessa. 'The merchandise is taken care of in each case. The goods is you, and here you are – integral and unmoved. Forget your show of suffering, and they'll forget how they provided an experience that you will stow away, in your attic, along with all the rest.'

'Helio was a joker,' says Petronia. 'He told those guys he was a leader, had mercenaries and super-weapons: obey him, they could have their state, their faith ... all sent from a table I had totted long ago, when it was left outside.... He messaged from it....'

'He wanted someone; he was lonely, I expect,' Vanessa says. 'You too ... and me. But what you wanted wasn't him....'

'Poor Nadia,' says Petronia. 'Her shame. It's not so much from falling, being broken up – it's having told us she was good, and good up high.... I suffer with her ... I felt short of someone, lots of people, myself too ... so I picked out Helio....'

'Yes,' Vanessa says, 'We suffer for each other and ourselves, and some people seem quite permanent and stable, and then....'

'They drop.' Petronia says. 'I never give the others an expectation, a hope....'

'That's so,' Vanessa says: 'You've always been consistent at it.'

*

It's so hard to get things done, Petronia thinks. If there's a boss, an emperor – you have no effect on anything, and if you are his confidant, you stand to end up bad ... at his hands, or along with him when down he goes.

These modern countries – full of laws and people who've been round for centuries more than you and yours ... They call you in, to check you walk the line. You'd think opinions were for free and only actions are controlled. It isn't so – there are the lists, the interviews. Not on the right side? – they can tell at the first sight ... some jail-time to soften you...?

Predict the worst and hope for solidarity? – forget it. It's imagination, and everyone has that, and sees catastrophe all day. Doomsters abound, they're quite correct, so they can be ignored.... If you are stressed – try something quite ridiculous – don't hector, don't campaign....

Dictators do only what they want. Democracies – they aren't a counter where you pay and order.... You are free, not to get anything you want. If you have the money, you can get what's needed anyway. The system works like that.

Democracies can take against the people they don't like – whether they're among you, like indigenes ... or, the guardians might come in stealthily by night, you may have robbed them long ago – they have the power to harass you, beat and shoot you ... all your lives, and long beyond....

Monsters – my Monster in particular, not just a person or the people – they are my world: my civilisation. That's my Monster. Civilisation – the only place where anything can happen – where it all happens.... where what has happened in the past – made my civilisation happen. My Monster made me, shapes me: my civilisation is my Monster, *my* Monster ... you will understand...!

With cash – you don't need convince anyone, or make a case. You are a mini-state. No wonder, Petronia thinks, things happen that can't be explained, that ought not to happen anyway but more and more they do ... and they keep on happening, until....

Until you have a heap of money. But how?

*

This may be how.

Takis says – 'You are a wonder, dear Petronia – a Cassandra who hits every happening – spot on...'

'I know I'll always be an enemy,' Petronia says. 'But I'm innocuous. Leave me alone. Don't threaten me....'

'You know,' says Takis. 'Political prisoners? You may think you're due for jail – but it's not an option. There are no prisoners. Yes, there are jails. For transiting. We need to keep our noses clean, and so – there's other ways to guarantee that we go steaming on ... just like that big ship that you stole ... You'll not be one of us, it's true – but there are many things you'd probably like to do, for due reward.... You, my dear, can help, serve, many sides. At once. Your body's of no interest – it's your future that's at risk ... even an advantage for you and us ... Your future's what we can dispose of, when we wish. Watch me fence, watch my sword and dagger, all around you, slash and sleuth ... – are you confused? Silent? Can you concentrate...?

'I think much broader than a side, a country. I offer you a share in my idea. What more could you desire? The future's – mine.'

'It's cash,' Petronia says. 'Present, not future. I've realised – my dangers come when I can't pay bills....'

Spies are eternal – not immortal, but it's not like Cold War times. There's no communists now, no destiny, not even a 'long-term' ... and almost all the countries inquisitive about what's going on are medium size; and spies are operatives – professionals and amateurs, but it's a career, or part of it, and not for dedicated traitors or romantics.... Nothing is simple, not justice, not equality – those, least of all. Petronia wouldn't need believe in one side more than any other – it's about the soldiers, nationalisms ... and cash that's given quite reluctantly. She's not a soldier, nor a diplomat, and not an expert in technology – so, where would she fit in? In a uniform?

THE OFFAL JOINT

Wars make you eat exotic stuff – gather snails and slugs, boil the cat and roast the dog. And afterwards – you miss it. Enterprising countries can stock foods that are no longer served in classy joints: – road kill, *carogna,* what is usually thrown away or taken by the workers in the abattoir to feed their kids ... if there is an abattoir.

Otherwise – it's evident. There *is* stuff the offal joint won't touch – seal flippers, bear's paws, deer's penis, porcupines squashed in smashes on the road. But bring on the black pudding and the white – aha! the sausages and who knows what goes in, the haggis and the *mortadella*, the humble pies the chitterlings the trotters .... Indeed, you might call it, all – 'smash' ... Then comes the tasty and forbidden stuff – the Romans with their cow's tail, calf's bowel: the entrails, sheep's brains; hearts and tongues, the *animelle, coratella* – but here we're into folklore, acceptable and rare... for the moment, passed out of fashion and necessity: and into larger, less fastidious, bellies.

'Pilchards in chocolate sauce' – a feast for Danes. 'Calves' foot jelly – mmmm.'

A shuffle on the dance-floor with a diplomat – the same with a Milanese with a taste for donkey flesh.

This is the last place where you'd find solidarity, *Kameradschaft*. No miners digging here – making a breakthrough for togetherness.

*

Spying? The dirt? It's a laugh! Petronia chats up the chef, the butchery guys are info'ed in – and so, away! Away, away! and on, on with details, evidence of every kind, the names! Photos and then pack-drill for the brassy military guys, who'd slunk off in the bushes with the passionate guardsmen, and the ministers of state....

Spying, blackmail ...

'I need a favour....' Petronia would say: and she's obliged, with a story, fresh, for Takis, for her boss.

'A surprise!' says Takis. 'A sex romp in Scandinavia – a premier, no less? Ministers in Italy – a whole table-full on the take...! Cardinals? No. No surprise, no interest. Old hats, those.'

'The fresh tittle-tattle will all be in tomorrow's news, I hope,' Petronia says.

'No, not at all,' says Takis. 'Everybody knows about the great, and their back stories – it's the photos that lend weight to this. The European Lady on the table, underneath the wolfhound – that is art....

'Generally, it's good old stuff – you've done well. They're all the banal ones, the suspects. The bosses are all documented now, and the pics will work as blackmail – enabling trade, exchange of info and of capital, lobbying, and trips for big guys ... science and wisdom, marketing and plans for atom bombs.... The ones who're fingered organise three days of feasting to avoid a boring time at home ... recriminations. Better banquets and orgies ... no shame, and so no blame.

'Well done, Petronia. Watch your back, and get some more....'

Gossip and dirt, snaps from the phones, a blue-print copied, or a statement from a bank ...

'This is it, is all?' Petronia asks. 'Spying? Orgies and banquets, just like we've heard...?'

Horrible, horrible, she thinks – although they're dead, the collateral, the martyred casualties: who once lived by their brains and paws ... the animals at the banquets! Cows, tapirs, peacocks and swans, with no farewell, no oration, no name not ever; no regret, just cupboard-love from farmers; no chorusing of brays and whinnies, clacking of hooves.... Where's the send-off, the real amazing gracefulness? – no! Nowhere, no love, just smacking of the lips. The knife, the plate. So justice requires it should be for us, Petronia thinks.

Larks' tongues, pressed and bound, singing on loops – talking books of blackbird arias ... their Goldberg variations infinitely varied ...

She weeps – for them, and for herself.

*

'That's the end for you, Petronia,' Vanessa says, with glee. 'A total sell-out. What next?'

'Oh,' Petronia says, not embarrassed. 'In the past, Takis would use his network to make an army, sell them arms, make them terrorists or counter – or just confuse. Drugs? You find a Kuomintang who needs the cash, and Mong to do the carrying. But that's been done, and all gone by. With Fentanyl – it's changed. You don't need farmers, fields, no prohibition, and no Scarface, the narco-states bring trouble to the country-masters, those states-men and -women who manipulate. For you – it's simple.... Just find a room and cook it up. That's all. And in the future – just the same. You'll only need another room, and different protagonists, experts: the cooks.

'And no, Takis isn't interested in the info wars. He knows what everybody thinks and plots: as everybody does. As for the secrets, "All too human" is his motto – what the other bosses do, it doesn't interest. Technology? – he barely recognises a big word. And he's only arms-lengths away from getting caught himself. Criminals, the real ones, scare him, they're so huge. So do big states, with all their tricks, their perseverance, and their courts.

'Now I have paid my debts, it's clear, if he wants me to advise him – the future fortunes lie in banks and food. Corner the market, rent the ships ... get financed....

'Trade the people, fight the wars – in person or by whispering round. Ship the people, fight the people, trade the wars ... and banks will pay for everything....'

For a moment – 'ship'. Petronia's mind flips back. Was hers, the great adventure – a portent? Have the ships, you have the trade ... the food. Rent the scientists – you have the drawings of the little fiddly pieces that make the world go round. Is she – was she – a rebel, victim, or accomplice?

Will Takis put together countries wide apart and have them, under the table, back a group of spoilers? Fundamentalists and warriors? Plotters? – 'None of this is me,' she tells Vanessa, 'but it's how it goes, year after year; an ugly infant grows and grows and in the end....'

'A bigger monster?' asks Vanessa. 'Bigger than your Monster? With unlikely parents? I don't care. I owe nothing, nothing to anybody. You did wrong, Petronia, when you paid your debts. Debt is the sea that makes us float. You can go broke, but still you'll live – it concentrates your mind, outwitting creditors and having them give you more cash. For those you owe to – if they sink, it's good, they were not worthy of your trust....

'You chose the solvent ones to ship you here and there – you are the subject, you reflect, you analyse what you have seen. You should be paid, my dear, not them ... for your intelligence.

'But now – you're in the sticky web that Takis spins. You have the choice – to be his master or his slave....'

'I have another option, I suppose – to be his mistress,' Petronia says and laughs. 'That's the worst choice I could make – a living death....'

'No, no,' Vanessa says. 'You were a radical, you wanted to repudiate what *was* – what seemed to be. You didn't want to be a boss, nor even prophet – but – you veered and gyred, a petrel in the storm ... tossed, but still aloft. You're lost? – but songbirds can't get lost. You'll perch somewhere, and someone will be seduced, and listen, charmed....'

'Banality,' Petronia says. 'I'm ending in it; triviality. No orgies and no banqueting ... and so, I didn't gain the confidences that would give me a position – and ... I fell....'

'Remember Nadia,' Vanessa says. 'As they say – "even dwarves started small", and all her siblings – small ... and getting smaller, and she, in her basket, curled up and powerless, like a beetle left with just its shell ... smaller than small, compressed by gravity. You fell, and alas – you felt you had become leviathan. Stuck on the sand.'

'I bet, apart from chagrin, Nadia's furious,' Petronia says.

'Emotions?' Vanessa says, stretching out her blotchy body, 'They are the scent of flowers – they go on when you're asleep, when it's dark, when your nose is blocked. It's good to know they're there, but after all – they're just attracting bees.'

'Honey and stings?' Petronia says, and laughs. 'Be serious, Vanessa. Takis and those like him – they know whatever happens: everything. They know.'

'How awful that must be! And even worse if many awful things – they make those happen too!' Vanessa says.

She's re-made her face – it's unlined, unblotched, unblebbed. But – after all, maybe it was better when it showed her ravages, her crumbly soul.

Petronia thinks: Vanessa's flesh – flaking like old plaster, those cave-like eyes, the cheeks poor wonky shelves bodged up, wavering on degraded two-by-twos.... It seemed more – honest? Human? Think of the brightness of the animal parts, the offal joint, blood-red – where all is consumed or binned, not like the wrecker's yard where you can find, re-use ... replacement parts. Spares. In the offal shop, those hearts and brains are served up double-quick, and then they're gone for good. Or ill. One-offs. Into your guts.

You even have to guess what animal they're taken from: there's no spirit of the wrecker's yard, no '– ah! I recognise a Peugeot lion ... a Trabant cadaver ... traces: a butterfly ... a fiddler....'

'Yes,' Petronia responds at last. 'That's what Takis says. Intelligence – it's on the label. They know it all, what happens, and who made it so. They know much more than God. They know who made God happen, that's for sure, because they've agents who have made it so.'

'Then,' says Vanessa, 'it's pointless to say you don't believe in God.'

'I think that's true,' Petronia says.

'And all the plots, the characters, the wit, the sentiment and reason – it's all been thought up, in an office on the seventh floor?' Vanessa says, playfully.

'You know, they also put The End,' Petronia says. 'They plan for it: the future – and naturally, planned it too. In the past ... But they can shift it, if something is resolved they thought was much too difficult for them....' and Petronia joshes her restored friend, but both of them are fearful ... oh, she thinks – the horrors ... the indeterminacy...! Oh for determinacy....

'I restored my face,' says Vanessa, in a low confidential tone, 'Because I have a public role. A tour guide. I've read up on it ... now, it's me.'

'Where?' Petronia asks, jealous and curious. 'There's nothing to see here, and you won't take them round the offal shop, I'm sure....'

'Oh,' says Vanessa, launching in. 'Archives, life stories.... There's steps – the ones where the pram went down, remember, in the movie: and those where you mustn't sit in Rome, the bridges where they threw Algerians off; the cyclodrome for deportees, the bullring where there was the massacre, not only of the bulls! – the ruins where the Romans had their sports ... the gate in Germany where the Russians stopped ... Those "Iron Gates" that are made of water and of stone. The ghettoes – one where there are only monuments, a labyrinth, no tombs.... Whole capitals where there's Africans who do the work and wish they were back home ... there's Syrians who do the same....'

'It sounds quite morbid,' says Petronia. 'If you come on holiday – it's orgies, banquets, that you want. And shopping too, of course.'

'Oh, that they do all day,' Vanessa says. 'They walk my tours at night, when it's less hot.'

They laugh. 'I'm sure they get their fill,' Petronia says. 'History is what we stroll within, tread on; each step is on another story – the basalt pavements from Vesuvius, hot dusty air from the Sahel, the bottles abandoned near the balustrade – the Tiger beer, the Stolichnaya, Pampero rum and bathtub gin.... The world's imported here to bring us cheer ... stone, dust and air ... and booze.... Whatever they are shown, my dear, they'll say it's beautiful ... there's people too, shipped in and picturesque....'

How she envies Vanessa ... a paying job, with tips....

'And you, Petronia – stuck at your keyhole, dishing dirt,' Vanessa says, delightedly.

*

'I only wanted,' Vinnie tells Petronia, 'To feel some human flesh, pressing against me, in desire if that's available....' He sweats, he trembles. He sneaks an arm around Petronia....

'Treasure your emotions, Vinnie dear,' Petronia says, thrusting him aside. 'I'm moving up a grade, into Intelligence.'

'Alas, we're many of us moving down,' says Vinnie. 'Poor Fritz – the robots come with orders stencilled in, there's nothing Fritz can say or make them do.

'So, maybe we shall never know about the ship. Is it a mystery? Are we? Was it designed and calculated ... those caravans of people from the sea, the land, and what they do and where they go?'

*

'You have to go to banquets,' Takis tells Petronia. 'Orgies is up to you. Don't complain – you have to show yourself, to have a public face ... or people might assume you're just a spy....'

'A guide?' Petronia asks. 'My friend says you get a public face, a guide's, by knowing history.'

'You only need a title,' Takis says. 'No history required to guide whatever. What shall it be?'

She thinks of the ship, the one they stole. High admiral.... High up the mast, that is, not on the pills.

'We rent our ships, we do not build,' he says. 'And we are land-locked too. Sharpen your wit, Petronia, refine your tired *boutades.*'

'"Historian", then,' says Petronia. 'I know the detail and the dross, and then, I guess, select what passes by. Expectations must be met – a scandal here and there, but also logic, and a plan....'

'Secretary of State,' says Takis. 'That's you. Write everything down, and file it where it's hard to find.'

She asks herself, 'but what's it for?' and doesn't question Takis.

There's tons of real, and tons of kitchen, French. Diplomacy and menus.... 'Was it for this,' she wonders, 'I recruited myself to be a trencherman? Plying my flatware in the Offal Joint, with honour, maybe even – a scrap of dignity?'

Vanessa mocks her – it irritates. Vanessa tells tales, no one knows if they're a spoof.

'Listen, Vanessa,' says Petronia. 'From now on – I'll invent. I'll be creative; post mortem – I'll be admired – like Mata Hari....'

'Even the Capitoline geese,' Vanessa says, much amused, 'were alarmed – even before people ate foie gras. Sound your trumpet, Petronia – look in the future, wake them up! Beware yourself....'

'My theme is lies,' Petronia says.

Invention: she improvises. A riff.

'Music, now: it's not its formal strength or innovation. Music written to be heard elicits emotion, that is all. Musicians see, imagine, structures, formal ones, and cloudy ones. The audience, however, listens for the sentiment – the passion, the skill of all those guys in suits and frocks who manage more or less to keep the time. Their dedication. Here comes the scherzo; the heart races, and the blood flows fast. The sorrowful bits, repeated themes, the solo that puts some guy high on the tightrope – what if she falls, and cracks a note, or whistles with her clarinet ...? what daring and what expectation ... mood follows mood, explosion follows elegy, a triple forte shakes the hall....

'Music is a structure for the musician. They know the architecture, what it looks like, how it stays vertical. They may, they must, sneak emotions in, and those are taken up by passive listeners. Emotion: – it's not structured, it's a sentiment, and so untranslatable; presumed, but can't be shared, measured, or foreseen. Each has her own reaction. Some have none.

'Prose – the novel. The writer has a fantasy – projected in the plot and characters. Her fantasy – she hopes it will chime with, engage, accelerate, what the reader fantasises. The writer draws the best part of a life lived there, in the book; and leaves the reader wanting more. She doesn't want, and cannot have, an exchange of fantasies with her fan. Whoa! – she thinks, my fantasy is mine, I don't want readers to start vocalising, and pushing their strangeness on to me! Read silently, and be far away ...! The hope is to create a fantasy which speaks to, engorges, combines with, enlivens, other fantasies. One page is printed with another, different, page, printed on its back....

'As with painting – an illusion. That the flat can be inhabited, the real seized, frozen – yet without decay and ageing. Time, motion, stopped: immortalised. The leer, the smirk – made permanent.

'So – our art's emotion; fantasy; illusion. The highest achievement or the airiest, and where does it stop? The judgement – is the receiver's: the amateur, the common type, not the creator. The paying public is what decides. The expert glimpses, dangles from, the structure: – everybody else apprehends a spirit. The structure – that's imaginary too. So – the map, the atlas, the way the earth's divided up – is fantasy, a fable – the spirit – air. The wind. And we, the people – blown this way and that, the power comes from our scythes and swords, our faces scarred to show where we belong ... all drift and rain and goats, conscription, mutiny – and now it's documents....

'Still, in art and life, we call this process "creation": not "a lie". Civilisations – they are tombs and painted shards. My creation – out of my head.... the Mind we don't believe in now ... the light-bulbs in our brains – invisible and flickering.... So – I'll create. And Takis should believe. My tales – he feels it as his reality, a true representation, structure – that he must pad out, pass on, – plated: with emotion. Then – yes, it's real ... it's credible....'

'And will that all be art?' Vanessa asks. 'All we take to be reality? All that is real originates in imagination, in tinkering with the palette, the thesaurus? What's false is true, because it's all there is?

'And can you convince your boss you are discovering *real* stuff? Your lies ... from out your head? Conventional types tell lies, but hate you telling whoppers in return.

'Remember – we're at war already, always: possessiveness and fear combine, into a clinging fast to what we love ... our life, possessions, and the blessed state of "nothing happening, not much at all". Peace: an illusion. A pregnant pause. An emotion: a time for puffing up and pretending to be brave and patriotic.... Is that your aim?

'So – everybody lies. And always will until the final victory. The biggest lie. Lies to themselves and to anyone at all who listens. The real's all lies. And is it art, Petronia, your lies? Does your boss care anyway?'

*

'If this did not have the sound of truth, Petronia, I'd say it was made up,' says Takis, on hearing Petronia's last tall tale. 'It's art, like our best liars make. It's structured excellently, the colour's right and fast, it makes us proud to fear the foe. We'll fight to save our leaking hut, neglected grannie, our corrupt establishment....

'It's art, and everything, it seems, is art – the sound, the colours and the narrative.... A stroll through smouldering woods? I hear you say – "it's Mahler's Sixth!" ... We live, and now we'll die, for art, Petronia.

'For sure, you'll end up with the rank of colonel, even as a general of the reserve....'

'It seems this solves my problem of the real, and why what happens cannot happen differently,' Petronia says. 'My ship? It's art, perhaps. Not really real. Not now.'

'You distinguish between what you think is there, experienced, and what you can create yourself,' he says. 'You don't lie, because you start off from your real. That's what you say: but there's no test. No one can doubt that what's created by you – is real...! But where it comes from.... Only the hidden, skulltight brains can tell what is the real ... from what is real.... Your universe contains no lies, because there's nothing else – the problem's solved. What is, is. Maybe the problem too was false....'

'I wouldn't lie to you, Takis,' Petronia says.

*

'I want you to keep your presence in the Offal Shop, Petronia,' Takis says. 'Don't try to tell them what's true and what is not and what is art. I'll do that, that is now my task. But you've been right about one thing – that what is boiling is not just heat and meat, but war, more and more, more general wars....'

'I know,' Petronia says. 'No one doesn't see that.

'At least I've paid my debts.'

They laugh. 'Don't say I've not been loyal to you, Takis,' Petronia says.

*

'It all sounds plausible, Petronia,' Takis says, listening to more tall stories. 'That biggish guy wants to fuck his sister, who for sure's the favourite of that next-door big dictator. She – the sibling of the biggish guy – is a rare, a juicy fruit. I don't blame him, not a bit. But – would the *echt* big guy next door take reprisals, shoot shells, so all the other big guy's guardsmen get knocked over in the counter-thrust? Then, there's all the allies falling out and sabotaging one another? Possible, but risky, don't you think?'

'I eavesdrop, Takis, I don't do strategy,' Petronia says, defending.

'It's like I think about the music,' Takis says. 'You do the emotions – I do structure. I make the story plausible. We two, we don't make music – not the popular kind at least – and not together. Most people make things up, and in war you have to, or you'd ask for peace. Remember anyway, Petronia – both sides have best boxes, starting off with little soldiers, airmen, watermen and firemen – all are knocked over regular, and don't get up. You can't feel emotional about them, though everybody in command, like me, we lie, and say we're sad. Structure! We need our war aims to be achieved or sort of ... after all, we started this, it's our parade.... Power? You say it's wind – that's tempests and tornadoes too. We ride it, maybe we invent it too, create. More power, more wind, more heat and steam and smoke, the strongest are the hottest and the windiest....

'"We" – not me, you understand, not me at all – the grammar's self-explanatory. So, Petronia – is it so, that allies start to fall apart because of friends' passes at their relatives? That's what you say.

'And, yes: we went to war because the others are our brothers, lost, the land's not theirs, but them we love, hope to embrace them, all that's left, and straighten out their thoughts, get rid of all their leadership, iron out our own reluctant awkward squads, recalcitrants and sceptics, make more weapons, bigger, sneakier ... we must trade emotions, sell, exchange, keep the wobbling structures for ourselves, the pros are us.... These guys, the stories that you bring ... brothers, sisters all, we know it, humans are a family, incestuous and murderous ... wrestling and intercourse – it all looks much the same, and of course – we're serious about our conflicts – but these tales, Petronia...? A war? Your story? Is it all for nooky among relatives?'

'That's the buzz,' Petronia says, much stressed, embarrassed by the quiz. 'It's what you've just described. Brothers, sisters all ... I'll check it out, of course....' She scuttles off ... emotions, the ephemeral. Her taradiddles – can they become a structure, and with what outcome for herself? She knows she lies – so, what is new? Is she naive, doing what we know and thinking she's the first?

'Which side am I on?' she asks herself. 'I don't feel anything for any of them – all are civilised and hope they can destroy the other's civilisation, which is theirs as well – and then they think the civilisation that is crushed and buried will be dug up and put on show – the bangles and the bows – bows for hair, and for archery.... I'll ask Vanessa,' she declares, then: 'Oh no! She educates! She takes you round, she guides. All's civilisation! Not structure nor emotion there, just tales and spectacles.... Leadership, her as the guide – and fables.'

*

Liar. She thinks. Let's polish it and make it – maybe not a creed, a profession, but something more than hobby, the fun-time of the architect who toys with poetry. I'll try it out. Write it, not on my passport or my tax return, perhaps – but on a notice on my door.

'Advocate....'

That's what you need – a lawyer who will tell lies for you. A lawyer-liar. The diplomats – it's known.... Lie's what they do.

Is there a liar's school, or must you improvise? Traditionally, a lie is in the liar's interest – but let's have a wider view.

I'll publicise: 'Establishing a new real – solid and reproducible as it's been, but now, professionally traduced by a qualified liar. Forgery and false witness a speciality. Reasonable rates. Commercial guarantees, reviews – rates on request.'

*

Try it out.

'Vanessa,' Petronia says. 'I'm a liar.'

'Of course you are, my love – you are a pro, much better than us amateurs,' Vanessa says.

Petronia says: 'I want to start off honestly: "I lie." And see who takes the risk with me....'

'Oh no!' Vanessa crows. 'The Cretan Paradox! Remember that – all liars lie, how do you discern the truth? Is everything a lie? True?'

'Stop there,' Petronia says. 'I've done all that, established it, my argument. Forget the Cretans. How in any case do we discern the truth, when there's no Cretans round? I'm lying so that lies will become the truth. Forget belief – it doesn't last. The Cretans – they can't all be Cretans ... someone must really lie, and not dissimulate, telling the truth. The point is, anyway – all concerned must know the lie, the truth – just as I say.

'I'll find a test to give me credit for my porkies ...'

*

Beware, Petronia. Test, attest, detest – all you can imagine, all you'll find, is that between the truth and lies there is a distance paper-thin ... between two truths – enormous space; between two lies – the same. Space, though – is nothing. And where's the metaphorical – seemingly outside the real, outside the lie...?And banquets, orgies, death, the lovers who you do not love – all yours, all evanescent ... untrue, death especially? Can you fit those in?

Intention. Does it all come down to that? Meaning's what we mean? No, for certain no.... But then, what?

*

'You are mistaken,' Vinnie says. 'You show your hand, or make as if you do. Yours – is treachery, letting down the side. If you say you are a traitor, even if you aren't – you'll end up really bad. You leave no space. You can't tell anyone you're loyal – you will not be believed. The commonplaces – all untrue. Just lies. Not true, not false. Just what you say.'

'Oh, people are so complicated,' Petronia says. 'So simple. They don't know how things work, and how they end....'

'Nothing ends,' says Vinnie. 'The ship – went on. Just – we weren't on it any more, and so we never know where it was destined....'

'It wasn't destined anywhere,' Petronia says. 'That's why the wheel was fixed. It was us who were not destined, but we climbed on....'

'It's not like that,' says Vinnie, wearily. 'You have a kinky brain, it leads you into cul de sacs, and places where you can't turn round.... We have to say we want to win a war, though fighting it's a monstrous deal, and winning will make us monstrous too, like losing will as well ... but there'd be different sceneries, different friends. Something changes everything – work? The will? The thing to do, Petronia, is hang on in. Teeter on the teeter board, stay there as long as possible ... you can't stop anyone's abominations, so don't try logic on them....'

'Those fish,' Petronia says. 'Poor things. In death, they were made to tell their lie ... the colour, the legality of their missing heads. Even....'

'Too late, Petronia,' Vinnie says. 'They're dead. And they don't care. They'd no image, no imagination, of how they would end up. You and I – must draw the consequence ... if there is one.'

But Petronia – already she's been shaken. Maybe Vinnie's right, and bringing in the fish – he's hit the spot. There's nothing to be done, and no one doing anything....

'Must I watch myself?' she asks.

'Don't risk the garrotte,' says Vinnie. 'Don't set puzzles that take time to solve....'

'What have you ever wanted of me, Vinnie?' asks Petronia. 'You only ever wanted someone different, and hoped to make me so....'

'I wanted to be loved,' he says, 'for myself. I didn't care who loved me, so long as I could tell them "that's myself you love"....'

'To be loved, you must be lovable, not just yourself,' Petronia says.

'It's not so easy now,' says Vinnie. 'You always preferred Fritz to me, and now – he's been replaced by robots.'

'Many of them?' Petronia asks. 'That would be quite a coup, if it took lots....'

'Not really,' Vinnie says. 'They're all similar, and all like him. They come off the line in multiples, standard, different shades....'

*

'I wonder how it works,' says Vanessa, when she's informed. 'Hundreds of orgasms, until you turn him off. Your randy robot. Do they repeat "and was it good for you?" each time, or maybe there's a button you can press....'

'I fear the skin,' Petronia says. 'Each one a little clammy. And you must watch they do not overheat. And robots may be good for orgies, but for afters – in the banquets – how do they adapt?

'I think we're being primitive in this. For instance – do they lie?'

'The more advanced ones do, I'm sure,' Vanessa says. 'Have lovers, second families – forget their children's names – claim to be sexual athletes for all tastes....'

'How strange; they look like Fritz, but are quite different,' Petronia says. 'And let's suppose they don't forget – not anything, and yet – they cannot solve a mystery.... Numbers are no difficulty, but – the ship....'

'You wouldn't want that solved by someone with a clammy skin,' Vanessa says. 'Who can't fall off the wire unless it's told....'

'They're making millions of him,' says Petronia. 'To fight the wars. The other side'll set theirs loose on us, for sure....'

'Will they have nationalities?' Vanessa asks. 'So many questions! Writing a novel, or a play – it seems to me, that's always been like making robots – maybe of an ancient kind.... They stumble, fall downstairs, some urinate on you – they do exactly what they've been designed to do ... although I guess you'd say they're useless, unadaptable outside the covers of the book, or off the boards – can't deviate or change a line....'

'Can't make coffee, turn the TV on,' Petronia says. 'Like poor old Nadia,' and despite themselves, they smile.

'Emotion, Petronia,' Vanessa says. 'That is the gift the humans pass to them, the Fritzes, all those robots, sent off to be blown up.... Humans' emotions come and go, and flicker on and off like glow-worms' glows ... so, take robots: will they be constant, unlike us? Or psychopaths?'

*

Publicity – Petronia has a camera, fits in a hand. She snaps Takis. Look! That shows he's real, and she is too, it must take two to make a photo – subject, object, she, behind the lens.

'I want reports, Petronia,' Takis says. 'But – stir the public up a little first....'

'Sing?' she asks.

'A little show,' he says. 'A little humanity. Remember – emotions, structure. Do a bit of both. These guys have risked extinction – some have fought, been wounded, others are on leave, and most are waiting to grow old enough to join the war....'

'I don't know songs,' Petronia says, terrified.

‘I’m philistine,’ says Takis. ‘There’s keywords, and then you draw out the vowels. I’ll send someone with you – Aurora. She knows about frocks and what to leave out of them to flaunt....’

‘Flesh?’ Petronia asks. ‘You want me like a butcher’s joints?’

He doesn’t answer. Off the two go – Aurora needs a lot of coca to keep her moving on. She’s golden, gold all over, her hair too ... and she wears gold, it must wear her down ... there’s an abundance ... Petronia asks ... ‘so, is it real?’

‘No, no, Petronia,’ Aurora says. ‘It’s colour. Gold is that – a colour. Fashion is about colours and the skin – our forest drapes, the green, the tan, a bark like leather.... I’ve been on the anvil, on the griddle. I’ve been converted – now, my faith is in the coca.’

‘I didn’t know humans could look like you, Aurora,’ Petronia says. ‘If only I....’

‘You won’t be, dear, not ever,’ says Aurora. ‘It’s class. Maybe you weren’t told. And the cash that keeps my class and me both floating high.’

They’ve seen where the armies clashed – the left-overs, it’s like the Offal Joint – villagers got in the way. Those cannonades!

And now, their audience is sitting there before them – Petronia warbles, and Aurora claps. The public: faces robotic, expressions identical, or similar: no grimace, no yawn, no *smorfia.* Not even a suggestive tonguing.... Robots: or the shell-shocked? The public and their war.

Petronia’s at a loss, she sings, ‘O horror’, and it comes out ‘Aurorroarrr’, a shout of envy and despair.

‘Do robots get off on medals and promotion?’ she asks Aurora.

‘Probably not,’ Aurora says, ‘but I’m sure their handlers do. You should be glad these machines can do the fighting. Only the old, the young, the cowardly, the handicapped – only they can’t run, escape. They go down – it doesn’t mean a thing. Officer and bureaucrats, the programmers, the interpreters, the engineers – it sounds it’s almost everyone is targeted....’

‘These tin and plastic guys resist the radiation too?’ Petronia asks. ‘I don’t see wounds, burns, all that....’

‘Oh,’ says Aurora, ‘They have them fight quite naked. They don’t mark, distort. The uniforms would burn. So, they’re taken off, and they fight nude: the drapes cost, and there’s not many spares.

‘I think the robots need a cunning shot to take them down – their works could be in a knee, a toe....’

I'm not an accomplice, Petronia thinks. I wasn't when the humans fought, and now – these guys are bought in thousands....

She finishes the song –

She and Aurora, they hear 'boo!' – not many, but. Enough.

'They've taste, those robots, a few at least, it seems,' Aurora says. 'The emotion passed them by, but, my dear, your structure is a wreck.... Remember, structure's their emotion.

'They mustn't think we are an enemy, or we'll need to run, run very fast....'

*

'Between us two, Aurora,' Petronia says, 'I feel there is a buzz....'

'I'll check the panel of control,' says Aurora. 'Each warrior has their feelings bared – those with "aggressive", "indifferent" – get sent out to fight. The "fearful" ones stay in the tent, to clean some terminals. And as for us – the buzz – it shows up as "envy" on your part.... It's usual when I meet a person who thinks civilisation's over, or should be. I am civilisation, naturally. Clearly, I go on.

'You can't sing, Petronia, but for this evening, you're my friend, and I promote my friends. If I don't do it, who else would?'

*

How shaming, thinks Petronia: all I'd renounced, condemned ... it seems I still crave the cloth of gold, Aida ornaments, the cash ... It also seems the robots, as they are refined, become more human. All too human. They aspire to taste....

Maybe they'll mutiny, take over everything.... The war aims: who grows beets and radishes and where the frontier lies – it's more refined, the earlier mechanical tommies weren't much interested. It's quite baroque, how we're set up to win a sliver here or there of boggy ground, straighten a kink of frontier, and oh! the cleaners find the offal underfoot, uneaten and inedible, old bones, exhausted brains.... Suppose the robots tire of trivial disputes – fight for the genres, become iconoclasts....

What was it all for, she wonders; is someone seeing what we can resist, or make of life, of mere existence, the useless spaciousness of the uninhabitable universe? The void. What can it mean to you? A huge set-up, set; made to terrify, humiliate, and come to nought – the weather, the eruptions, earthquakes ... and the wars, thousands gone by, all past, nothing resolved – a test, abomination, and for what? If we are tested, as you could expect – we mostly can't take much, don't understand, go crazy, cry, can't sleep, die. A day – and we are done. So – stop! The point is made.

It was a folly, ludicrous when the humans fought, and now – it's robots.... Is the aim to see if they are humanised, if they can take the strain, or break down in the fields and weep?

'Those tin soldiers,' Petronia says. 'They remind me of souls. Souls can't die a second time, can't be sacrificed, and yet ... if you believe in residues, in purposes unclear, in lives unresolved and dutifully pointless – in memory, the past, there must be souls. They're yours, you die – and then your soul is on the loose. We've seen them bundled up, they play dead too, for sale in quantities. "And yet", one asks. "Why?" And then again, "Why not?"'

'I was once on a ship, that sailed – though there were no sails – like a ship that's made to carry souls, from here to there, to land them, and then – on and on they trek, ship, souls, but there's nowhere at all for them to go because they lack the wherewithal to see one place is different from another place.... One fate is different from another fate. But – they've already had their fate!

'Like these soldiers we have made – see, this hybrid public can't applaud ... the almost humans and the traumatised.... Even if they can distinguish pseudo-life from pseudo-death, the blood, the current with its fits and starts – what is their point? The fighting – it means nothing to them; war – a word.... Unless – they create ranks, generals ... strategy ... map-reading and aiming off for wind. The big parade, the putsch – what then? They might be fundamentalists ... discriminating against us organic crowd ... Add more human traits, more circuits, on and on ... Is this our altruistic resolution – making soldiers that will torch our homes and rape us ... is there no limit to our self-harm, to our excess? And do we liberate our soul only when we're dead – and meanwhile it's just a sycamore seed that flits around, our blood is like its swimming pool, it does the butterfly, shouts out encouragement to other souls, gives pins-and-needles to our feet – songs of the leprechaun, a *ppp* that we can't hear – a viola improvisation, muted, played off-stage.... What depravity, transgression, will we devise to pass the dreary time while we're alive ... to keep our souls fired up?'

'You went aboard a vessel not intended for you?' Aurora asks. 'Maybe there'd been enjoyment in the past, if you had wanted whoopee:

you wanted good times afloat ... but souls – they don't have wills. Or destinations. They wait, they're carried, they are nude.'

'Then,' Petronia says, 'I am a soul.'

'Love me,' says Aurora, 'and that will give you destination and a will. Alas, it won't give you a voice....' They laugh.

'Listen,' says Aurora. 'They do applaud!'

There's a kind of windy buffeting noise. 'They rub their shoulders against their neighbours',' Aurora says. 'They share. They – they are in common ... they recognise what is identical to themselves.... Don't try to live with them, that's all – community with them is like the everywhere you cannot stand....'

'I thought that would be precious,' Petronia says. 'Humane, humanity – that's a link, but then, these warriors are not alive. They're order-bound, but unlike us – they don't refuse, don't disobey....'

'No,' Aurora says, 'Petronia, you are too late, too little. You think "humanity". It seems a principle, a peak. It is the height to which the common lot aspire. But it meant demotion for me, so – I started streaking ahead of all the rest, the pack. The soldiers – far ahead of us....'

'All fake,' Petronia says. 'My dear. That's you. Smeared, clipped, on. Just gold and sunshine, stuff you find in any hole and on every beach. There's no transcendence, trust me ...'

'Is that what you'll tell Takis?' Aurora asks. 'He thinks I'm tops. I'm not a robot, but I've left humanity behind. I act the parts, though. Everyone likes fake.'

'What Takis wants? Not human? More or less?' Petronia says. 'I'll sound him. He wants to win the war, it means long life, children a-plenty. Any war. Good luck to him!'

'I could make you a celebrity, Petronia,' Aurora says. 'It's not as grand as being me, you won't have gold, a tan, and forest clothes. You'll die; meanwhile, your raddled face, decaying body, will make your audience nauseous.

'Not like me. I smell eternally of red sandalwood and myrrh, but natch – being dead's no fun for anyone. Celebrity? Just say the word ... it can be you.'

The words that come to Petronia's mind are 'banquets', 'orgies' and 'garrotte'. 'It's only principle, Aurora, that makes me turn you down,' she says. 'It's nothing personal....'

*

'Well,' Takis says. 'If we win here, like you say we can, we can win anywhere. Being as we are, but larger. If we lose – a village once again, an immense one. All of us still simple, simple we can never cease to be – the village run by whispering bullies, gangs and fencing off the grass, the grass-roots chattering like rooks, the fruit encaged – all private no-go where once we went. A castle with a well-filled jail, water coming through the roof.

'Better to win and dress in silk ...'

'But there's no sacrifice,' Petronia says. 'That takes the lustre out of victory.'

'Maybe,' he says, 'but that is so for everything. The cheap is king, you know: more stuff. Stuff you can't appreciate. Beating us – it would mean nothing – except that we are weak, we can't turn out the soldiers quicker than they can. Don't worry about that, Petronia, it's nothing, no significance. What matters is your being loyal – back to the offal shop with you, and spin some tales....'

'Who will win, Takis?' Petronia asks. 'I know no one ever enquires – forgive me for doing so....'

'People who have more to lose have more to spend,' he says. 'Attack might pay. The less you have, the less you think you have to gain. So – you defend. You might. But then – it all depends on how you go about it: bit by bit or all at once. It takes time, longer than you can imagine, and all the people who set off – they none of them return, not ever, and there's never even a postcard comes ... the commentators likewise, all guesses contradicted....

'Remember – there's more poor people in the world than rich. Add them up! Where is their bet? Winning the war, backing the bosses, or changing them? Democrats with empires – that's what they want to be! The creed, the hope, their dream: dream of the past, or present? Square circles, Petronia, that's what people seek ... Things do not compute...! Things – people want those, I promise you!'

'I've no idea about that,' Petronia says. 'Do you, Takis? Must I pretend to understand, and share my speculations? Must I propose that everything is up for grabs, although – all's pain and loss, erosion....'

'No,' he says. 'Of course not. You're on the team. You must work hard, be optimistic.'

'Ignoring stuff....' she says.

'You don't have options, Petronia,' he says. 'You never did, you're on my team: for you, there is no choice. There never was, and when there was, you didn't take it. Being on the team means – you stop thinking "win or lose". It's quite irrelevant.'

'Aurora was the only one who made an offer,' says Petronia. 'It didn't seem quite me. But – my question – who will win? I didn't ask who ought to, or when – you could have tried to analyse my question that you didn't start to answer.... I know who's team I'm on....'

'Then that is where we leave it,' Takis says. 'History's not made by vulgar little skirmishes, and boastful popinjays.'

*

'Singing is clagged around with memories – rejoicing, keening, just sitting, sitting waiting to sing,' Petronia says, '... the next step on from apache dance and soft-shoe shuffle. If I'm to give another concert, I thought of a low croon. Evocative, a "speaking-feeling mode", a *Sprachgefühl.'*

'Go right ahead,' Aurora says.

Petronia asks, 'Should I sing "sorrow" like "Sarroow", or "Sorraahh"?'

'They'll watch your frock,' Aurora says. 'Your tits. Do exactly what you want.'

*

'Why do you toy with me, Takis?' Petronia asks. 'Vinnie was passive. You are passive, but you make me look an idiot.'

'You're funny, Petronia,' he says. 'The funniest thing since someone invented falling on their bum on stage.'

'It's the uniform, I'm sure,' she says. 'It lets you think you're someone else. An angry person? Like me? I could make the soldiers mutiny.... Do they cry? They didn't when I sang. Aurora says "the audience, their passion, is not about me, it's about my lovers and my cars." Cheap stuff for kids....'

'Of course,' he says. 'But crying comes later. Firing them up is first – flames and sparklers, gun rage.... Repentance? Reconciliation – an hypothesis that we might come to – but not now, with you in your spasm, pique or spite; but after: when it leads to where we want to go.'

'Not me,' she says. 'I'm not coming. I want to do it all backwards – life as a revelation, ending with the shore, seeing the ship, apocalypse, the flames ... then back: having beside me all the people I have lost, Angelo, Mirkat ... even Nadia- made-whole....'

'It shows you up,' he says. 'As trivial. And it's not those people that you want, it's *any* people you remember. Can other people make you seem fulfilled and interesting anyway?

'Life – you have to do it all yourself.'

'I don't want victims,' she says. 'Killing people is squalid. I want something huge to be my vehicle. My city, pantheon, billboard ... an opera? A Turandot? A Traviata?'

'You'd not be in them,' Takis says. 'With your voice's bark and howl.'

'Too bad,' she says. 'I saw you as a footman in the entr'acte ... lighting hundreds of candles in the chandeliers, a weak flame on a pole. Light! Drinks all round. Then the big snuff ... your task again. The dark.'

He waves to silence her.

'I must be large,' she says. 'My past life: I've always been a puzzled element. Without plot and character, no choice and no psychology. What could be my packaging, my envelope?

'I know – a novel!'

'Out of fashion. And you'd be only half alive....' he says. 'Written and re-written.'

'But immortal,' she says.

'You do nothing,' he says. 'Books have spines. You don't – you would be flesh, not bone. People think "yum-yum", they chew you ... you're tough, implausible: many spit you out.'

'I go on board,' she says. 'Give life and substance. Sing. Implore. Imprisoned, escaped, cast down, thrown up – peace, war, *en fleur,* smart and ingenuous. So what I don't do photographs?'

'Even if.... Even if....' he says, half captivated.... 'Even if you were there, safely pasted in a famous book: fashion, taste will always be against you. Unread for centuries, a Gilgamesh, a huge "so what?" Limits, cautionary fingerings.... They'll think that you wear crinolines.'

'Everything continues,' she says. 'I'm not responsible for anything. Not past or future – not the present, so you say. You know what I think; I left my orders. I judge. Nothing happens, nothing that I do – you have free will. All of you, do and be damned; it's academic, what you do to one another.

'And when you close the book – I'm still there, and can't be removed.'

They reflect on this. 'And when's your mutiny?' she asks. 'The paint thrown around, graffiti: statues with their penises knocked off...?'

'When we start to win or lose,' he says. '*My* side. You'll see it. Serious stuff.'

*

'It's normal,' Aurora says. 'Intelligence tells you to think of aftermaths. Takis knows it's best to win, whatever anybody else may do.

'You, Petronia – *don't sing*! It doesn't entertain – especially not those poor machines. Live high and be prepared to run – pack a small case with useful stuff – no clothes or toothpaste, dear! Pack what you can spend.

'Takis may end up as top dog – but dogs are opportunists.... He is the heir, but in this play, the heir must kill the king, the boss. A flourish and it's done? Or scorpions battling to the death? There's no guarantee he'll stick by you.'

It's true – the worse will always trump the bad.

Petronia asks Aurora, 'Have I joined myself to Takis? His success....'

'What does success mean to you, Petronia?' Aurora asks. 'Takis will end on a catafalque or a rope's end. What does that mean to you? You can't be born again, rich and talented, or even generous like me. The mistakes you made – can't be undone. What's left – eternal peace? We all get that and fight against it to the end.'

'Incident, Aurora,' says Petronia. 'Orgies and banquets. Things happening. Avoiding being useful to a fantasist, a true creative. No walk-on parts. No famous people up above me, with their thunder clouds and moods.... No – maybe it's the ship ... a destiny....'

'Finding a purpose? Or a pattern,' Aurora asks.

'No,' says Petronia. 'There's no purpose, or it would have shown itself – a chain. Consequences. Logic and reason. No – there's a pattern, like the bower-bird's. You arrange things, giving comfort to your brain, and hope the right arrangement brings you happiness.'

'Selfishness, self-satisfaction? Knowing that being happy is an end – for you, if for no one else? You're more convinced than me,' Aurora says.

'I think, yes, there is something rather than nothing, and it's no use asking "why?" But then, it's all a mystery. I knew – I had to go on board the ship,' Petronia says.

'No,' Aurora says. 'You need not. That's exactly what you're telling me.'

And they leave it there.

*

Takis makes his move. He has friends everywhere, on every side. No one likes him.

His argument is: if we win, we'll have to go to war again within a year. Then, we might lose. Or ... if we lose, we'll have to go to war again.... Either way, no one would be content. They're not content now, and so ... if the clock won't stop, hit it with a hammer.

He makes his move – some days too soon. It's a conspiracy, that everybody's talked about for months. However, it's now that Takis makes the move.

The fighting's now done by mechanicals, so no one sheds a tear for them – the human casualties are 'by the way'; in their beds; or underneath the stairs, if they've two floors. Thousands or millions? No-one counts. There's rivers everywhere, so it's too damp to dig a cellar out – that's the worst thing you can say about the territory. If you conquer mountains, cellars are a boon, especially if there's trees, and you can store the wood down there for winter fires.

There's no call from Takis to Petronia. She is his dog, she knows, she doesn't need a whistle to remember.

Fritz and Vinnie call her – best to have a contact, even a contact on both sides, and maybe a contact for winning, and one for losing.

The three meet in the Offal Joint. There's a mazurka, rowdy, lots – down below, where you can join in, dance: 'Oh,' she says, 'I remember it, being taught at school!'

Together – they cut a rug!

'It just takes everyone to say "ok",' Petronia says. 'And there'll be peace, or maybe more decisive war. The important thing – is "get it done"!'

Napoleon, not Robespierre. Then Metternich and not Napoleon. That's all there's time for; no one remembers Marshal Ney, or they confuse him with the Champ de Mai ... 'Let history judge' is best, and so.... Takis stops some people flying here and there, the generals can't access their Mercedes – but then ... you do it, everything, from your little screen, and so, and so: it goes. And so. There is a pause, a lull, when you can speculate. It almost certainly has been a putsch ... or maybe a computer went agley.... You check what everybody thinks. You fret.

During a mazurka, unknown to Petronia and her friends, Aurora flies off to a safer place. She has friends everywhere, so does not need to tell the friends she leaves – besides, if you don't know mazurkas, and you're in a crowded space, you jostle and there's *bagarres* with other dancers. Best change the scene.

Takis has made quite a disturbance, though he wouldn't care....

The rhythm quite defeats Vinnie, he ends up furious, stamping there and here. 'If you had even gathered absent friends, or comrades,' he tells Petronia. 'In arms or in the brig with you, you would not have been so isolated. Now, only the complicated rhythm keeps you moving on ... a figment of activity....'

'I'd never thought that, Vinnie,' Petronia says, 'that not attaching on to you meant that I was isolated.'

'Takis will abandon you,' Fritz says, trying to help but merely sounding threatening....

'Oh, I do hope so,' Petronia says. 'Trust from the powerful, or complicity with the falling – help me to avoid them both!'

*

'The dancing was fantastic!' Petronia says, flushed, excited, 'If only we could go and see Nadia, in her glory days....'

'You should concentrate on your future,' Vanessa says, quite stern. 'Finding a writer to put you in their book...' and she smiles.

'This Takis. How is he, Petronia, what does he see in you?' Vanessa goes on, quite envious. 'A summary! See if I concur.... And is he bully, or a democrat, a boss, authoritarian, moderate or radical?'

'Oh yes,' Petronia says, 'that describes him well. He sticks to rules and precedents, but doesn't let you make a fool of him – as for me, he likes to be entertained. If you're a little scattered – he loves that, and if you like the things he likes, the doing things a-right, the porcelain, the *griffes*, the cloth well cut, the right name on your stuff ... you're in. And yet, he's still a person of the people: parades, a stadium – those are his elements ... but he's discrete. He talks incessantly, to other top guys too, part of his work ... it is his element, a drone of reasonableness and sense.'

'He sounds a total horror,' Vanessa says. Petronia winks.

'And is he trustworthy?' Vanessa goes on, playing her game.

'It's best to keep your business separate from him, and not ask favours. Give him presents – for the gesture, not for the thing,' Petronia says. 'He has ambitions – building stuff, and monuments and special days for honouring and not....'

'And does he want our good?' Vanessa asks.

'That's difficult,' Petronia says. 'It's rather – our goodness, more than good.'

'Well,' Vanessa says, 'I can't wait to vote for him – if he gets his way, of course. And we shan't know – did we win or lose, and does our being paupers in a desolation make up for it....'

'Of course,' Petronia says, 'I wish all this could go away, being bossed and voting for it, spies and soldiers, being chosen, being not....'

'We don't know anything,' Vanessa says, quite sadly.'Of anything that happens anywhere. But you, Petronia – you have given in and....'

'Nothing,' says Petronia, sharply. 'I have no allegiance, no party and no card – except maybe the joker.'

They laugh. Petronia wishes Vanessa were not a stiff old stick and they could dance around the room together, like they used ...

Vanessa says, 'You think like a historian, Petronia, but you don't act like one. Someone must have trained you to hold back, be prudent.... And yet – you've looked inside the motor, you've see the engine, ridden on it. It's not possible you didn't recognise ... it moves! And you must too, or else.'

'I don't remember anyone who told me that,' says Petronia. 'Who told me anything worth listening to, still less offered me a training....' but she thinks, maybe that's why the adventure, the Ship, bothers me so. Motion eternal, determined, pointless and unchanged – like Time.

'The real, as it is, as it will be, is ineluctable ... or may it be a revelation? As for history – I might be a historian, but if history came and bit me, I'd not know who or what it was....'

*

Takis – is in the balance.

'You should watch yourself, Petronia,' Vanessa says. 'I thought you'd be a radical. Instead – you drift and climb, like a fruit fly, observed aspiring – clambering in an alembic ... slipping down ... lost, beyond salvation.'

They laugh: 'Who is radical now, Vanessa?' Petronia asks. 'You weigh up Takis, find him wanting. Beware: you are exposed, you suffer.

You protest – you're beaten, jailed. I understand the tides – you can't go against them. Not to speak of nets – I saw the fish ... and not their heads. How were they hoisted up on board?'

'Oh,' Vanessa says. 'We're all on course to be the fish. Except – here, we're in a favoured place. We make integration happen everywhere, people forget, they think they're all the same – and it's us, the guides, that profit. The more the world is one, the better it is to be in the top rank, and watch the others fight, and scrum for food.'

'I'm sure you're right,' Petronia says, 'but some things – it's better not to see. You sound so moralistic, but we're rather stuck.... The situation ... the more you know, the more there is that you suspect. Stay clear of currents, storms and tempests ... seek protection if you can ...

'I had a choice – Vinnie or Takis, and the option wasn't great, but with Takis – you're swept up, you should see the panorama way below ... too bad there's mist and clouds....'

'And do you eat enough, Petronia?' Vanessa asks, thinking that the banquets never fill you up and orgies take it out of you.

'I don't eat in the Offal Joint,' Petronia says. 'I don't like seeing what they take in, through the back door.'

'So long as it's not you!' Vanessa says, and laughs. 'You're so delicate, not for this world. And I can't follow you, when you trance off – in your metaphysical mode....'

'Oh,' Petronia says, 'it's mood, not mode. There's problems, and solutions, but we'll never put the two together – people are exhausted, if it's not the wind, then it's the sun....'

'I know,' Vanessa says. 'Our time has paused, if ever it was ripe for us. The war we women won – it didn't bring the peace.

'And now – you suffer speaking out. And keeping it inside – it comes out in boils and stuff....'

'I know, I know,' Petronia says, 'we suffered so for you.'

Vanessa – she can't make a choice: or rather – she sees the choices are all bad. What use is that, you'll ask.

*

'Tokay! The best – what a treat,' says Takis. 'Five *puts...*'

'You've left your apparatus in the street, I see,' says Jan. 'Your spooks. And brought Petronia. You arrive together, leave together, but you're not "together". How appropriate for days like these, when we wait to see if anyone's "together" now.'

'There's fewer want to wait for anything,' says Takis. 'To see, to watch. They sing along and that is all. Over the years, we beat the "people" – in the good old sense – quite flat. It's only us, the players at the masters' table, that anybody cares to watch. And – we watch them!'

'It's all so delicate,' says Eva, who's with Jan. 'I scarcely breathe. Will we be occupied, or are we occupied in picking up the spoils? As they say "to the victor, the spoils". All's spoilt, Takis.... All those people, put in jail, for being sceptical....'

'I tidy up, that's all,' says Takis, and they all smile. Dead, alive, jailed, freed – it all depends ... on if you seem untidy.

He makes a statement. 'Doing what's right – it's always treachery …to something that *seems* wrong. Being oneself – the same. Betraying what you might become, have been.

'There's always a higher something that means all treachery is really loyalty to something else – never tangible, apparent, present, but that's there, and everyone salutes it, as if it's *really* there. The flag, the standard. It's what you cherish most. It is inherent, like the circulation of your blood.'

Jan now has his say in full because the wine, the apartment, is all his. So is his job, his title.

He's in a different tree from Takis: both – proud monkeys, too proud to shout insults at one another. So, they socialise.

'What do you say, Petronia?' he asks, as she stands mutely like a block.... 'And what a lovely curious name. Your father, now – a big player, in his day....' He takes a book, and reads, '*When his treachery was discovered, or invented and admitted to, as if he intended to die in the same profligate and careless manner as he'd lived – he had his veins opened and then closed – not so much to postpone his end, but to let him continue to tell the tall stories and louche tales as he was wont to, in his happier days ... His veins were opened and closed, and so on, until....*'

'I never knew him, and they told me,' Petronia says, making a sad face, so the subject could be changed discretely, 'I had no father, and they chose my name from lists.'

'I'm sure my veins are a revolving door,' says Takis. 'Life flows in and out without a pause....'

He drinks down the Tokay. 'All the eggs are in the pan – there's nothing I can do until the omelette's cooked, and anyway, I'm doing nothing; nothing of what people say I do....'

They leave it there. There's nothing to eat, nothing prepared, except impressions. And soundings-out.

'Jan and Eva,' Takis wonders, 'after all, are they on my side?' He doesn't know. 'They invited me....'

'What did Eva say?' he asks Petronia when they've left.

'She said I didn't eat enough,' Petronia says. 'Looked at my thin wrists. I like them so.... But maybe, while I'm waiting here to see who'll be administering the peace or continuing the war, I ought to plan another of my journeys, like last time when they rescued me again!'

They laugh.

'I leave you to decide,' she says. 'A bad peace or a better war.'

'There's not much to decide,' he says.

'Everywhere's still different,' she says. 'And I don't acknowledge countries and their changing shapes. Perhaps there's zones ... continents – that's stable: even if they drift. The atlas has been changed to accommodate the sides – we cut out enemies and journey on, way down south – with compasses and boundary stakes, and submarines. But power – all over in the north, power could work out very much the same. And south....'

Takis says, 'That's juvenile. You'll say, "In the rough South – where everything's for sale and money doesn't count, won't stick there – there's a special power, affinity, for despots, permanently."

'Down South you always need to be prepared to run. But in the North – they come for you.

'We're thinking how – there could be something different. Power homogeneous, silky, efficacious....'

Petronia backs off, avoids a criticism.

'I know. I told you, everywhere is always different, and we back our side, and suffer terribly....' she starts. 'The strong – they need the weak, and bully them, exploit. Peace and war, like it always is, means everything is always open, always closed – nothing to stop you, Takis. The future comes without a preconception, but its feet in chains. Revolutions always start quite small but lucid, and as they go on, you find "the means will justify the means". Continuity prevails until it breaks. The past makes the difference, and no one has found how you can undo it.'

It sprawls out from her, her reservation, which is all she has the courage to say to Takis, who's trying not to fall, go underneath the wheels of his own diligence.

You can't be loyal to everyone, can you be disloyal to everyone? Being loyal to your side means you want your enemies to be crushed – even if you're one of them ... but that's absurd – so you must want the other side to be held in, and holding in means they couldn't threaten you, your allies or your interests, your economy, what you call your culture and your conversations.... We all said that many years ago, and so – there's no point in saying it all again, now that everything is scarcer and more dangerous than it was when we started out to end the scarcity and the danger to ourselves, and everyone.

... What Takis wants – is so much power, no one resists. Not fighting enemies; does 'holding them in' mean winning the war you didn't want to have with them? That's 'peace'? Take some, lose few, are you a Monster or do you preen and purr? That five-colour map – suppose it's four or two – will it be one? Try it? Imagine it? You might not – others will, others already live in it ... Who pays it, the price, for the war you don't want to undertake? When you win, is there the peace you had before, or something indescribable, beyond our understanding – pearly dawns. And savage sunsets?

'I've won my war. Now, it's my time to lose it,' Petronia says. 'That is the moral. Just for me. I don't believe, don't trust. All power, so you do what you want? The logic's good, the history too, I guess – but it's not me.... I've been bitten other times.... All Power to...? the Party? The Soviets? We'll see how it goes wrong this time, and then, my time will come again....'

She's prudent, and she knows force is the midwife, but she's fastidious and squeamish, couldn't use the force herself and wouldn't easily accept what happens everywhere and always and doesn't take her into its consideration. Hers is alarm, a precognition, nothing more. Takis laughs.

'Be prudent when you look for me, when you come back,' says Takis. 'Look up and down, follow your instinct, and don't ask, don't say my name – my nickname, that is.... Consolidate a continent, that's the key ... try it again, this time the humans will agree ... remember, now, there's machines to stop our projects turning sour....'

*

'I'll go on foot this time,' she says. 'And, it's safer underground.'

There's catacombs. France, Italy, Ukraine – all similar. Mongolia, Siberia, Syria and Turkey.... A near infinity – the little cubicle, just snug for when your flesh is sloughed and you are just some shabby sticks, a bowling ball – a cartoon phiz – 'big eyes' and hungry teeth.

All martyrs for some cause, she thinks, and spools her voiced-out thoughts behind her as she walks, a thread that's undisturbed, will lead her back, she thinks, except there's just one path, nothing is lost, there's nothing left to lose. 'To China' says the sign, but might it also say 'From China', depending on the way you pass.

Cool and odourless, you walk and walk, until you wonder if there's space left vacant somewhere, every cubicle chiselled out, unlabelled, everyone a martyr, and you despair of ever finding space to lie down in, though you might have no cause, except not wanting peace eternal with these dumb old sticks ... silent, ahead, behind.

'And where are Mirkat, Angelo, and the rest?' she wonders. Not down here, probably. Here no one is numbered, singled out, virgins are prone, aligned with everybody else, no credits and demerits given here to martyrs, irrespective of their cause ... they asked for it, for sure....

No! My friends – they'll still be in the camps. Or on the move from one to other, de-classified in one, re-numbered in the next – displacement is for ever, but you're sometimes on the move.... 'undesirable' is permanent – not just 'not desired' by Jack or Jill, but an irrevocable judgement that the species makes upon itself....

She walks and walks – under the sea? The Black, the Caspian ... and above, the great river, Amu-Darya, and the great tomb: Timur's, in Samarkand ... and on and on ... ah! The Amur....

It's to be doubted. There's no waterproofing.

Catacombs are dull, after the first few kilometres ... they seem to go on for ever, and they could, but don't.

She sees a guy – 'Guide' … on his hat. He doesn't look at all like Vanessa, but his hat's identical to hers. He looks like Vinnie, so much that she touches him, and he turns.... They say old men look alike. They don't. Middle-aged men look alike, and it's not Vinnie, who fell into disrepute and hard times, until Fritz took him in to share his room, and both hated the arrangement, but there was no way back.

The guy says, 'You've come a long way. That may mean – you'll stay. Thousands of these cubicles – we'll have to make them share, two in a bunk, the poor old broomsticks. Don't walk any further – it says "to China" but it's not so. And in China, they don't want you, won't welcome you, they'll treat you bad, and if you find one of these breathing holes – you can pop your head up, like a gopher's – and see, the places round here are ruined, they don't want you either.

'You're a tourist, I see that, just like every other tourist. You think they're games, the history, the digging out, the martyrdoms, the architecture and the big empires, bigger than you'll find now, even with all the soldiers and the machines for making more and more, and arms going everywhere, and not just the Scythian bows but real strong stuff – you think it's games, the past, the present, where you can watch and not join in, not belong, like when there were the lines of people playing chess, the top board with the master, and guys crowding round to try their luck against him....'

'Yes,' says Petronia. 'I've been very clear. I'm not part of this, the game, you call it. I call it "the civilisation". For instance, I'm against violence, but it's true – nothing changes without it. Be ready to destroy everything and start again as you would want.... I don't think people are capable of that: the people who can must depend on all the many other people – who can't. And the martyrs, the best....' She meanders on....

'Pop our heads out,' says the guy, 'and I'll teach you how to snipe. Start with a real big target. That way no one sees you shoot – they watch the big guy, as he drops ... and there are other tricks to learn as well – how history really works and how you can ride it as though it was a camel. How to put street lamps out of action: how to stencil slogans on a wall....

'You seem to be a tourist, but you've seen more martyrs and their ends than almost any tourists that I've come across.... You may have made some dirty deals, because you don't know which side you're on....'

'Oh,' says Petronia, 'no problem. My side lost long ago, long before it could be "mine", besides – I don't believe in sides, not that there is a side that wins and keeps on winning....'

'You must be right,' the guide says. 'I agree. But that's where you belong: a side. You have a side, and everyone but you can see you on it. You've always been there even when you were betraying it.... All you have done, all you say you didn't understand: you could be a child and still understand ... everything.... You don't want to lose, so you must want to win....'

The Guide seems to know it all, and he hops along, eagerly; he has a lantern jaw, and as he speaks, as if he's chewing 'baccy, it swivels round, sags down, like a pelican's beak; his scraggy neck – could hold a catch of tiddlers, and you think how maybe he could dive, a string around that neck, like cormorants have so they don't swallow what they catch, and Petronia says –

'Hey, comrade Guide! You're not supposed to guide the visitors to "inside themselves", but at the most, you should explain what they have seen!'

'There's really nothing to explain,' he says. 'If you have eyes, you see. That's it. I grant you – if you'd learn to snipe, you must know there is a condition called the "nonconformity of eyes". A sniper keeps both eyes open, and so sees two different images.... It can't be corrected, but you can allow for it. If you only see one picture, one-dimensional – it's a deformity but it means you never ever miss what you are aiming at....'

'All this,' Petronia says, 'is quite irrelevant. Maybe – untrue. The catacombs are just a filler-up, while I wait to join my companions on another of my journeys.... Your special pleading – is just casuistry. And you choose a place that's foolish to display yourself – the martyrs' highway ... everyone who got caught and terminated, for the cause.'

She wavers, totters. No chance of going up the ladder, taking down the guy the guide points out.... It must be the Tokay, the finest – makes you hallucinate, and slip. Nothing, nothing whatever, has been resolved.... Beware the booze!

He thinks he is my conscience, Petronia thinks. I don't trust anybody, anything – still less my conscience, which I don't believe in anyway.

'Take the gun,' the guide says. 'Do what you know you must and take him down....'

She doesn't move. 'You haven't been as far as you might think,' the guide says, shoving her towards the ladder and the gopher hole above.... You've seen a little sample, wandered round and round, it being an illusion that the path is straight – it winds and doubles back ... you may have seen what's left of all the good citizens of Lvov, but there's no sign; they could be from Bomako or Port au Prince or Badajoz....'

It's all confusion. Petronia thinks – I need companions to start the motor, set the compass, tell the jokes, the tallest tales.... I need to start again....

And so, remembering that's exactly what she thought when she first saw the ship, the tide advancing ... she turns around, and scuttles back, back to where she climbed down the ladder, strolled along the catacombs of Martyrdom....

*

Near the mouth of the catacombs, there's a small elite group, who've paid much for the tour. Some may have won it as a prize, or because they work in the right office – get a discount, pay when they want.... Petronia picks out Robbie, dressed for the running track, Rita – ready for a fashion shot ... and a frail wind-tossed figure, Malek, stretching out.

She'll be expected to keep him upright if his heart gives in – too bad for him, she thinks.... We're here to see with our own eyes what we've been told, what we already know ... the battlefronts where we are fighting nature; harassing the poor voyagers, the hopeful, the wretched, the precarious....

'Our side is much too weak to fight barbarians,' says Robbie. 'We have reason, science, on our side, but we need severity. Takis – not one of us, an appeaser and hampered by the rules – and prudence.... They all strive for a stalemate, all sides, waiting for the final push....' 'or putsch....' Rita jumps in.

In friendliness, Petronia whispers to Malek, 'Robbie shouldn't be allowed near nature....' And Malek laughs, at once tells Robbie who scowls black back at Petronia.

'When we go up the high mountain,' Malek says. 'I hope I'll be left there. Dead. That's my last wish, it was the first.... The panorama. No trees, no green, no animals. No worms roaming in your gut.'

'It's near to paradise?' Petronia asks, indulging.

'No,' Malek says, earnestly. 'Paradise is low, by a lake; you walk across the water to the island, and they give you some clean clothes and blow your brains out through a hollow stick of ebony, and give you new ones, fresh from the scriptures.'

'How do you get down from the mountain?' Petronia asks. 'Are there sherpas who transport souls?'

'Oh,' Malek says. 'There'll be a service. And there's funiculars. Avalanches, glaciers. We're here to check them out. Cadavers find it easy getting down.'

'I didn't come on this trip to attend funerals,' Petronia tells Rita, 'The guides should find another way....'

'This is the guide,' says Rita, showing Petronia a pamphlet. 'The mountain's there –': it's tall, above them, and has a point. 'What more do you need?'

Robbie joins in: 'Malek has had a life in jail. First a nationalist, prisoner of those Brits, and then a spiritual chief unwelcome to the secularists. Never complaining, always following his star.... And now, we owe him. His last mission....'

'We must not miss a word, not a word of his deep wisdom....' says Rita.

'Was it so wise, to spend those years in jail?' Petronia asks, and then regrets ... how do you spend a life, in fact?

*

They climb and climb, they drag up Malek, a dead weight. And he expires – he's much attenuated, slimmed down – he doesn't tell them if imprisonment was worth it, and what wisdom he is taking to the paradise that lies below.... They leave him on a ledge, hoping the wind will catch him, land him – he's already filleted. They brew up lichens in a rusty can. Hallucinate. It's terrifying – all the monsters of the mountain come and sniff them out.

'Help, help,' Petronia shouts. 'Where are our flags, the prayer flags, to frighten off the beasts?'

'No, no,' Robbie shouts back. 'There's only North and South, not East or West. It's patronising, speaking of an Eastern spirituality – the spirit's everywhere....'

Petronia doubts it, and in any case, it is irrelevant. 'How'll we get down?' she asks. 'The casualties occur in downhill ...' and as she speaks and helplessly she looks around – the upward path was traced upon the leaflet 'Guide', but winds and snows erase it when it comes to getting down.

Robbie's blown off. He's tense, an athlete till the last, but hasn't enough weight to keep him sticking to the mountainside. His body's curved, like waiting for the starting gun, he doesn't straighten up and there's no corresponding recess in the rock where he might fit, a piece in Petronia's puzzle. He bounces here and there, it seems to add to him, his energy; he stretches out, is beaten by the stone – a piece of steak you pound to make it thin and easily digestible....

Rita says, 'Robbie was the genius who started every sentence, knew where it would end, but left it up to me to set the *clou,* complete *boutades*, the peg of wit that gives authority, the hammer-blow that strikes up the royal face and so the coin's attested, ready to circulate....'

'... and hoard,' Petronia concludes.

They laugh. For, after all, Robbie was a bore, his sex demoted, pushed down into ankles, running shoes....

*

'I hadn't thought,' Petronia says, 'this trip eliminated guys. We two, Rita – we must make it down.... There's only cadavers remembering their stuff up here....'

The leaflet-guide has blown away. Petronia says, 'There is no map. We are alone, we two: the rest are girding up their guts for combat....

'War, war – who whom? Who's with us, who has doubts, we'll scare them – threats and promises, re-cycle ploughshares, the forty acre field is mined – we're off to fight the boche, the reds, the whites, the blacks....

'Everyone desires a fight, it is the logical result of what has gone before; and then we'll see.... Will all the continents look the same? Suppose it doesn't stop ... Will there be people left to draw the boundaries and change the city names? If there's no crops, the poor will go to war for sure, and we will beat them at their game....'

She thunders.

*

And Takis, bonding East and West, the North, the South: Petronia begins to formulate a question for Rita, requiring her opinions....

And then.... Oh no! Rita has loosed her hold and down she goes, curled up into a full stop. And bounces down the outcrops like a tennis ball....

Rita – a neutral sort, Petronia thinks. Asexual? Maybe not an orgiastic type, but one to cuddle up with when it snows....

Compromise and adverse winds, she thinks: it toughens you. I used to think I had the choice – to be an intellectual, maybe popular and loved, a source of bawdy tales ... or have adventures, as a militant. Go where there's fighting, and record, be witness of the massacres. I'd take my side, but would not fight. I'd administer, intercede, make settlements. Make a name.

Better a martyr, die for a cause? – or be a virgin, innocent, untouched? Die where you're inducted? In your fresh uniform?

Or – accidentally, drop off?

'Malek was both, martyr and virgin. Choosing where you die, clasping your virginity, it's a good last statement, an epitaph. 'Here I lie, the place chosen by me, cost what it may.'

'Robbie and Rita, always collateral, free samples, as it were,' she says, and no one hears.

*

She thinks – I'm like Takis, who they hope will solve everything, everything with honour: war and peace, a continent exploded, re-designed, bristly like a gorse-bush, growing from a single stem. Armed thoroughly, and rich: and poor. Friend and exploiter of the weak. And I'm like Takis too – dead, alive, dead, alive ... and unavailing....

'How do I get down?' she asks aloud. No one here but her to answer....

Down the chimney, across the face, then the ledge, slippery with eagle shit, then a dangling rope – check that it's firm, and so, and so, but quick, before it's dark and snows....

*

If you alone survive your group, they waive your fee. You wouldn't pay it anyway.

I, like justice, and like destiny, am always on the side of doubt, she thinks. Vanessa – the trustworthy. My only friend. She's determined, resolved now to see it to the end: life. The basic principle of uncertainty.

Sometimes, you step back and don't fall off – you're a spectator. I'm a survivor. I have risked ... this time it went well for me....

*

'I wonder,' says Vanessa, 'if all those who bet on communism and lost, lost totally, from the first day – went on to bet on something more, like everybody else who doesn't win.'

'You think Takis planned his ploy?' Petronia asks. 'From free choice, or constraint?'

'Only lunatics think that choice is free,' Vanessa says. 'Who ever went to the track, made a free choice, and thought that's what betting means? You win that way?'

'Oh,' Petronia says. 'All these tall poppies, they've been lots of things, and will be more of everything.... Since I'm his dog, if I want, I could bite and run away. That's all. Communism – too simple: simplicity can't work.'

'Everyone is fascism-lite, these days. It's the default flavour, easy to like and lick, doesn't cause a stir,' Vanessa says, cocking her head, and putting on a sage expression. 'Doesn't scent the breath. Alcohol-free, drink all you want, stay lucid. Fascism from nature, not conviction, not from being literate, informed....'

*

'Climbing down the mountain,' says Petronia. 'I knew I had to be careful, very very careful, or I'd fall.'

'Anyone could see that,' Vanessa says. 'How much you wanted – not to fall! That's a surprise. You're sentimental – dogs, children ... spiritual leaders.... But, you cling on the mountain.... It must be love!'

'My sentiments are limited,' Petronia says.

'I'd not thought it was a climbing trip,' Vanessa says, insisting. 'And nature? Refugees? The mountain, toughening you up – then home you trot, without a breath of why you went....'

'I can climb up, not down,' Petronia says. 'The rest – is on TV. It's lost its interest.

'The trip was tough enough. Three out of four did not come back. It was a rout, no war has casualties like that.

'Nature. Desperate people. They're plaited round like bind-weed. Those two make thick chains that started small, and wind and bind. They grow like boa constrictors, they feed on one another, swallow and regurgitate. They are huge, unstoppably voracious, we have no way of stopping them because they consume each other without pause, becoming one, there is no limit to the size. The two resemble one another ... and now, we see they *are* the one.... The malady of nature is the malady of us, ourselves....'

'And yet you worry about your treachery,' Vanessa says. 'Who cares? The odds are – you'll tumble; fall whatever course you take. Worry about truth: you'll find there, too, that "who cares?" is the response.

'Do; don't think; keep climbing up, don't think of climbing down.

'It's unavailing, you are right, we're in a bind. Those two chains, that grow as one, that feed on one another, like constrictors – can't be stopped or separated.... Yes, it's so: a chain reaction. Our war on nature is an attack upon ourselves: the monsters prosper.... The mastery of nature, human victory – destroys what it must feed on....

'And when they've eaten everything, the birds and beasts, the creeping things, the bugs – the monsters die. The rest's already dead. We have consumed ourselves. Devouring nature- there are ever more depending on it ... if we abstain from kids – we force nature to go small, and smaller, to specialise in what's inedible, to take the drugs that make it impotent. We eat our food – it's gone!...'

'I know all that,' Petronia says. 'You tell the stories and sing songs because ... there's nothing left to do. It's a relief when Jack and Jill go up the hill, and then fall down. It's a clean ending, needs no explanation.

'My epic – help me find a worthy writer, dear Vanessa, enshrine me, and have done....'

'You slagged off almost everyone, like no one was to care – and you expect a writer to give you top spot in their book?' Vanessa asks, incredulous. 'A sculptor – glue you on her plinth? A Belle Hélène in operetta, except you don't have the looks?'

'Or the voice,' says Petronia.

'Writers once were critical,' says Vanessa, with decision. 'Now, you're right to give short shrift to them.'

'It's visibility I want,' Petronia says. 'Not judgement. Not jokes.'

'You're a monster, Petronia,' Vanessa says, and they laugh.

*

'MAGIC MOUNTAIN: CURES.' says the sign on the clinic. Petronia and Vanessa find Vinnie helpless in a narrow bed. He's unconcerned and garrulous –

'You want to win the war?' he asks, pulling at the sheets, at the clothes of visitors – 'Bring on more men and women! If there's a defensive line – more and more pile on, attack without respite, someone must get through, survive ... have them walk over the bodies of their friends to reach the enemy trench....'

'We're not into that,' Vanessa says.

'If they retreat, then shoot them. If they surrender, shoot their families,' he says.

'We've come to say goodbye and comfort you,' Vanessa says, coolly.

'If they succeed and shoot our enemies, then – give them their medals,' Vinnie says.

'Do you want to sell your medals?' asks Petronia. 'That might pay a doctor to have a look at you.'

'No, no,' he says. 'There's Fritz who's looking after me.'

Vanessa asks; the archivist looks Fritz up. 'If he's not here, he's dead,' she says. 'And if he's dead, where he ended up – we do not know.'

'And Nadia?' Petronia asks.

They find her, in her iron crib – inverted like a tortoise, feebly waving her front paws.

Vanessa and Petronia – they scuttle out: 'We couldn't think it would be a happy time,' Vanessa says. 'When I was very young, we had a pig. It was our light, our friend, our future: and when we had him killed for meat, the old ones cried, but I had never eaten pork or ham. Or sausages,' and she smiles, she laughs. 'He was delicious! I must have eaten half of him that day, and had a rack of ribs beside my bed in case the hunger came at night.... Happy? I've never again been so happy....

'Remember, Petronia – happiness is relative. Your relatives – they may be sentimental, but you come first, it's up to you, and no one else will care....'

'Had he a name?' Petronia asks.

'His name was Sam,' Vanessa says.

'Should we go back to Vinnie?' asks Petronia, as they reach the outer door.

'We mustn't scotch his hopes,' Vanessa says, pushing Petronia down the street. 'He reached the trench, and that was victory for him, and now....'

Into the trench he goes, Petronia thinks.

Where can he have fought? Vanessa wonders. That trunk beneath his cot – medals for sure. Explosives – possibly. Which side ... or sides? I'll shake Petronia off, go back and see if Vinnie's hiding wealth beneath the bed....

'The geographic centre of the continent,' Petronia says. 'Is Lwow. If he came from there, he'll have been in the midst of everything. He didn't seem that old.... I wonder, what side did he end up on....'

'For sure,' Vanessa says. 'That's why we, why everybody's, here. We're all into something, but I'm sure it cannot be "the midst".'

'I'm sure the midst of everything's the Offal Joint,' Petronia says.

They laugh. Vanessa scurries off. Petronia shouts – 'Help me, Vanessa! The visit's salutary. Help me to live with all these dead!'

Vanessa shouts back, 'The trunk, the trunk. Medals and orders, jewels, citations....' and she's gone. Enchanted, taken over by the gold, the emeralds, her hope: off she goes, and hammers on the clinic's doors to get back in.

Petronia realises there's no one left to ask about the ship.

ORGIES, BANQUETS

'I'm called on to complete the stories of three now non-combatant friends: Fritz, Vinnie, Nadia. Poor souls. Wind up their existences, make a plot, assert conclusions. What was their work? I ask myself,' Petronia asks, waits for no response. 'The lesson I have learnt is that what is inexplicable can be explained. Explained in many ways, so many – no one seems to care which one is plausible.

'I thought I moved to responsibility from excess, from indulgence to punishment, making a last gesture – to Venus? More likely, to Dionysius....

'It isn't so. The movement is away from responsibility to banqueting ... as they've said, the orgies are an option....'

Takis – like a paper flower, dropped in water: a text – he unfolds into many chapters – in jail, in triumph. Acclaimed and then derided by the countries that think they're good; derided and hunted down by those that think they're in the right.

Every empire has its Monster. If you aren't an empire, or in one – what do you do? Don't ask for a Monster, that's for sure.

*

Petronia finds a new young friend, Ivan. Too mousey to know about the orgies, so she thinks, too ratty to sit still in banquets for the toasts and speeches....

'Clubbing in Mumbai, Ivan? I'd love to, but I look odd in fancy dress, besides....' she says.

'It's the karaoke makes you tremble?' Ivan asks. 'You're so transparent, dear Petronia, like a tumblerful of gin.... You needn't say you're gay. You needn't say you're anything.'

They laugh, they laugh a lot, although Petronia won't relax, and Ivan is a staffer, once of Takis,

Now – apparently – a free radical, keeping his nose clean.... his snout, Petronia thinks, while hugging him and praising his turn-out.

'We'll just sit here, Ivan, and talk each other through,' Petronia says. 'My last travels – a disappointment. That guy Malek – in jail for wanting independence, then for the religious turn – starvation, flagellation, resurrection ... of course, no rational regime could let him out.... And let's set things as clear as possible. With Takis ... a continental policy, a plan to solve the conflicts here ... transposing them to somewhere else....'

'Oh,' Ivan interrupts, 'Takis has vision. He's a true European, thinks "continents" not countries, just like you....'

'Ivan!' Petronia interrupts. 'Takis does deals, and one deal that he's made is having what he calls *his* continent at war with all the rest. China and India first, and then America. Then – I suppose – back to the little local spats. What's the sacrifice he's offered up? Budapest? A noble city, and that marvellous empty synagogue, built like a cathedral.... For holidays – there's a few enclaves in Africa, but it isn't safe. The Europeans said he'd solved the problem – a new division of the world, but working not much better than the old ... Africa? No comment yet on anything.

'And as for me – my! I could make you weep – my history will make you grind your teeth and rend your classy clothes.... I have despaired, my friend, taken any route at all so's to escape. It's like a box of tricks, of mirroring perspectives ... the corridors, the maze, when you must ascertain exactly what you are, and then you try to pass as what you've said you were ... but, you're still in the labyrinth. All changes, Ivan. If this is civilisation – better to let it drop, let it become an archaeology, all skeletons and bling. 'How clever they all were, despite the human sacrifice....' the diggers say.... Let's bring on our buried phase as quick as quick: the good stuff in glass cases; build on the rest....

'When you run, you don't escape – there is another box, a hedge, a wall, another turn. I've tried them all, tried to reject each one. No use!

'I know from my experience – the continents are fluid – until they go to war and spin the tale how, kept separate, they are contented ... and at fisticuffs with everyone....'

'Petronia,' says Ivan. 'Stop! You and I – it's to be a fun time, a joyous ending to your fabulous life.... Forget the stuff about the culture, history, all that. We'll tear each other's eyes out trying to decide. Have your last fling, powder up, fill in your cracks and wear two wigs. Dump your conscience: Vanessa, that's to say! Don't contact Takis – you're a spy, remember, people with secrets shouldn't trust you.... "Love me for myself, if love you must...."'

I'm archaeology already, Petronia thinks. I should have booked my place ... those catacombs, so quiet and fresh ... Vanessa – crazed by metamorphoses and now by hopes for stolen wealth –

Locked in the Clinic, tubes up her nose, sectioned ... diagnosis: 'fear and greed'.

She tells Ivan about the Ship. He doesn't understand, he doesn't see there is a mystery of where it started, if it ended – where, and how?

'It's how it is,' says Ivan. 'It happened. We're like that, and so are the accessories, the people moving here and there, a swirl of happenings and being loaded into trucks....

'Being given guns and told who you are to shoot. Trying to understand the languages.'

'I thought,' Petronia says. 'That everything that's here should be accommodated, made permanent – people like me and you, the little animals, all that – and now it seems that no! we're on the slide, unlabelled and unloved, unwanted – more: we're disappearing, and there's no fiddler or trumpeter to play memorials ... last post....'

Ivan laughs. 'What a sentimental bear you are,' he says. 'They say the servant's like the master, only more severe – and you are slave to Takis!' and he laughs some more.

'I've a suspicion,' Petronia says. 'I seem to be living someone else's life, but backwards – someone who must be dead, and in a book, like I am trying to be. The only immortality – is to be a friend of Proust, a dancing partner of Tolstoy. Those – are who counts. All the other writers could have saved their ink.'

'You're smart, Petronia,' Ivan says. 'As for spies – you're right. Takis sets me to spy on you, that's what spies do, spies spy on spies. You noticed that – but smart is out. Not fashionable.

'What's in – is conviction, determination: awkwardness and simple words. You don't have those. You saw what History was, and climbed aboard – it's people moving round. With bows and arrows and sharp sticks – they drive the settled, known as civilised, off – and then ... they settle in their place until the next new bunch of guys with bows and sticks arrive ... stripped off. You found their clothes ... except! We live in times of fashion togs – that's cheap as cheap! Used clothes abound.

'They're not nomads, but they move around, they don't have flocks – those died of thirst ... but, they're as smart, determined and convinced, as you should be. They're qualified, which you are not....'

'All this is true,' Petronia says. 'But there is more. There's conflict, which I didn't see. Real people, threatening. Seeming to threaten. That I haven't met, or haven't recognised....'

Ivan will have his say: he goes on, 'South against North, poor against rich. Like America – their economic war with China ... no opium this time, just millions programmed to live in poverty, those economic missiles sent as emails ... their hope is to inspire a counter-revolution, another one, and make some friends until the next time when they feel a threat. Those Yankee bosses – provoking wars if they don't feel like fighting them themselves! They aren't so good at winning scuffles, although they try and try. 'It's better to provoke the friends you make, so they will take up arms to save what you have given them....'

'They use the language of democracy – democracy is what creates complicity. Join in, speak out – and you are complicit in everything: vote – it's "*placet*" with reserve, for all the decisions that are made.... My! What a tool.

'I'm glad Takis doesn't play that card, and I don't live where there's an overpowering democracy. I let tall poppies have their say ... They're everywhere ... they say and do exactly what they mean. Exactly what the rest of us believe. Enough hypocrisy – the rich democracies use their voters to exploit the poor, the world's, their own, the other half ... stifling and excluding them....'

'But you will suffer, Ivan,' Petronia cuts in.... 'Tall poppies – everywhere – send you to the sausage factory. So do the others – that is so as well. They're carnivores. They're like Vanessa said – they're quite insatiable – the smell of roasting pig and crackling they exude – it makes you weep....'

'That's why I prefer to spy,' says Ivan: 'On somebody like you, Petronia – a squeamish gourmet, sceptical of what is called her civilisation ... and so, subversive! Nihilist and anarchist – much more a danger – a dry rot, a death-watch beetle in the floor – more than communists, who only wanted everyone to work, work better, and work more ... communists all over, had their chance ... and disappeared.

'You attract, Petronia: people watch you, as you conceal your skills, flaunt your *accidie*. You slump and query, join the parade and beat a muffled drum.... You survive, seem fearless and convinced – the Monsters don't fear you, but you seem so tall – taller than the emperor, taller than the corporation, its offices, committee rooms....'

'You come to these conclusions much too late,' Petronia says, pinching both Ivan's ruddy cheeks.

'That's why I turned my back on revolution and reform. That way there lay, at best, a comfortable death. Now – moderate banquets, orgies with discrimination – that's my game. My partner – Ivan, that is you!'

They gaze at one another. 'You're not Chinese, I suppose?' Petronia asks.

'It's irrelevant,' says Ivan. 'Truth has no nationality. Trust me, Petronia. My country is – the truth.

'Trust Takis: he'll get us out the war he started, with honour, medals too. He will be friends with all who want. You can't shoot at your friends, you know.

'He has in mind a war to end the little wars, and maybe – he'll finesse and fund us all....'

Petronia reflects. It's rhetoric, she thinks. A banquet or an orgy – there's no questions asked, it's rare that anybody attending them would pack a gun. They are the safest places....

'No, Ivan,' she says. 'You're fanciful, and vulgar. You have a tabloid mind. A ship is not "history", people move around, but we were not awaiting anything: the people we met up with were going nowhere in particular, with no plan – no sticks, no bows – no nomadic empires there, they were abandoned people; like we were. For nomads, conquerors and empire-makers, there were settlements and traffic, songs and edicts – and appointments made and kept. The Scythians were organised, and did not want to leave a trace, even a name – nothing written, carved, and yet – they took along their goldsmiths, who made their ornaments, they bet on making fortunes, had a goal.... The Yueh Chi....'

'Yes, yes,' Ivan cuts in. 'I know all that. It's you, Petronia, you want to snuggle in a book, you're terrified you'll go on boats and drift for ever, trafficked without aim or sustenance – no book to hold you, no immovable print to give you shelter, no plot, no character and outfits fresh designed, supplied.... All that, a desolation, where you know: you lack everything! You are alone....'

She shouts at him, that she is in control, that being hostile to your civilisation doesn't mean you have no substance, no personality yourself....

But Ivan's right. She has no history, no peace, no home and no return, eternal or metaphorical.

'Both of us,' Ivan says, pressing her to himself. 'We have no clue. We have no means allowing an interpretation, an optimistic one, of what is happening to us. We're not on that revolving drum that spins, you see the horses run, the bodies having intercourse – it holds the movement, draws the sequence and it shows us how we might travel in our little space, return to the beginning – spin, spin, and start and end again. Most people watch the spin....

'Instead – we move, but – there are no strings that hold us upright, no tape, no celluloid that guarantees our permanence, a place.'

Petronia weeps. 'The fish,' she wails. 'It was the fish, made the impression....'

'Your comrades,' Ivan says, thrusting along. 'How were they?'

'Vinnie, the old soldier – had half of everything shot away. Fritz – wore a corset, waxed his beard – and had an atlas of the world, tattooed upon his rear. Nadia – you only saw her way way up, so you don't know if she was big or small. You saw her very very small....' Petronia improvises, then, decisively. 'Forget the physical, Ivan, it doesn't cut with me. Your paws? – keep off, and strum your mandolin elsewhere – I am impervious to your come-ons. What could interest me in some sex is me, not you....'

'Oh, how you sound your trumpet, Petronia,' Ivan says, canoodling. 'I go where love calls, that's all.'

'And are we – us two, or generally – in danger, Ivan?' Petronia asks, cooled down, alarmed.

'Takis? In general? Of course,' he says. 'His enemies? Naturally. The world, from bugs to bombs to lack of air – you know it's so. You have to learn – enjoy the risks! Learn to steer, you're in a cockleshell, forever on the rapids, white water all around.... You won't destroy at first, you're tough – think "dodgem car".... You have resilience, you'll puncture and you'll dent, but each of us – it takes a lot to send us down. Besides – you know that's where we all will end – scotched on the rocks!'

'Oh Ivan,' Petronia says, amused but not relieved. 'Call friends, and let the banqueting begin! Me – I don't eat most things, but I'll sit here and criticise you guys, who'd eat the world if it came in sauce....'

'No,' Ivan says. 'The world's flambé, not broiled,' they laugh, and hope their friends, and friends who're now their enemies, prolong the conflict, but hold off the serious bombs....

'How did this start?' Petronia asks. 'It was the mountains, and the green fields we thought must lie beyond our magnificent horizon, blocked by fog....'

'You were Takis's victim, then his confidant, and then his spy,' says Ivan. 'And obviously all those three at once. "I think, therefore I am" whatever Takis makes of me: that is the quote! And "I am, therefore I'm not" whatever else I think I am. Unroll your flag, Petronia, up in the air it goes, at dawn and dusk – show you're alive!'

It's hot, their chairs were on the beach – they haven't moved, and now they're in the sea ... 'Oh no,' Petronia says. 'The clichés! They swarm in like locusts as the planet melts – they've reached up to my knees.'

'There is a plan,' Ivan says, lowering his voice, 'to make a demo, make a sacrifice. Bomb one of our own cities, just to show the consequences ... a pre-emptive destination ... can you believe? Shock! ... or pass it off as an atrocity...? Not ours.... Takis will save Russia, save us all. There must never be a victim. The final curtain – everyone's alive, applauding and applauded.'

'Which city?' asks Petronia. 'It wouldn't be Lwow, Lviv, that has been done. Besides, it isn't clear where Takis stands. Which way he leans. He's "in between". Paris? Or Moscow? Or Washington? Beijing?

'He's not a worker, but he has no country ... any capital will do. They're all potential allies, targets too. Or maybe both of those; go splash a dash of Tabasco on them, just to show how hot is hot....

'Cities – they're always full of people moving through or moving out, they don't stand anywhere....'

*

The sea – is swelling, at their feet.

'Forget I mentioned it,' says Ivan, harvesting up their drinks, and moving everything beyond the line of tide. 'It's all turning into commonplace; no one takes notice now of anything.'

'I'll tell you why,' Petronia says. 'The difference between a calculation and a miscalculation – where does it lie? Not in the formulation, not the action – but in the result. And what's a result? The result of revolution – Charles the Tenth...?

'When do you start counting? ... miscalculating is inherent in a calculation....'

'Oh, you're so solemn, Petronia, reactionary as well,' says Ivan, scrolling up some friends who love him, and love fun as well ....

'I want some certainty, that's all,' Petronia says: 'That what I want won't turn quite soon into something I don't want.'

'Takis is a nationalist,' says Ivan, 'He belongs to many nations. None must be defeated, all must rise up to something larger, and more powerful. No nation, or its allies, should be humiliated, still less disappear. Each one is sacred, even when you flatten it. Out of the rubble – will arise – the phoenix: the roast turkey. Bigger, much bigger – poorer, but immense. Europe. All in, all countries, every dialect.

'The future, yes: like Bluebeard's wives – "all alive". He believes in believing everything, in lots. He's Europe, the full continent – he ties together East and West to make a proper North. The South? We have to hope ... for something good....

'He loves fans, loves to make a spectacle, but he's sensitive: hates being booed. So – can you predict, now, what he'll do?'

'Let's start ordering the banquet,' says Petronia. 'Non-destructive food, in moderation.'

'That's no fun,' says Takis. 'Maybe you don't know what fun's about, Petronia?'

*

'This looks good,' says Petronia.

It's a pink club – the 'flaming-O', and there's welcomers, dressed as pink birds, with pine torches, beckoning them in.

'No,' says Ivan, 'not there. This part of town – there's music gangs. They're rivals, and while you're jumping, fun-timing in the wrong spot, they could shoot it up. Let's find a place where there is truce – they don't welcome you, because it's full already, you stand in line. It's safe.'

'I hope they know about running banquets,' Petronia says.

They stand outside and someone works the queue, a youth in a top that says 'Sorbonne'. 'He's looking for a sponsor,' Ivan says. 'Gold mines. They need people to go down in the bowels, but if they hit a vein – or emeralds! – it's happy days. You're in, in big! Stones, not dust: those are the best deal that there is, but you need spades and chemicals, and cash to spring people out of jails and pay for licences....'

'Your friends, Ivan,' Petronia says. 'I hope they won't bring us grief....'

'They are the best,' says Ivan. 'They're in security, but they dodged the draft. The soldiers' uniforms are shabby – and they're full of holes. They had another occupant,' he laughs. 'We'll have fun times with them.'

The two guards sit down with Petronia and Ivan. They're much excited, primed with anticipatory booze.

'This is Teri, like in teriyaki, comes from Surabaya,' Ivan says.

'What's this place?' asks Teri.

'It's FAMO-us', says Ivan.

'I'll look them up,' says Asia – that's her name. She looks up everything. 'FAMO – a gang, a music gang, from South Africa,' she says. '"No danger now."'

Teri and Asia make everything move fast, in quick-quick time, the danger too.

'I knew an Asia once,' Petronia says. 'You might be....'

'She knows she comes from Asia,' Ivan says. 'But doesn't know the people there. Or here.'

'It all comes back,' Petronia says. 'The guy that sold gold scrip ... his brown bag, for the races ... or was it black?' Asia? Could this be someone known and dead?

Mirkat's friend, Kaufmann's love impossible.... Asia....

Petronia goes outside. She hears the music – what nostalgia! – the electric *ehu* rings out in a pause – the headline group is from Amhara, but it does fusion, no one gets off on them....

She asks the gold-mine guy, 'My friend, my master, inspiration – do you know him – Mirkat? Your competitor?' But he doesn't hear. Maybe he doesn't listen, doesn't know. Doesn't want to share.... 'Asia'? There must be more than one ...

Teri and Asia – they are revving up. They wear parts of their work-clothes, and Petronia sees – they both have body armour on. Their webbing smells of gunny oil.

They wear tops, similar, with equations Petronia doesn't understand: 'Ends of the earth' – they must show the air, the water, their compositions needed to sustain our life – though not, Petronia thinks, life as I have tried to live ... life as I have lived.

'You're lovely people, Asia, Teri, but I'm too old for you,' she says, quite near to tears. 'I'm sure you'll give your lives for me – I wouldn't think of it, if I were you.'

They stare, the other three. A false, a premature, disclaimer. Miscalculation.

'Well, then,' Petronia goes on, 'who are you, exactly?'

'Oh,' Asia says. '"The power that wills forever evil, yet does forever good," that's us.'

'I recognise that,' Petronia says, confused. 'But not exactly. The idea, not the quote.'

It doesn't fit with what she knows. Indifference, cruelty: her life. Self-pity, too.

Another pause. 'The Malagasy *valiha*,' says Petronia, 'I recognise that.'

The others don't, maybe they do, and everybody else, the population of the world, they all do and are embarrassed by what the snobby tyro, Petronia, proclaims as hers: familiarity.

Who gets a money prize for recognising the Stones?

She pauses.

An orgy with us four – it's insipid, stagey, Petronia thinks. How can we recuperate? The importations, food: the manioc and bird-nest soup – those chime with what the banquets used to be. The orgies? – I'm sure when they were full of food, the ancients will have brought the scrubbers in. Picked off the street, for fat old gentlemen. The question is, it seems to me, what shall we eat? I don't like the sticky stuff. What is the meaning of a banquet nowadays?

'We eat and drink, but – different times,' says Asia. 'Food soaks up drink, so it's a waste, and if you eat and drink, you puke, another waste.... You seem to be a picky-pick, Petronia!' She laughs.

'That's very true,' Petronia says. 'It means then – no banquets if I have to pay the bill, including a regurgitation ending down the tubes....'

No orgies either, if you're not paid. Or pay. If you're a lady, you don't count; you won't have sex unless you are a pro....

'Ivan,' she says, despairing. 'I'll buy a round for you, your friends, and then we'll split – off to the barracks for these two, and we – to our chaste beds.'

'You can't afford drinks here,' he says. 'Petronia – the scheme is this.... Listen: the barracks. That's where orgies happen. After, they call up every take-away of every nation's food, and there's the banquet! Global mix. The only limit is – you mustn't drink – at dawn there's target practise, and you mustn't shake....'

Asia and Teri laugh, relax. 'I didn't know,' Petronia says. 'I had a different panorama, and of course – we're here to listen to the music ... only that.'

'No offence,' says Asia. 'We think you oughtn't come back with us, not to the barracks. We think you are a spy, and so you're on all sides. You are a risk to you and us....

'Stay here and listen to the music – it comes from everywhere, so you are not a suspect – it's the universal language, not communicating anything, nothing you can be responsible for....'

'It isn't about age, Petronia,' Ivan says. 'Don't think you're lumpy-frumpy – it isn't that. It's politics. Both sides, or none – you raise an awkward hum. Look back – you've always tried to keep a nose that's super clean, and yet – you stick it into everywhere, the grubbier the better....'

'If anyone would like to dance,' Petronia says – 'I do a neat mazurka....'

'This isn't music for a dance,' says Teri, patting Asia's thigh. 'Not one you know, at least.'

There is more silence. 'Tell them, Petronia,' Ivan says. 'Why you sit with mouth agape and staring, wanting what you cannot have? ... excuse me – "what you cannot know"?'

'It's finding links,' Petronia says, reluctantly, but wanting to share, to let it out. 'Events, why they are and what they mean, where do they come from. They impinge. I verify them, through my experience – quite weak and passive. It might authenticate – but it is weak – it vacillates. Hallucinates.

'And ideas – where do *they* come from? From nothing ... inspiring, creating, all decisions and all action, for you, Ivan – mouse; or me – lizard.... Example –

'On the page and in the drawer – music is soundless. Find some guys with lengths of wood and brass – and they'll construct for you a sonic pile of shelves, a building with no roof, a host of empty cans.... Silence into sound: trust them! A structure – ephemeral, won't bear your weight but ... it holds its shape, is recognisable – Ave Maria, Nellie Dean – you hear the difference ... each bears a weight.... A structure, like your silence had imagined? Possibly....

'I'm talking of the serious stuff, of course, not ditties, shanties, all that rote, and jingles....

'It comes from nothing, the idea, and yet something – comes forth. But – not an idea, not more ideas, or not only that: something quite other – a heap, call it a structure ... chipboard and tin – in sound. Feel it, touch, listen – *how* is it there? Why is it? What's it made of, what's it left behind, for use another time?

'I thought I knew, knew about emotions and the real. Maybe I did – it's like you say – 'I know that horse – it wins!' Perhaps it does – not always. So – you must change your mind about it, your belief. Back it with caution, don't recriminate.... It's a horse, not fortune....'

'It's complicated,' Ivan says, excusing her. 'When it comes to doing things, the appropriate – it used to be the good, the true. You did both those. But obviously what's good and true today to you and me – tomorrow is quite different for both of us....'

'I'm so far from answering,' Petronia says. 'And even having questions formulated, I thought I'd find a writer who'd put me in her book – and then I'd be the product of her idea, her creative nothingness.... Would I not?

'But – I'd be immortal: even if the book's unread. Especially. So, I lie there on the page, experiencing just that. And so – it's pointless. I'd not be me. It'd not be my idea, my nothingness, my having-been – but hers! The link....'

'You're wrong,' says Asia, 'to look for links. Why should there be, and how'd you know? Suppose I say: "Ideas spring from your nothing; then comes, stirred in, your experience of keeping chickens, then writing silent music, and finally – having your symphony performed by guys unknown, unseen" ... It's madness! Nothing is nothing, everything is something.... All different! Varieties of stuff, tangible or fluff.... It's all destiny, like planting baobab trees. Find the book, open it – lie down – for ever. Perhaps you *are* immortal – a pressed flower? A name, with nothing left but that – the name?

'The important thing is this, dear Petronia: as you're on a list, can you get off it, to get in to orgies and to banqueting – not on the menu everywhere – in the barracks where, it's obvious, you don't belong?'

Is there somewhere they'll let Petronia in?

*

Petronia and Asia: they've broken up the evening. Petronia has left the Ship behind ... but that's what she wants to be explained –

'You guys go on,' she says. 'And leave me here, I'll join you....'

'I'd no idea you kept chickens, Asia,' Teri says.

'Not in barracks, naturally,' she says, flustered. 'And I've not written the symphony yet. Maybe one'll pop out like an egg....'

'I made a fortune betting on cocks,' says Ivan. 'Fighting cocks. Then the guys ganged up on me, and I lost big.'

'Cocks is treacherous,' Teri says, nudging Asia and winking at Ivan.

'*Damkol* – let's hear this,' says Asia. 'Kurdish. Maybe they'll send us there to fight....'

They fidget, till it's done. It's unrelenting.

This is belittling, Petronia thinks: if I can't solve problems, at least I could become one.

*

'Teri and Asia,' Ivan says. 'They're safe. They fight, and if they run, they run to where it's safe. You and I – we are not safe at all. We don't know where to run: – we put our trust in Takis – and it's not reciprocal. He put his trust in the big boss, the machines the big boss thinks he understands, the population which goes along with him until it's quite impossible to trust him; so – he'll change. Or maybe he will not.

'But – we are never safe. No one trusts us, because we trust big poppies who don't trust us. We're fall-guys. We should listen to the music, go home, get drunk where no one sees us....'

*

Petronia says – 'How did I get here? I know this is how it is, would be – and yet I schemed to get inside, to get protection. It seemed the only thing to do – except I knew, it was the civilisation that was wrong. I couldn't shout, I couldn't leave....'

'Don't whine, Petronia,' Ivan says. 'You were curious, you climbed on board, you didn't understand where everything was sailing to, who was with you, who next would climb on board, and where you'd beach and find a host of guys abandoned there.... Pictures, Petronia: you ignored them. You feared there might be nothing – and didn't see how difficult the "something" was.

'It's true, no thinker has got further than you have....'

'Useless, Ivan,' Petronia says.

They peer into the dormitory – the barracks stretches out, it's huge, it fills where once there was a park, with follies, hahas, tall birds with fragile legs....

There's Asia, Teri – cuddled down and fast asleep. There's bunk beds, and the floor is covered in white boxes – 'Mmm,' says Ivan, 'there's crispy pork abandoned there,' and Petronia – she shudders.

'Those two kids,' she says, 'are safe until they're not – what moves me, Ivan, is the crispy pork – the nameless ones....'

'They're all called Sam,' says Ivan. 'It's for security – a default. A single name – they all count as one casualty – thousands of them, long pigs in fatigues, tripping on the sea, on land, and dossing down in strangers' shacks and in the flowerbeds – lost, but command knows where they are, and why. There! A paradox for you, Petronia. Lost and on the map.

'Everybody in the settlements – they have a code, to show the mailman where they are. They think they have a settled place: it's just a code....'

'That's poetry, Ivan,' Petronia says, impressed. 'I almost hope I'll end up crisped, a quick snack for the innocents before they wake and board the trucks and planes, go to their work.... Having professionals kill you – that's the best. All within the rules, and clean....'

She hums the start of *Damkol*: 'I fear I shall die and never attain happiness....'

'Teri and Asia – they seem to have attained happiness....' she says, uncertainly.

Ivan doesn't reply.

'These guys, bosses of continents, they've all invaded countries, crushed peoples – for this pretext or that. Do you suppose,' Petronia asks, alarmed at what she's guessed, remembering what Ivan said. 'They each have pictures in their head – of sacrifice. To win, to hold firm, not to concede: has each in secret, by their will, decided how much, how many, they can spend of us? We, the resources of their life-world, the living world?

'We think of you and I as vulnerable – but in reality, the question for the bosses, is 'up to what point is it worthwhile to live, defeated, humiliated? And, further – what is it worth, for the species as a whole to live?'

'Bring it all down! Risk! Dare! Be strong, determined – we sacrifice our armies, why not all the enemy? Or us? The shoppers in the cut-price supermart?'

'There's classes in the war academies that discuss the end-game,' says Ivan. 'It's a test for first-years in the military. How far will you go? Bet, and lose a country? The big poppies – they've all done that. A continent? They all risk that. When you say you disclaim the civilisation, Petronia – remember, that everything alive already has a price, fixed by the will of someone who will stake it and its creatures on a losing hand....'

'And Takis?' asks Petronia.

'Oh,' says Ivan. 'Among the first-years, he was the paragon. No stake too high for him ... no bug or bomb too perilous that he'd refuse its use. But, of course – that was to impress the staff, a boast made to puff himself.

'That is the only way to graduate, Petronia. Loyalty is total, or it's treachery in waiting. The big boss, or the team of them: they live by that. For you, the End – it's the extreme act. Yours, yours alone. For them, they live with it all day ... it comforts them. Ultimately, it will conceal their failures....'

In the banquet, waiting for the orgy to begin.... Petronia thinks. Not just letting the planet die through their indifference, their impotence – but all of us, all living things, exploded. Blown to tiny bits, too small to fossilise. This is what the story is about? Original for sure – the story of our species, of each one – nothing. Ending in nothing, no trace, no memory, no dragons becoming screech owls? Nothing at all?

'And you, Ivan,' she asks. 'Are you loyal, totally, to Takis – who's not loyal?'

'Yes, Petronia,' Ivan says. 'Absolutely.'

*

There's another pause. Then Ivan says, 'Is it possible, Petronia, you didn't know all this. Everybody knows it and everyone goes on as though it had no consequence. It doesn't need explaining, no one but you designated it "the inexplicable". All is explained, and if nothing is explained, it makes no difference at all to anyone, not to you, to me, to Teri, Asia, or to anyone. Even what's not known has been explained. Explain or not – it's the same. Explaining gets you nowhere, Petronia, and you're made so you don't believe in explanations anyway.'

'Everything is difficult,' she says, randomly. 'You're right, though – I ask "why" even when something is explained, though nothing happening to me has never even been explained.'

'We'd all go together, at once,' Ivan says, tired of following her.

'That's the worst part, Ivan,' says Petronia.

'No one to close our eyes?' he says.

'You're a strange person, Ivan,' Petronia says.

*

'So, Takis, you won,' Petronia says.

'Yes,' he says.

'I'd congratulate you,' she says, 'but nothing seems quite at an end. You being here – is good for you, but kind of indeterminate....'

'Oh,' he says – 'my metaphor is this ... the problem was to balance more cards, make the paper castle taller: to fit more legs on to the milking stool. Think of the continents – the problem comes when you leave people out, a leg – that's why we have the war, and all the rest.... A stool with two legs cannot stand, with three – uncertain.... Four – it's too conventional, there's legs that gang up: – that won't do, to isolate the one and leave three legs: five legs is eccentric, so we carry on, adding what we must.... Now, there's lots of legs, I've glued them, it should be stable, but there's a question of their lengths....'

'So the green fields....' she starts, 'waiting for us....'

'A metaphor. And one meets so many people when there is a war,' he says. 'It's like you fall asleep during an opera, and when you wake – that one's over and they're into Götterdämmerung. Above all – there's been corruption. People paying not to be involved, and people paying to be cut in.... I couldn't pay you, Petronia, because it seems corrupt....'

'You never paid me, Takis,' she says. 'My payment was avoiding punishment by you.'

'Well,' he says, 'don't do jail-time. It does no one any good, it's not intended to. And now, you've had the best part of your life, Petronia – you should spend the rest avoiding ends. Especially the big, the silent, one. Survivors – the best profession that there is – the ones who're left – they live and live, even if they're sorry for it....'

'Yes,' she says. 'The history says – there's emperors who're very young and very old. And, Takis, you are left with one who has survived. You are his confidant, his prop, and his successor too, perhaps. Friends and enemies – they accused him of all atrocities, and yet – maybe he just liked his job ... stayed on, made peace and war.... Found reasons and excuses for the deaths. He's ballast, as you know.... A ship is steadied by it, but weighed down....'

'Countries are built on earth,' says Takis. 'Topsoil. Don't mine too deep, don't let what's frozen, melt ... don't dig for gold. Dirt is what we stand on and are buried in.... Dirt, muck, ballast....'

'That's amazing,' says Petronia. 'We never thought to look beneath, in the bilge – down there, a clue ... steadying the ship....'

'Oh,' he says, 'they put all kinds of stuff in there – brass cannons, broken porcelain – all signed, if you had cared to look.'

'It wouldn't speak,' she says. 'It's trafficked, traded, dredged up....'

'Your life,' he says, 'is it acquiring shape? If you don't sell yourself, how do you know what you are worth? You can't live on, hoping your question-marks will hook a fish!'

'Someone will have caught those fish,' she says. 'That sounds like an explanation. River, sea or lake? But – it's not the right kind of explaining, it's another mystery. A piece of a puzzle, but – which one, which puzzle?'

'Most mysteries, says Takis. 'Are such because reality has been well covered up. You have a trivial obscurity to face, Petronia: your life, just one. I have the war – a mass grave of mysteries and cover-ups. No witnesses, for sure. Just – unanswered questions. Bodies galore.

'For you, no payment, and no punishment – you don't exist, Petronia. I don't see you!'

'You watch me, but don't see me, I'm out of context, I don't exist. I'm your wish, your figment,' she says.

Too big to swallow, just big enough to go in a mouth?

'The war, Takis,' she says. 'The soldiers, the robots – they don't need break anything. I know you smash things, and the people, to show them – war is tough, tough business, don't fool around, don't play, don't underestimate, machines won't do your suffering, that's still your part. Winning costs, it's good, losing's bad, it costs even more. Losing might be good – but costs the same. The war.... It's frozen now, but everything's destroyed...!'

'When it's up again,' he says, 'it will be more beautiful and clean. I shan't pay for it, and nor will you. It will be marvellous – full of memories, ghosts, shades, thoughts and poems: plum blossom. I shan't want a monument, and nor should you, Petronia. What comes after – is superior. Mimes will come – more life-like than a statue – and more fun.'

'So, this hello is a farewell?' she asks.

'Nothing is owed,' he says, 'Nothing. Except....'

'Loyalty,' she says.

'Absolute loyalty,' he says. 'Besides, you signed the paper....'

'... took the oath,' Petronia says.

*

'And are we more secure?' she asks Ivan. 'The map has changed, but it doesn't show the people, where they come and go.'

'We're lions, Petronia,' Ivan says. 'They aren't on the map. We'll be the top, so long as there is something weaker left to eat. And rain, of course.'

'Your side won, Ivan, so it's time for you to do jail-time,' she says. 'Collect your medals, get the new office, the secretary and the job. I hope you understand what you must do – in the cell, the office.... Most jobs – you don't know what they're for – unless it's sweeping streets and pulling beets.'

'You know how it works, it worked, Petronia, but you don't know anything that counts,' says Ivan. 'You should feel worried – though it won't change a thing. Big people get buried in the earth, and little ones like you – maybe like me – end up just buried. In the villages, the little houses and the shacks: in the big cities and the lines for handouts – all get buried, if they're not dust. Don't complain: there's nothing personal in anything. Somewhere you don't think of, isn't you, don't want to be in, don't know how you'd get out, what you did to be born there, put on a list for punishment, wearing someone else's shoes ... can't think of anywhere better, not where they'd have you, and it's too big to get out by running ... Somewhere, Petronia, somewhere is yours, or rather: it is not. It's special for you. Look for it, take a room, order Pastis and *rillettes.* Your special place – don't linger. It has no special meaning for you, but you feel at home: people – are people. You can boss them. Imagine you have money. Money may come by post. You're big here: they hate you. You eat well, there's dancing – not for you. Happy? Yes, you're happy. Think "Oklahoma" – the state; that's not like the musical, not at all. Be glad you are not there.

'That's it. All you'll get, all you need to know. It doesn't last long at all.'

'Teri and Asia,' Petronia asks. 'What news?'

'Security's a strange business,' Ivan says. 'The more you hope to get, the more you have to endure, risk and suffer ... the more you're insecure. And so is everybody else.'

'So, where are they, those two?' asks Petronia.

'Over the hills and far away,' says Ivan.

'It's dangerous?' Petronia asks. 'Why aren't they machines?'

'They're the next best thing,' he says. 'And we know for sure what side they're on.'

'Is it a side I'd want to be on?' she asks. 'And now, it's dangerous, more dangerous?'

'For everyone,' he says, and there it rests.

*

This is where we used to dance, and now it's changed. Quite different.

The meat place, my nest of spies and dupes, Petronia thinks – is quite transformed. 'The Minerva Project': 'make your contribution', say the signs.

'Oh,' says Petronia, 'I've got no cash. I never carry cash....'

'No,' says the lady. 'We need your thought. Your pansy.'

'My thought is this,' says Petronia. 'I'm thinking about soldiers: – robots. They're simple souls. But there must be bigger machines that know much more about winning ever bigger wars....'

'Oh yes, for sure,' the lady says. 'But this idea diverts you, soothes your fears. No one will steal a march on you....'

'It's a rocket, I believe,' Petronia says. 'The idea is – we send it to the nearest star, and colonise, convert, plant "the flag", all that – so we can be evacuated there. You wouldn't want to go unless you're forced ... maybe the rocket trip's for criminals. We could put the presidents in – a punishment for greed and war, the preparation for the conflict, provoking it, and spending all our cash on fighting it....'

The lady laughs: 'Oh no! It takes a hundred years to create the fusion thrust. Then, the journey takes another fifty years. The bunch of guys you're thinking of for punishment – they'll all be dead, long dead. Besides – the ship is not for people – it's enormous, empty, heavy. It drops a kind of tent, when it arrives. That's empty too.

'The project cannot serve as punishment: we might find nothing there. It's easier to execute the bad guys here. Maybe strange people will hop aboard when they see it landing, and fly right back here – maybe the alien starmen live for centuries.... We might not appreciate them, nor the smart machines they bring along....'

'What is the nub, then,' Petronia asks. 'Of this idea?'

'I'm sure it has its military use,' the lady says. 'Most all things do. Don't think of that, but just enjoy!... All we ask of you and yours – is "write a poem we can send: – a pensée, or a joke" – and if there's people who can read ... they'll know we're cultivated types, creative brains – each slightly different.... You represent the human side....'

'So, just publicity,' Petronia says. 'Distraction....'

'Good for anxiety,' the lady says. 'It gives you hope, humanity....'

'Oh, I'm not cynical, not like you,' Petronia says. 'I go along with things.'

Work here, if this is work? ... she used to know the customers, the music ... the dirt. She remembers – 'the dirt', that every country's built on....

Work here, get rid of Ivan, hide from Takis.

'No,' the lady says: 'No openings, my dear.'

*

Nothing to be done – a foolish type of work, and so, so what? You do it or you don't – who cares? No one but you.

*

Could it be, Petronia wonders – that my ship had some kind of resonance, a common theme – with space. Space: it's full of 'ships'. The search for people just like us, but fifty years away, forward or back. What a perverse trip! Are they like us? They'll take the ship to bits and steal the fuel.... But – my ship, the one that seemed to come for us, we boarded it, and then.... The absence of a crew, apparently... Just clothes ...

Is it possible the creatures we would find in space, long after everyone on earth is dead – are clothes? Is it possible – our underwear comes from a star beyond our ken, our system: it's alive. Life-forms – thinking threads, like trees and mushrooms have. Our trousers, in real life they possibly were managers of an outfitters on Beetlejuice, who got sent off to sniff us out and start an empire.... 'kill the earthlings, fuzzi-wuzzis' they'd be told ... 'their land is our land, the people ... not of interest: savages and poorly armed.'

We wear them, alien beasts; they're on, around us, when we sleep and wake, they read our thoughts ... we buy them, wear holes in them, wash them, mend and hand them down....

'No,' Petronia says aloud. 'It isn't possible. I saw the shipwrecked tailors sewing them, the clothes – clothes couldn't be alive, dropped down from space.... The clothes, fast fashion, they will finish up as pollutants, dross, in Thailand, or Nigeria – without a sign of life. And then – there's the Nutella to explain. Surely, it isn't made on other galaxies? And the fish....

'That's all too like the crap book I'd probably have found to feature in, and finish up, unable to get out ... a graphic novel, with my super face made conventional, banal ... and it would be impossible to exercise and move my legs....'

The dancing days are done, she thinks: quick polkas, tarantellas – farewell all!... What sticks in my mind is – people moving, leaving their cities and their faith, running for their lives, over the frontiers, choosing, re-choosing, sides and hoping it will, somewhere, be noted and the skies informed – not to drop anything at all on them ... not even take their photographs, not assign them with names and numbers to a group that you can smear and target, then eliminate.... Let them move into empty countries, pass themselves off as residents and carry on until it is decided – that the regime's no good, so everyone will be invaded, as we four had thought, when we first saw the ship, aimed straight at us. We four – as heterogeneous as you will find – at once alerted, knew by instinct we must move – leave everything and take the risk ... go where the journey, quite by chance, will end.... Or not by chance. It ends by running into empty land, that temporarily fills, and must, in turn, be emptied, so's to fit in others like us, then off we go again....

And she thinks, quite fondly, of her 'Angelo', bitter and suspicious of her as he'd always been ... trucked off, saluting her with his fluent umbrella gesture as they all were trundled out....

*

Hurrah! Asia and Teri, both are back. Scoundrels, probably, but their work consists in surviving and not making a fuss about the ways it's done.

'You do look similar,' Petronia says to Asia. 'To Asia, my kidnapped friend. I think they couldn't fix a price, and so – no one bought her. Now....'

'There's lots of us called Asia,' Asia says. 'If you're an orphan or just don't have a name. There's the music too, we can't all be called Aida.

'We're not from here, I know. Does it matter? Are you from here, Petronia? It might help you if you changed where you are from ... and all your expectations. Suppose you knew someone like me – identical. I didn't ask you where you came from, nor did you ask me. It isn't done. Where you find yourself – gives you its attributes....'

'That's so true,' Petronia says. 'Stick to your principles. I used to travel, but I'm not going anywhere on a space-ship that weighs a million tons, and nothing yet invented that will power it....'

People mature. If Asia is the Asia that Petronia knew – she won't admit it. What's the point? Another story you can't believe? Stories aren't made to be believed. An older person has left behind the younger one they were ... somewhere, but where? Unfindable.

'Teri was hurt real bad,' says Asia. 'Fell off the truck and broke his voice. His tales? He carries them – a box of discs. For common needs – he points.'

A talking book? Petronia thinks. I could have ended up in there.

'You're still searching, I see, Petronia,' says Asia. 'It's good, but let's suppose you find an answer to the "why do things happen to what there is and they become quite other things...." Situations, that is ... not only "things" ... "without our willing it or knowing the results, or causes...." Let's say you find it out: it's one of the mysteries of us-in-the-world. We all see it. It happens. Why worry about it? There's an explanation – the right one, that you're looking for. It's like the multi-coloured map – it can't be solved until it is, then everybody does it. Who will you tell, who wants to know?'

'It would be complicated,' Petronia says. 'The answer would be something so unlike the question, I don't think that it would satisfy. I've no idea how it would come to me, the answer – yet, it lies below all that I do, the wonder at surviving in a life that has no clue regarding change and movement.... Who shares my itch? Ivan? It wouldn't make a difference. Not to Takis, certainly....'

Hearing the word 'Takis', Teri springs to life.

Pointing is useful – wanting food, a pee, some sex, – but not for the complexity of the one word – Takis....

'Teri feels Takis is the hero,' Asia says. 'The greatest in the modern world. And yet – we were betrayed by him. On purpose; not as a by-blow, a mistake. The people we were fighting – he gave them stuff that made them win. The other side – we think they'd done the same for us....

'It's always indirect, we know. The truck: we were on it. Teri saw the bundles, what was in them, said "doomsday" and fell off....'

'That's what I suspect,' Petronia says. 'The real: the real story – it's always indirect. Unless – it's just the boss who shafts you.... In my quest – it's the real tale that lies beneath ... there's always one ... in front....

'You, Asia, you were lucky not to be eliminated. Perhaps you're known. Or liked....'

'I know my price,' Asia says. 'I won it. It's too high now, for anyone to pay. The black birds came for Teri – he's been '*hybirdised*'. We've lost our shine, Petronia. And you – you were never likable. Always the questioning, the discontent. You're poison, no one would trip with you. You make me feel for you, you can't stretch out to anyone....'

'That's very well,' Petronia says. 'It's true, I've played all sides. But you and Teri – not even opportunists. He's robotic: you are charmed....'

*

The Americans gave my grandmother gum and nylons, the Russians gave her a ride on a tank.

'That decided it,' says Petronia. 'Takis – has given nothing yet.'

*

'All this business you've been involved with, Asia,' says Petronia, 'The risks, the sacrifices, loyalty – the oaths, the jail time that you risk in breaking them – does it seem important to you, in your scheme of things? If you have a scheme, of course, and it explains, like I want explanations, but not, maybe, an explanation given in a book that I can't feature in, by someone who answers tricksy questions, but not mine....'

'You don't take the trips, Petronia,' Asia says. 'Don't meet the big boss who tells you what the question is, since you evidently do not know....'

'Clubbing!' Ivan shouts. 'A good time, a noisy time. Time! It's time for time, time lost, to lose, as you watch the spool unwind!'

'Gin fizz,' says Petronia: 'And as there's faith and no alcohol – just the fizz.'

The others take their Shirley Temples, Teri tries for kvass, or kumiss, but has to settle for kefir.

Teri puts on a disc, during a pause, using his dead hand: a voice, rotund and actorly, says, 'You know – the continents are like gangs of lemurs – ghosts. They're rivals, fight over food, but keep separate ... until there's an escapade, a pregnancy, and you see them – eyeing each other up, squabbling over young ones, how to bring them up, and then a common danger – reluctantly, they will cooperate, but if a gang is weak – because it isn't warlike, it's disorganised – it lives in poverty and the other gangs take what they want from it, intimidate .... They try to keep the conflicts, the big wars, settled on the weakest links, those invaded, poorly resourced, factions and too much philosophy.... But in the end – they're gangs. Boastful bosses, punishments, all that. Some are hard, some less so – but in the end, they're all lemurs, hop-hop and all with tails of bottle-brush ... black, white, off-white, brown, but their behaviour is identical, except here, there, their clocks run fast and slow, the terrain changes –but, in the end....'

'That's Takis, fooling,' Asia says. 'He sees himself as one who could unite the sides, or at least seem palatable to all – while having secret yearnings – unconfessed, and so you can't believe him. No one ever wants to give a centimetre, even when they're for ever on the move ... appealing to people, it's a fraud....'

*

'Takis is a poet,' Ivan says. 'He doesn't talk direct to you ... often he departs – a riff on love or envy....'

It's a dream. Imagine! One boss for one continent, let alone for many, let alone for all.... No one's come near....

'Just philosophy,' Petronia says: 'I've seen him close to ... and he's....' Unworthy, deceitful, cruel? – she wonders which to say.

It's a relaxing evening, comrades all, and so she says, 'he's fanciful.'

'One civilisation – one community,' says Ivan. 'And yet – all us lemurs, threatened, in one small spot – on the way to their extinction ... a species, that lives in gangs, autocracies with rights ephemeral ... walks upright, has a number....'

'Music ho!' says Teri, hoping. Music there is.

'Ivan caught a jack-fish, but his wife insisted "it's a lobster" – Be it so, or be it not, Let the jackfish be a lobster' – sang the kozba and its master-musician. The friends join in; even Teri, up to a point.

'Faith is emotion,' Ivan says, when the song is done. 'Belief is something else – harder, tougher, but provisional. It's the unpredictable killer.'

'Be it so,' says Petronia. 'No rocket for me, no shipping into space. No new Fritz who can't steer me where I want.'

Asia weeps. 'I'm stressed,' she says, 'and Teri can't console me, nor can I console him.'

'We're all fucked up,' says Ivan. 'No one wants to serve under some boss, not even under Takis. Especially.'

They sit, sober, disgruntled, out of love.

*

With no alcohol, they look round sober at each other, cool and disenchanted. Petronia, dark of mood and insatiable, gobbling wisdom like a chicken hooked on corn. Asia – a soldier-volunteer. Who knows what atrocities she's committed? Ivan – a preening stooly, and Teri – oh no! Teri is further into silence, gone irreparable, his discs are scattered ... his part is done....

He croaks, a raven's epilogue, his nevermore: and then – he's croaked!

'We can't involve ourselves with guys here,' Ivan whispers. 'Carry Teri outside. No autopsy ... lay him on the tram-tracks, and scamper off. We know all there needs to know about him, don't involve the rest.'

And that they do.

'He'll be sliced up like a *mortadella*,' Asia says.

That doesn't take them anywhere.

*

Teri doesn't linger. He's edged himself out, on the margin, then off and on the carpet. Leaves no manuscript.

'Best not name names,' says Asia, 'Cover up, forget your experiences.'

'There's lots we don't know,' says Petronia, 'Lots more that we forget. Not to mention interpretations. We're all on lists – best not be on too many. Best be of the wrong age to fit in anywhere. Do like the Syrians did under the French – don't ever reach conscription age.

'What countries do, and continents, the exclamations – "busy busy and help help!" ... and everybody watching porn or filming it, buying watches and pricey cognac, and selling tanks and giving English lessons and recitals on the theorbo – I admit.... I couldn't keep in touch. Too many running, and too quick. That's why I turned my back on everything, but you have to eat, and so – you have to compromise.... That's so, Ivan...?'

She waits for his continued silence to break and give a go-ahead.

'It doesn't do to be too smart,' eventually Ivan puts in. 'You see the other side, its point – and you are sucked in, into the quick, the quicker, sands.... You aren't so smart, it seems, the deserts and the peat-bogs seem to have a life that's bigger, more informed, than yours. Much longer, too. And down you go.'

'Ivan, you send us off,' Asia joins in. 'To fight and rescue; mostly to knock stuff down. I thought you had a plan, you guys – it seems you have a wish, a vision, that you hope we'll make come true.'

'Exactly,' Ivan says. 'We wish, and you're the genie who we hope will serve us unreservedly, and grant us – everything. Anything. We give you armoured dodgem cars to travel in, full of bangs and maps: a lamp, if you'd prefer. Then, "sort it out, dear Asia!"' And he laughs: '"Policy" is dreamland, and you, you soldiers, are the enchanted brooms who should sweep the sandman and the nightmare monsters out of sight.

'Good for you, and let's hope that when they're needed, your shining swords are sharp and cut the bad guys into pieces, quick as quick....'

'Oh they are,' says Asia. 'A hundred, or a thousand bits and each piece shoots up and becomes a newborn warrior. So there is work, and wishes to fulfil, for all eternity....'

*

'You said it, Asia,' says Petronia. 'You're happy with your mission – destroying, losing, till like Teri, you fall off the truck. Me – I had an adventure, a puzzle, that you cannot contemplate. My trip. And – in the last resort, I do not care if you win or lose, dear Asia. I don't care which side goes top – it's fiddle-faddle, playing endless games of football or of chess while you could be ... or rather couldn't be ... being me....

'Alas – you're cheap, Asia. All people in the stream – are cheap and ignorant: following their choice. Your trade is cheap, and stupid too. This vainglory – it reminds me of what Takis said, that he'd do anything to leave his mark, to reach an eminence, even if it meant a sacrifice ... even of himself ... of us....'

'Oh yes,' says Ivan. 'That has been his plan. To sacrifice himself, to let his friends or enemies – in the end, they're much the same – pin him, dismember him, make him an example, humiliate him in any way.... Then, in extremis – save him, love him, acknowledge him, offer him their kidney....'

'Burn it all down, and throw himself like water on the pyre?' Petronia says. 'They never do. Not even scorch themselves. I know the sort – and I despise them, vulgar, showy, bad actors and singers -stentorian and out-of-tune....

'It's why I take myself out of this bison-horde, the scamper after water-holes, the fall-guy playing rear-guard to the lions, a movement of the horned and horny – of the gullible.... Enough! Enough of the wavering human fronds, who twist to east and west with every breeze.... Enough of sacrifice, of valour in a trivial cause; enough destruction in the name of sacred goals.

'I'm through. I'm back to my first principle – withdrawal, retreat from what they call their civilisation. I will betray these foolish evil guys, but not be betrayed by them....

'I am the only one who saw the ship and its trajectory as epic, mythic; a revelation intimate and labyrinthine. The others thought only of the rescue, of what they could loot and carry off, and of the wonder of the landsmen when we returned to shore....

'Enough of you, Ivan, enough of Asia, of all the victims slipping off and falling underneath the chariot wheels.... My experience was majestic, to be forever questioned, used as the key to living, acting and to thought....'

'That makes you sound crass, Petronia,' Asia says, tartly. 'A case. Swollen, rather than puffed up.'

Ivan smiles, embarrassed.

'And do you have the answers, Petronia,' Asia insists, 'to why things are as they are, and when some happen to you, what does it signify?'

'There's no answer in the philosophical mode. At a point,' Petronia says. 'You must accept – "there it is, that's what there is". When you stand up in a breeze, why don't you fall over? Why is there breeze, not a tornado? You'd be exhausted, answering all that.

'And you, Asia, can't answer anything. You gave up. You took orders. End.'

'Regarding what Takis proposed?' Ivan asks. 'A comment's due.'

'It's not possible, and he's not the one to try and fail. It's not instructive,' Petronia says. 'Because one big boss kills more than the rest – it doesn't signify a thing. He – she – had found it possible, that's all. Alone or with a vote, threat or promise. Rich buddies or the bigots.'

'I accept your judgement,' Asia says. 'I'm dross. Too bad. I don't understand you, not a bit.

'But you've gone nowhere, nowhere at all, Petronia. Trying one thing, then another – quite inconclusively.'

*

They're lucky – about Teri. But then, soldiers are expected to kill, be killed, lie on the rails – be dealt with by a special authority which has its special ways.... Soldiers – they bury soldiers.

'Atrocities, Asia,' Petronia says, and Asia laughs – she says, 'It's a funny thing to say, to want to know....'

'Well,' says Petronia, 'as you say, I've done nothing, ducked everything through casuistry. But you –'

'We're taught to stand – stand still, stand our ground. And let them come on you,' says Asia. 'And that they do. They're afraid, for sure, but they know – it scares you, if they keep on coming straight at you. It is a plan, but when they disappear, and you go on – you find they're hunkered out of sight instead ... in houses.'

'I understand, Asia,' Petronia says. 'It's plans. Atrocities.'

'To you it seems atrocious,' Asia says. 'You have to stand firm, and not think of what they think, what drives them. You don't want it, that conviction.'

'There's lots of places been invaded,' says Petronia. 'All over, and not concluded well. Georgia, Iraq, Afghanistan, and Iran soon, or maybe not, and then there's Africa: today there's Libya, and to the West, the Sahel. To the East, Sudan – and then there's Egypt, full of people like an egg....'

'Full as a river with a hatch of fry,' says Asia.

'Takis – feels he's needed,' says Petronia, fishing.

'He knows both sides,' says Asia. 'Except there's many more than two. And then there's neutrals and the undecided, and places where they've been at it for decades, grinding each other, that we don't put on the active list. There's Africa, of course.

'Ukraine, that's almost gutted out ...'

'Takis says he's ready to sacrifice, but really,' Petronia says. 'He's like all of them, they've nothing of their own to give or have destroyed. It's just another idea on top of all the others....

'He may be right, that someone like him would be needed, but he's not that person and he complicates....

'It's fantasy, Asia. It won't proceed like that, with everybody looking for a compromise that's really just a loss, and living with the enemy. You've knocked it down, where you were sent.... People remember them, the smaller things that you forget....'

'Yes,' Asia says, 'it's so – there's all the other things, like money ... and the food. Enforcing peace? That's really empires' job ... you need lots of force, brass bands. Takis has none of those.'

'On my trip,' Petronia says, 'they rescued us, and it seems a symbolic end, a proof of restoration – but when you think, it's a reflex ... searching for what's lost. And where did all the others go?'

'You were in luck,' says Asia. 'Luck comes once, not twice.'

'Luck's not Takis, that is evident,' Petronia says. 'He's not the end. There is an end, that's why it's not a book. A book is always "there", it doesn't disappear, or die. It could be a movie, where you can cut and cut, and re-shoot, I suppose.... But, a solution that is acceptable to everyone? A boss of bosses, or a friend to all? A happy end?'

'There isn't one,' says Asia, 'or else the story wouldn't have a start.'

'The ship – invaded us, but we four went aboard, so it was us, invading; except we didn't know the how and why,' Petronia says. 'We were the innocents, especially me. I didn't know how it would turn out, and who the people were we ran across....'

'All the rest knew, Petronia,' Asia says.

'We were rescued,' Petronia says. 'Just us four.'

'Teri and I – we weren't,' says Asia. 'We weren't like you, wanting to end up in a book, safe.'

'You didn't understand,' Petronia says. 'It's territory. Land and borders, that's what counts, and nothing else – except maybe for water and the cash. The rest is rhetoric. Romans and Huns, the Mongols – they showed another way – perpetual advance, ignoring boundaries and who's the citizens. Making slaves, then freeing them and roaming round, on and on, giving away the lands to relatives – that is the only way if you want alternatives.

'And now – the lady in the former Offal Joint, she says that who gets up first and takes the nearest star – has everything that circles round: whoever is prepared to fight to plant their flag, if there is somewhere where it sticks.... Up there, down here, it's much the same.'

'Well,' Asia says. 'We've seen it all before – Takis as a Chinggis or a Timur-i Lang? ... those had a cost, but in the end, they're in the books; and Takis too – he'd be remembered.... It's about force and power, Petronia, not inclusion. Empire, Petronia, not eternal peace.'

'Takis?' Petronia asks. 'Does he have hidden hordes? Or legionaries? That's the mystery.... Of course, the wretched of the earth are always waiting, expecting to be fed, conscripted in return; given the bows and staves....

'It's fantasy, of course, but it is bleak. It's rise and fall.... The universal ruler, like eternal wisdom – often proclaimed, but like the mercury, it runs, divides, pollutes....

'All Europe, already mobilised – to take Africa again.

'Europe, from Sakhalin to Aran is already naturally one ... resources, intellect, imaginary.... America is easy then to choke, the Northern part will drop through civil war, the South will take what's left. Parrots and banana groves – in Manhattan and the Bronx ... China and India are the souk; they can sell stuff, they know how. I've hope for Mongolia, that they'll be left aside....

'Add the long tail of islands to Asia, with the paradises drowned... all compatible. Along with Africa – the South.

'The desert lands – abandoned – maybe to stage a beach volley tournament from time to time....'

Asia laughs. She says, 'That is the plan: with Takis, the historic pacifier....

'Continents. Even a small piece achieved – would be amazing. Are you ready, Petronia – the new era ... at your door?'

'It's all so nineteenth century,' Petronia says. 'Big Europe – Engels and Schopenhauer! The US now – militias and the Klan ... Spying on us all, provoking, slapping down ... invading. Russia – a sickly giant, a sprawl....

'Has Takis ever read a book?

'Now Teri's gone, we've lost our source, he was the enthusiast for order, even the new one....'

'It goes like that,' says Asia. 'Death. Some you will lose, along the way. You say what Teri used to say – "There'll be atrocities, but there's atrocities all the time." Spies and soldiers! – running big shows, as ignorant as carp. And those who're not the soldiers or the spooks – those bosses are eccentrics, refugees from show-business: – comics on the pier. They played with soldiers in the nursery, now the soldiers play with them....'

'I've no opinion,' Ivan says. 'It all sounds very strange to me.'

'Tell us, Ivan,' Asia says.

'Everything,' he says. 'Sounds like kids' stuff. Wanting to finish countries. It sounds so ... like so long ago.... Not nearby countries, they said – don't fight those. "We'll have a blow-out: colonies for everyone who counts!"

'And will there be Esperanto, I ask you? French Revolution stuff....'

'It's true,' Petronia says. 'A gallimaufry. Reminds me of the offal shop – but possibly ... might it be the future? Eternal return to the enlightenment, the great illusion...? Or the great change ... animal spirits .... do it, do it loud ... excess, elephants sitting on your face....

'Maybe, if they hadn't rescued us, we'd have sailed on, found Happy Island, or the golden steppe, where horses don't need breaking and it only rains at night....'

'The more the trend is to consolidate,' says Asia, wisely, so it seems, 'the greater grow the conflicts.'

'We weep for you, Asia,' says Petronia. 'Your loss. Ivan – comes out as an apostate. But as for Teri – he might be a prophet, but it's hard to feel respect for him.'

'He gave the finger to respect,' says Asia, starting to cry again, remembering. 'He wanted credence, that is all. And scepticism too – you do no credit to yourself, Petronia, believing what the lady says about those stars.'

'It's what Ivan said: belief is powerful, but runs off – like water that was ice,' Petronia says. 'The Offal Joint – it always was a knocking shop, where the fox-trot led us to the bosky groves.... Now, it's the stars who lead the dance....'

'That's hearsay,' Ivan says. 'It was diplomats and politicos said that – they frequented, they're the gourmets, no impropriety there.... Stardust twinkles in their eyes....'

The other two – they let it rest.

Nature's not to be gainsaid, when it comes to having fun.

*

'Don't go along with Asia, Petronia,' Ivan whispers: 'It isn't you – you are a prickly fruit ... those two, Teri and Asia, they were with Takis.... Not like me and you, with reservations, blackmailed and disillusioned; but they were in it for the whole, the project. Stay away! Takis has the great ambition ... the continent, and after ... And as he fails, is thwarted, he'll be more demanding, tricky, treacherous. You know it, you've worked with him ... he's poison, there's no antidote.... An emperor of Europe, another of America? Us – the West, become Byzantium, the East. The West – Rome – America, pagan, invaded and cast down. Byzance: who'd not prefer it...? Or emperors everywhere, with senates, legions – and those capitals, always being built and looted ... Syria, the Maghreb.... Imagine, imagine – there's infinite space for that....'

'Tell me, Ivan,' Petronia says, anxiously ignoring his fancy fugue. 'Are we occupied? Is it a "lite" invasion, or ... there's soldiers everywhere, they're foreign, but I'm quite unsure....'

'Oh,' Ivan says, nervously. 'Don't be alarmed. There's foreign soldiers everywhere, except they're friends and allies, so they aren't, in the real sense – foreign. Soldiers – it's trivial ... they could be just the start of Takis and his project ... or, of course – maybe it's the end....'

'It could be up to someone similar, who has a different plan....' Petronia insists. 'Big European countries – they've all had bosses; centuries, where they thought they'd boss the whole, the universe ... and had God as their fan.

'It usually turns sour. They handed it, the parcel, continent ... the hot potato, to the Americans. It wasn't wise.

'It's natural that what Takis wants is copied by a host of copycats.... Restoration, revolution and reform – a customs union or arms sales ... most everything's been tried....'

'Don't be a xenophobic,' Ivan says. 'Not everything can be explained, it's all too complicated. You should know ....' And he laughs. 'It's unity, or wars eternal. Better wars on the outside than within, I'd say....'

He scans Petronia and Asia. They're not too sure. 'We didn't go to Europe,' Asia says: 'We were in between, we thought: between there, and further still.... Petronia, where did you sail?'

'Oh,' she says, 'the instruments were broken – we went everywhere, but we weren't registered from where we started, though it's true – the language was quite similar. They hadn't heard of Schopenhauer....' It sounds a little lame. 'I thought I recognised the fish,' she says.

'Well,' Ivan says, shrugging off their scepticism, 'of course, you live on a round planet, and round and round the story goes. On a square, a triangle – the picture'd change decisively. Maybe the offal lady thinks the rockets find the planets where all's different – gas, or acid, where you'd need rubber boots, lead suits.'

They laugh, relieved.

'The Romans went to India,' says Asia, 'but the Greeks stayed within their magic sea. "Takis" took a Greek nickname, to show he's moderate, inclusive – but I'm not sure that it works. The Macedonians....'

'Look,' says Ivan, interrupting. 'There's a light! I'm sure we'll get a proper drink....'

*

There's only beer. The barman says – 'There's Phix or Bud. The best beer is Romanian, but we can't serve it here.'

'You look stressed out,' he says.... They are.

'It's politics,' he says. 'The Lethe fountain has gone dry, I fear,' and he laughs roundly at his little joke.

Petronia weeps. 'I do not understand these conversations all the same. The people – they look different, their tattoos vary, their colour, timbres – all seems different, but the content ... always identical ... power and governance, the *pari mutuel*, Beethoven, the stock exchange, the guns and planes....'

'You'll find that what's in the bottles is just the same as well,' the barman says. 'Same as always, by the label. The poems and the symphonies, the bodies that you long for, lust with – the eats: pouting chicken breasts, the flaming lobsters and their desperate cries – all, all the same as always were or very similar....

'German, French, American or Russian – bosses all the same, and in comes India and China, and waiting in the wings....' He lists.... 'It must end in South against the North: resources against predators....'

They all look, feel, speechlessly depressed.

He reaches down – down past the baseball bat, the sawn-off gun – 'Here,' he says, reaching way down.

'I make this for myself, and for really desperate guys....'

The demi-john is almost full. It brings to Asia, Ivan, and Petronia – the place. It's not the Golden Steppe – but similar. It seems a mountain, smooth and shapely, set up on pillars.... Are those lions that purr? And plum trees – some in blossom, some with purple fruit – blue and red birds, they don't sing, they caw, but then – even when you're pissed or drugged, you can't have everything ... too much, and it would all seem – a hallucination....

'I don't want cash,' the barman says, when they come down from high, where they've been lofted. 'But I would ask you to clean out my cellar down below....'

They have no choice, and find – the cellar's like Petronia's catacomb. It stretches on for kilometers, there's everything you've ever thrown away, no human corpses, but remains of everything that ever ran or slithered on the world....

'Where do we put it, and in what?' asks Ivan.

'You'll need to dig much further,' the barman says. 'Don't bring that crap up here – dig out some more kilometers, and shift the stuff into the new space. I'm expecting a fresh load of beer.

'In time, archaeologists will come and dig up all this junk, and put it on display.... Until then...'

*

It's quite conclusive, useful too. It ends the speculation troubling them, the geopolitics; it makes them forget poor Teri; and the digging puts them in good physical shape. The liquid in the demi-john is better than a secret currency, than digital gold *solidi.* It's worth different sums for everyone, and so better than freedom, which, presumably, is the same for everyone.

'It's a fortune,' says Ivan. 'Stored in demi-johns.'

'But,' says Asia, 'it's the barman's. We can't take it. And the digging part! Ouff!'

The barman's 'special' – it's a great success.

'I could have had sex with everyone, like on a computer,' Ivan says. 'In the plush salon. The promise – was sensational.... I'm impotent – I seek those promises....'

'I was a great hit,' says Asia. 'In my second career as singer. I was on the stage – the Mariinsky. Or Woodstock. Now, I've managed to identify the "la" crouched in my throat: – the rest is all downhill, they say.'

Petronia stays schtum. It's vanity, all vanity. Sadness – returns for her.

*

'Opposing,' Asia says, 'without doing jail time – is a wonderful thing. We should tell Takis that. Opposing, failing, being wrong – all those things. Do it, and bless you! So long as you don't push it; stay within the frontiers, knowing the rules ... not going abroad. Expecting trouble, maybe getting roughed up. Cops, the law – it's not a paradise, but....'

'I'm not sure,' says Petronia. 'Opposing must mean you are seeking power – not freedom. Try real hard – and you'll be made to suffer. Power is exactly what I don't want, won't get.'

'Oh,' Asia says, laughing. 'It'd be no good for you. You're opposed, but you must fail, you know you will: you hope. "It's the civilisation...!" That's what you oppose.

'Almost all opposition fails. Revolutions, putsches – fail before they start or on the way.... Besides, for power there is no "way" to follow, no end, and so ... the power you'd get might wither away, unless you change the rules.

'You know *you* can't change those, Petronia, and there is nothing that will guarantee you if you're forever on the outside.... Try living here, but incommunicable, silent.'

*

'They're starting the dancing in the Starshot,' Petronia says. 'The ex-Offal Joint. Dancing's a compromise for me, although I love it.

'Dancing – it's the epitome of civilisation, I would say. Silent too, probably incommunicable.'

'People are a problem for everybody,' Asia says, quite kindly.

'No,' says Petronia. 'Everyone is fine. Me too. I might illustrate what you say, but I am not the picture, not the movie. I'm a still.'

'Who betrays, is betrayed,' Asia says. 'Who doesn't betray – is betrayed. That's the safest way to look at it. Orgies and banquets – never hurt anyone, on the contrary. It's the profile, the generosity you should watch ... you are exposed ... the poisoned wine-cups. Being too much in the flow. It attracts malignity. A suicide enforced....'

'That's hypothetical,' says Petronia. 'You need cash for banquets. I am skint.

'Orgies – you can set those up quite cheap. It's not significant, but I hate that clammy artificial skin you may attract....'

We might all agree on that. Jail time too; avoid it, if at all that's possible....

'This is the beginning,' says Asia. 'The booze – it's cleaned us out inside. Our brains ... on a safari....'

'This is where we sight the ship,' Petronia says. They hug.

*

'I feel I owe it to Teri,' Asia says.

She'll do a tour. She doesn't say, but it must be Syria.

'Takis mustn't win and mustn't lose,' she says. 'He's a monster, but the other monsters taking over.... I wouldn't want to hasten that.'

'It's your profession,' says Petronia. 'Finding your comrades, going to fight monsters on the orders of monsters. For you, immediately, it's all about the people that you like.'

'Comrades: does it surprise you?' she asks.

'Not coming back, would be a surprise,' Petronia says. 'You should survive me, so I needn't worry about you. I feel my years, no one comes after me....'

'That's your nutshell, ready for you to curl up in it....' Asia says, and they laugh.

A tortoise, living for a century – it must wish it could slough its shell, run free and naked. But the shell's its skeleton.

*

Asia and her mates: the soldiers in the other wars are machines, but she must risk her life in person, just like civilians do.

The question is: 'the right kind of Kurds' and 'the wrong kinds of belief'. How to identify, and reconcile, them?

Robots take to people who have strong beliefs: – they make friends with them, pray with them, even play football with them. Asia – she must not.

Some Kurds are in the wrong place – Iran, Iraq – and then there's those in Syria and Turkey – how do they draw a frontier around them all, make – hypothetically – a bordered country they might want in live in? Sykes–Picot drew a line, but that was on a map – Asia and her comrades have to make decisions quick, while they're on the run, or on a truck. It's tricky. Are they better at it than machines? They're cheaper, that's the point.

Who but the Kurds wants anything for Kurds? Maybe Asia does, but she's a lance-jack, nothing more.

*

'We are the future of mankind,' Asia writes to Petronia, 'but though that fires us up in combat – it's quite insignificant.

'No one believes we'll make a place out there for Kurds who'd trust us and would like to live amid the dunes, all waterless....'

'Machines can't give up, Asia,' Petronia writes back. 'Humans can. I've persuaded the Starshot lady that robots could be shot up to the stars to colonise their planets. Robots live longer than we do, but until a way is found to cut the space journey-times, we'd be without them for a hundred years at least....

'As for you, Asia – you can surrender, or run off – you don't need programming or a code.... Do you know who you're fighting for, by the way? Which side? You can't see much, where you are.'

And then, of course, she realises – letters don't get to warriors. To message them, you need to follow a procedure that she doesn't understand.

Asia wrote her note before she left: it took months to get through to Petronia: Maybe the robot postie fell into a hole, Petronia thinks, and laughs.

*

The dancers in the Starshot are mostly human, though it's hard to tell who's who, and none look obviously like they're spies.

There's nothing harder to perform there than mambos, anyone can do those if they try....

Petronia finds the other dancers lacking – in class, in ingenuity. Most of the dodgy deals are done for lines of code, or documents in blue, or lists of dreary guys in offices ... provocateurs who get you lifetime sentences for stepping out of line.... If you name them, that's too bad: if you denounce them, it will cost you jail....

*

'I don't like you, Ivan,' Petronia says. 'In olden times, friends would play Bizet on the pianola, more recently – they dealt in arms and drugs. You don't do anything except – you watch me. Are we supposed to like each other? Are we robots? Do robots have affections? Is courting all a spoof – the conventions, tender things you say and find on *billets doux* for sale on florists' stalls?'

He giggles nervously. 'It's just a job, Petronia,' he says. 'Loyalty's the only human thing that counts.'

'You've finished here, Ivan,' Petronia says. 'You can report back, "nothing to report".'

'I'd need at least to describe where you have come to stand,' Ivan says. 'Whether you represent another civilisation, or none. Perhaps you'd prefer "post-civilisation".

'Each of these positions is a fantasy, but plausible. The species is finished, run its course? Have you found its successor? Something which transcends it – a technology, a brain that reproduces and expands, while ours decays? Plays with itself?

'Perhaps a personal stasis? Waiting for something different – something, someone, like Takis, who you could oppose without passing to another side?

'Or – are you inventing that new side? A new civilisation – imperial, that passes for a global one? The pacific solution, actually – militarised. And what you will create, you will disclaim.'

'I hadn't thought: well done, Ivan,' Petronia says. 'I thought betrayal was enough – but maybe when you leave the labyrinth of puzzlement, there is a causeway leading out, beyond the bog.... I'm on the shifting boards, tectonic plates – the elves dance round, confuse me – their lamps on poles, that flicker and go out.... I could almost turn to you for help, my dear....'

They laugh.

'I don't innovate, can't invent,' Petronia says. 'I'm stuck with you and yours, Ivan, and you with me.'

'It's disappointing,' Ivan says. 'I can't make a report that says you are a burned-out case.'

'Then say I'm proud to be what you call me: "barbarian",' she says.

'I'm doubtful,' Ivan says. 'Civilisation – however many, what sort they might be, you're in one. Like that or not.

'"Post-" is always good for conversation, "anti-" will work as a polemic. "Alternative" attracts a crowd. Add "civilisation" to any one of these – you're a celebrity.'

'Then "Barbarian" for me,' Petronia says. 'It is. And let them work it out. Strange practices, or none, appalling ones....'

'I'll pass it on,' says Ivan. 'That – you've retired, no longer in the game. You could have done great things, but there must have been a sneak, the boss, who tripped you up.

'And still, where you were hung up, starting your adventure, is the fish.'

'A beginning gone wrong,' she says. 'Persisting. The fish, decapitated; made anonymous, illegal, robbed of their life, their element....'

ASIA

Asia ... 'where imagination sleeps like an empress...'

Tristan Klingsor

Of all the powers we have, enabling us to move, to leave, to change, Petronia thinks, the body is the one that promises the most ... oiled and hairless, smooth and randy. And yet ... it falls, it freezes, wrinkles. Coughs.

My time, my vision's passing, past, without my ever being in it....

If you search real hard, or pay a guy to look – you may find the casualty, your friend. Or someone very like. A body, or a name.

Poor Asia.

'Friendly fire, that's what I hope it was,' Petronia says. 'My Asia – so unlike me. My warrior, obedient, unquiet. Armed and alarmed.'

It isn't that Asia sleeps – that's just what they say.

*

The lady says, 'You can be "Mistress of the Dance"' – in the basement of the Starshot.

The pay is tiny, but Petronia sells tickets to make up, like in a *té dansant.* Puts the records on. It could be her vocation. She's the Madam. Running the men is easy, running the girls – is harder, but it's rewarding. They say all the cats in a cat-house must be grey – it isn't so at all.

'Just selling tickets – like the hat-check girl' the lady says.

It's a way of cheating destiny, Petronia thinks: No one would expect to find me here.

There's a cubby-hole to sleep in. The dancing – it can go on and on.

Petronia thinks of Asia, and sometimes weeps, remembers how Asia remembered Teri and his bawdy tales; how sometimes Asia wept when missing him, or missing sex.

The job – it palls. There's barons, overmastering. Some are real barons – powerful types who can't be denied, and want things laid out, easy. There's barons who are merely office types, but they have gangs and *claques* – a following of scribes and fixers, ushers and turnstyle johnnies, cap-tipping types.... And baronesses, fussy ones ... all want the best and best there never is, nor has been, can be, and it wouldn't be for them, no, not at all, however much they're well-connected, hard-nosed, and rude, but all Petronia, and the rocket lady, Camelia, can suggest is put them on a list.

If the robots cost too much, uppity humans will be loaded in the rocket, and up, up, away. It's not an honour or advantage, but the bully bosses can boast about most anything, even being pioneers fired into an oblivion, a void.

Her work, Petronia fears – has soured.

'It's only been a week,' the rocket lady says.

'I learn quick,' says Petronia. 'I disgust, I'm bored, Camelia. It's too easy, the simplest job of all .... Sweet nothings, hugs and kisses – that's the best anyone can hope in life ... I dispense it, and it leaves me quite indifferent.'

There's no reaction. 'I know the Plan,' Petronia says.

Camelia laughs, Petronia goes on, 'I know what they – Takis, his rivals – propose. The continental union. A settlement that makes a whole, a continent; and yet each unit, "nation" still lives, struts, and can threaten all the rest. The dream of Europe, united, each village with its nationalist emotions – Napoleon and Hitler justified.... Bringing Russia in or crushing it? And will there be more or fewer European, Euro-Russian, Russo-European wars? And will each continent live in harmony with the rest – where most of the resources and the populations will be?

'I don't want that,' she tells Camelia, 'but – I have no country. I abhor the "Takis" plan. "Make peace to make a bigger war."

'It's true, I'm not a worker – but the formula still holds: I have no country, and I have no chains. I am a horde of one, without a destination ... wait, and see what I can do!'

They laugh.

'You sound quite Celtic, Petronia, my dear,' Camelia says. 'They were so orderly. Present for centuries, thousands and thousands of them – then, tidied themselves away. And human sacrifice is quite the thing today....'

'This fighting,' says Petronia. 'I'm not part of it, and it costs me friends. It's not my thing. My spying brought me grief, and even a responsibility. I don't start these wars and they don't stop for me.'

The Starshot should be a good new place to look for friends who don't fight wars, just fantasise.

*

'What do I mean to you, Camelia?' asks Petronia. 'I'm used to Ivan watching me – and now it's your eyes over me. What do you expect?'

'You're a repository, dear,' Camelia says, scuttling back upstairs: 'Of confidences, suspicions – losing friends and finding spooks. Try keeping your nose clean. The beat. Remember that – keep it hot and audible, and there should be no consequences....'

'I want an answer, that is all,' Petronia says. 'It's true – I am a suspect, victim and transgressor ... give me just one, a clue, an answer....'

'Oh, get wise, Petronia,' Camelia shouts down. 'The answer if it came – would unravel everything. The universe, its being there: and here.

'Meanwhile – you know the Plan! The Continental peaces and the wars. Wars to restore the peace. Until it fails – you are a suspect. And if it succeeds, you'd be the tallest poppy, its guru. Except – success and failure – they look very much the same....'

'I'm not interested,' says Petronia: 'I'm not a Celt, I don't want to start new bloody civilisations....'

'Be very very careful, Petronia,' Camelia says.

'Are you a friend, to be advising that, Camelia?' Petronia asks.

'Don't risk the law,' Camelia says. 'It will not serve. Don't criticise, or you'll get jail time, lots and lots, all in the one cell with many others. Or solitary. Neither one is preferable to the other.... Don't make a fuss, or you will lose your job, the landlord will not keep you on....'

'You're my landlord, Camelia,' Petronia interrupts. 'Employer too.'

'Oh,' says Camelia, 'here, we value justice, freedom. You don't seem convinced of that, my dear: – you want answers as to "why"? ... everybody does, but you're fixated. It sounds like a philosophy, but really – it's psychosis.'

*

'It's not that,' Petronia says. 'It's Takis, and the Plan. Nothing might happen, except – I know I shall be watched.'

'For some people, being in the eye is what they want,' Camelia says.

'You make me feel uncomfortable,' Petronia says. 'This shooting at the stars – I guess there is security involved, we must be cleared and vetted, have clean sheets....'

'Clean sheets – they are essential,' Camelia says, and giggles. 'Respectable places – must guarantee they've laundered, at the start.'

'I'll ask around,' Petronia says. 'Maybe there's others who would like a speedy trip....'

'Your companions, they often don't come back,' Camelia says. 'Whose fault is that?'

'I just get rescued,' says Petronia. 'Others don't.'

KONRAD

'Bad things happen over there,' Petronia says. 'Not here. Not now. They happen elsewhere: distant from us like distant stars.... Fifty years? It's nothing – go back in time, there's bad things everywhere, atrocious and unmentionable, but all's been cured, and where they happen still, once more – it's distant from us, as though they're happening on far-off stars.'

'I know all that, Petronia,' says Konrad. 'I just want a trip – a holiday. Curiosity to satisfy – abundant. Away, away...!'

He does a pirouette.

'I've watched you, Konrad, and I've chosen you,' Petronia says. 'Because you shake a leg – nay, both – with spirit, spirit of abandon, and of joy....'

'I study you, Petronia,' says Konrad. 'And I am dispirited. You're typical of half-informed and superficial folk. Your forte lies in travellers' tales, in speculative fictions ... while we, who trudge the internet all day, and watch the falsities hatch out – in thousands, millions ... we see you, credulous and easily fooled. You're like those children buried by the spotted Piper in the silver mine, to dig and dig for all eternity....'

'It's true,' she says. 'I'm barely literate, I follow what I see, am told.... I seek the truth, cost what it may.'

She hopes she's humouring him.

'There's two mistakes at once,' he says. 'Trust in others, trust in your own impressions. For instance – you should know – the Starshot is a joke, a stalking horse. There are no means to make a shot, no fuel: and nowhere, nothing, that will ever justify the time, expense, the risk, the deep uncertainty of shooting up, or down.

'It's an old myth, seeking "people like us" – a folly! If there were, it's gazing in the mirror, dear Petronia. Like us? And *do* they like us? Are *we* like us, and do we like us, ourselves? Who'd ever want to see the aliens, if all they want's – to see us?'

'Besides, you can't get there anyway, it's far too far. When you have the means – then, you might choose a hypothetical goal. Before – there is no point. It's out of reach and quite unnecessary.

'Then, you speak of Takis, and the plan to consolidate, to end the nations, form the continents as units ready for a universal war. You saw an operative, just one, called "Takis", who bullied you, seduced and lied

. He had you follow him as if he were a Bonaparte. You're wrong, Petronia.

'"Takis" is a group, a party, club – profession – a brigade of thousands, scattered everywhere, on every continent, but Europe is their base. They are a band of agents, diplomats, politicos and makers of opinion, their aim – to oversee the organisation of the world in continents. Your Takis – taking Europe. All are attached to national intelligences, security – a masonry, a cult, that's infiltrated, infiltrates; a fake gruyère, made by sly goats with lazy goatherds. Each member is a visionary....'

'How can I trust you, Konrad?' Petronia asks. 'What you say is plausible – I'm never taken in, but....'

'Oh,' he says. 'I want to test you. Are you reliable? If we take the journey – will you pick me up and carry me? Can you resist the truth, the odds against you, and back me? Believe me?'

'I've always got through,' Petronia says. 'It's not alarming, what you say. I know the rocket is a punishment, a con, publicity, a death-trap. "Takis" too – they're everybody looking for a plan, and then for holes in it.'

'So, you'd think it better to believe in nothing, not anything, not what you want or what you see?' he asks. 'Remember all the friends who trusted you, and were not rescued. Where are they? Did you keep a score? Some went the way you pointed out, and it was wrong, you saw....'

'It started off quite different,' she says. 'The ship: it was a way to leave. We had no plan, it was provided, intended for us, we supposed. And – in the end – it worked. We travelled, and we all made land – the four of us, that is.'

'Well,' Konrad says. 'It doesn't matter now. And what you thought were fish, the headless ones in sailcloth in the troughs, laid out like torpedoes in their pods ... those stick in your mind, your frivolous mind. So what; what do you do with images? You can't unpick them, turn them over, to see if there's a date, a signature....'

'You make me breathless, Konrad,' says Petronia trying to stop his flow, to move him out. 'Where could we go, for R and R? You're so much more up-to-date, informed, than me.'

'Oh, anywhere,' says Konrad, 'I've heard your discs, danced all that stuff. Go? Somewhere without music, without dancing, if that's possible, Petronia. A place without tall poppies and security; a place where everybody tells the truth and does so without threats....'

Konrad is competent – but, oh no! – his tweed suits, the *loden*, and the porkpie hat ... he's horrible to see ...

'Oh, I've already taken care of that,' he says. 'I think for starters – just us two....'

*

The room is bare – a picture of the lake, Lucerne; a bed, a hanger on the door for the tweed suit, the hat.

Konrad knows all the tricks, and some he's invented, trying out.

'Classical studies. You're a conscript, Petronia – I'm the gladiator,' he says. 'I'm the emperor Nero – I can send you off to war – as you say, attack and defence, when you're in the trench, they are identical. No crimes get punished when they're far in the past, in another language, a Latin now you only hear in church – excess is normal but it's titillating too. I get off on this ... forget the banquets, share my order of the day. Dying for your country – sweet and decorous. It's war, Petronia, watch out! Beware ... they'll send you in.... You could be casualty or heroine, it's up to you....'

He persists. He waves his arms, pretends to be a monster.

My body seems to get off on this, Petronia thinks. Unwanted sex: the body's said to thirst for it, the bitch. But, for me – this will satisfy for all my time that's left. No citation for bravery, thanks – I'll throw my medals to the crowd....

*

Technically, for orgies you need more than two – for Petronia, what goes on, yes, shows Descartes is right, the body's a machine. Hers gets its oil and grease, Konrad seems inexhaustible, and in Petronia's head, the questions and the revelations swirl. She cogitates.

We should have looked more closely at the fish, she thinks. The doubt arises – but then it's clear – a fish's body is quite different from ours. No, there was no mistake. Fish. That's what they were. The shape, the smell....

But then the bigger question comes, why do things happen, *those* things, how all things are, not otherwise, and what they signify.... What weight do we give them? And can humans take a lesson from them, concerning their own nature, their behaviour? Do we leave reactions, consequences, down to civilisation, and if it's lacking, as we think –

what then do *we* do? Inculpate ourselves? What, in a life where things will happen – do we do?

Do we see life as a test or – just step back, go with the flow? Cultivate what grows in the sand and on the dunes, and call it gardening?

'Enough, Konrad,' she says aloud. 'That was some trip. You pay the room and if you dance again, don't expect discounted tickets on the house....'

'I know,' he says. 'It's me. It's just too bad – there's nothing I can do.... I am a warrior, and I do Marathon. Take heart, Petronia, you've been satisfying. If it was a slog for you – that also is too bad.

'I told the truth – it has a price. Including clammy skin, and me repeating "was it good for you?" We've much to learn from robots, especially since they decided they'd be gendered, and almost all chose male. It was their wish, they voted....

'The war is coming, Petronia, and the robots – they must be on our side ... whole continents, allied, hostile – and battles into space.... All – under arms. Civilians? There's no such thing – we'll all be targets now....'

'We always were,' Petronia says.

But Konrad is unstoppable: the truth – a torrent, flecked with gore....

'Find a hole, Petronia,' he says. 'Hide. Resist the draft. Do not think of dancing through. Today, my carefree passion – that is just the start ... invasions are the norm! Watch out! A sample, your old ship....'

He laughs.

'The Monsters – all over, they are heating up,' he says. 'Loins girded ... quite to plan. We're ready, but you aren't.

'Barbarians? They're unlike you, Petronia. New uncompromising types, for sure.

'Everybody now's convinced – we need a conflict to eliminate the civilisation as we thought it was. You were right, Petronia, in your special way – away, away with everything. The dancing days are done....'

*

He disappears. He doesn't show up at the dance, nor upstairs at the scam-shop, where they collect the payments to develop rocket fuel, all – all is left, abandoned. For Petronia – the questions stand: is Takis really 'Takis' a huge conspiracy that augurs peace but thinks to get there through intensifying, spreading, preparing wars?

That the rocket is a scam – it doesn't disconcert. Even if guys get shot up – down – in the sky, and don't come back, it doesn't bother her. She knows no potential crew. The friends who've disappeared – her old-time lover, Vinnie; Mirkat, the two Asias ... and Kaufmann – dear Kaufmann, so protective of the earth – they wouldn't make it halfway to another star.

*

'It's just too bad,' Camelia says. 'Petronia – you do attract the ghastly types – Vinnie, and even Fritz, Ivan the wondrous boy, now Konrad. Top guy in rocketry, does dancing on TV. An expert in how to treat our fellows in another galaxy.... Dinner? He knows the etiquette for aliens ... maybe they squirt food in through somewhere odd, an orifice that we don't have.... Sex? Maybe they lay a thousand eggs at once – beware of one-night stands with those... He does the ethics too.'

'I know,' Petronia says: 'I'm used to monsters of the dragon type ... Konrad is one of the small crawling things – one bite, you're itching everywhere for weeks.'

'Oh,' Camelia says. 'He's well-connected. His colleagues come from every side.'

'That's what I fear,' Petronia says. 'Betray him, and it seems you have betrayed the world.'

*

'You should change, Petronia, change utterly,' says Camelia. 'Konrad may decide to come back, take another trip with you, slobber over you again, like the dog you didn't want. You can't stay here, exposed....'

'Oh, I couldn't move,' Petronia says. 'I live higgledy-piggledy, so it may seem to you – but I must be in touch.... I need *here*! Philosophy requires.... This is quite the apex, the forefront. To you, it's business. The Offal Joint, now the Starshot, Ivan and the others – you meet them here and only here. They are my life.

'My history is lived here, Camelia, from when it was the cake shop.... How it's transformed! This is my theme, my object ... my study.... I've had an explanation of my Ship. Unverified, but plausible. And so – the world: everything that is, it doesn't answer me. There's no explanation, not at all....'

'It's just cash,' Camelia says. 'Cash and Intelligence. *Panta rhei* – it all melts, becomes an other thing. Here is the dance, and the rustling that you hear is tail-feathers of our military. Rearming to defend our humble hearths, our civilisation. Of course, we need those missiles to perpetuate ourselves.'

'Oh yes,' Petronia says, and laughs. 'I remember – we had Rusyn neighbours – were they Ukrainian or Russian or a bit of both, of neither…? That was the topic long ago. The whole street questioned – what would they choose, those Lemkos and the rest – our side? And which was that?'

They laugh. 'You went in deep, Petronia,' Camelia says, 'and now you can't get out. You might stay here disguised, of course ... You're mistaken, of course – you fell into the treacle net and stayed there not because of what you'd done. All the blame and guilt, it's not because there is a mystery you can't solve, and don't know how, or what. You are to blame not because of what you've done, which is nothing, – it's because of what you know.'

'Disguise is commonplace, I know,' Petronia says, ignoring Camelia. 'The social – isn't social, not at all, it's people pretending to be animals or other people, or scraps of something else. It's true – I could pass as something pasted in – Doktor Caligari, Queen Zenobia of Palmyra, the black Magus – but who'd believe it, if I'm standing here, a roll of tickets for the dance, hot in my hand...?'

'We could change your look,' Camelia says, 'If it matters so to you.'

'The face? The body? The soul and its experience? The obstacles ... ignore them,' Petronia says.... 'Change everything and start again?'

'Oh fuck you, Petronia,' Camelia, losing patience, shouts, 'Understand! No one matters. Not one of us, not you, not questions, answers, not your rackety life. No one!'

'I'm amazed,' Petronia starts.

'It doesn't matter, I told you,' Camelia shrieks. 'Who caught the so-called fish, who cut those people's heads off. Know or not know – it's irrelevant. The ship came – a mystery. Or being dumped. It's the same, it's finished. Don't expose yourself, if you want a quiet life.

'If you want high office, bawds and banquets, tales for the lads – plus recognition for your gallops, then – this planet's not for you. Sign up for the star-shot, fiddle your time away and land with all the other cadavers that were packed in and looked for something better, richer, more original ....'

'I could wear a veil,' Petronia says. 'If you'd let me keep the job, I'm really desperate for cash....'

'I know you,' says Camelia. 'You haven't given up – you want significance. Even – you want meaning!'

Petronia gets to keep the job, for now.

*

Curiosity? Or justice. Petronia wonders. Best not separate those too quick, and all the while remembering – the big question: 'how much does anything matter'? If we don't matter, like Camelia says – what does, and what steps do we – I – take, to do exactly what?

For the moment, we have to hope Konrad is satisfied, digests me like a boa renders down a sheep, Petronia thinks. As for my adventure, I could sketch a story, bring in the clothes, the tailors – but there it would end. Explained. I shall have done everything, had everything done to me. I'm finished – but not over, still here but fading out.

And still, Camelia's right – is there significance? The explanation?

I'll set it down, although it's clumsy, doesn't sound quite right....

*

It went like this. There were executions: people so important to be put on show, the headless cadavers weren't thrown overboard, not like the people, those stripped naked, tossed in the sea, their clothes left in the hold. Captives, followers? Witnesses: a surplus anyway. The corpses of the notables, decapitated, set aside, wound in shrouds like tuna, all nine: – something intervened, instead of being put on show, the gang, the crew, the winners – they jumped ship, left it to motor on, end up anywhere, in straight lines, fixed wheel and rudder ... to beach itself, where maybe all eventually would be unravelled and revealed. No time to scuttle the ship, nothing, no messages.... Instead – we four, we unsuspecting, took the ship over – and on the sea, that blank space, the wetness, saliva, that will swallow you, not leave a trace – we met up with the silent human transhumance ... there's labour, work, mortality – traded to and fro. The qualified, who're wanted, miners, welders, drivers, soldiers – get a berth, reach land. The poor, they drift away, panicked, displaced: the really poor, the unskilled, unemployed – excluded and insulted: women, the worn-out men, the very young, the young, the grannies and the seers, farmers, herders, shamans, players of the oud and singers, poets, prophets ... they're really useless, without a use, surplus – shipped, trucked off, abandoned: survivors, if they're lucky ... mostly they walk. Some swim. We picked a cargo of the skilled ones up – and they worked incessantly, and went on to work some more when they were landed.

And we are rescued ... so. Hurrah for us! That was the good part!

We assumed those were fish, in the slots made for them, and so – we didn't look. We burned the bodies, thinking they were stinking fish. And who were they, those cadavers, so valuable, so dangerous: what made them so significant? We just found them, waiting for exposure ... revelation. Or a ceremonial burial at sea? Liberators or oppressors? And all the rest – followers? – stripped, thrown into the waves, naked. Leaving behind their poor clothes. And we were ignorant, and missed the mystery – completely....

Who's behind all this? You are, I am for sure. I've taken sides – I love California, Russia is part of my life and I hope the Chinese make it, and the Touaregs get what they need .... and so, and so.

I'm behind all the executions and the trafficking, and so are you. Think. It's not difficult.

Why all this? – oh, many different reasons that are probably the one, the same, all in time a futility, academic, archaeology, but now – watch it! Not knowing, not composing the picture, not looking at the cadavers, not asking, not surmising, not hypothesising. It means you don't live your life – many other lives swirl on around you, and nothing you see can you explain.

Keep your head securely on its neck. A conspiracy? that if you knew it existed maybe you'd be in, and then, from fear and prudence you'd be out zippy quick; a conspiracy of ghosts and fireflies like our leaders fear. There's wrong guys all around, believing the wrong things, having the wrong grandfathers, reading and forgetting the wrong books and leaflets ... And guys trying to get your job or not giving you a livelihood and driving off your animals or having you live like starving goats, cutting off your head, throttling you, jailing you for life, drowning you, starving you, having you die in deserts and containers....

You're obvious, you drifters – wrong languages, wrong colour, wrong thinking ... wanting to get in or out your country or theirs ... in the way, threatening, resisting.... And then there's everybody who makes it happen.'

*

Yes, Petronia thinks. The Ship. Something like that, I guess. Unless it was all just happenstance, and all the context hangs upon it like a discarded shirt – because the context is exactly what everybody lives in and they know it through its smallest part that is always clear and bright, a thread of tinsel that is all you ever see, the moment you lift up the sacking that's the front door of your shack, or you exit the glass door with gold lettering that says – 'The Starshot' where I live and am the mistress of the dance. You know the context, so the corpses, the fish – they fade into it, what they did, wanted, sink, swim, heroes, traitors ... just scenery.

*

'We'll never know, Camelia,' Petronia says. 'What Konrad knows, and I shan't ever ask him for the proof! There's no proof. How can you prove a context? How come I'm part of this, my life is banquets, orgies, high places and high treason, and I don't want any of it, it's not me, and it will be the death of me.'

'Listen, you goose,' says Camelia. 'Your answer has been given. "The world is everything that happens." There!'

'That's terrible,' Petronia says. 'To you, it's an answer, to me – my question.'

'But you're not an expert,' says Camelia. 'You're as ignorant as the rest of us, when it comes to "why". "How" is difficult – take shooting at a star. The "why" to that is easy – to make money, hollow out more planets, make a weapon – create problems for other generations to bother with: annihilation, exhaustion of resources, warring colonies a lifetime away ... an expedition....'

'Why are we here? Because we can't stop ourselves,' says Petronia. 'But for me – it's gathering up the pieces that you've dropped.... Red-hood, the cap of liberty, the natural man – running through the forest, the mushrooms he has gathered spilling from his basket. Should he stop and bury the cadavers lying there, beneath the trees? Wait! See what you've done, undo it ... start digging....'

'We will go on until we can't go any further,' says Camelia, cheerfully. 'We, the human species. Until there's nothing left. Nothing more that we can reach, spoil, consume. Exhausted everything.... And then the end: done. Finished.'

'You're probably right, Camelia,' Petronia says. 'I am not satisfied....'

'No one is,' Camelia says. 'That's what I told you. And stay clear of all of those who try to suck you in – Takis, Konrad, Ivan – the whole lot. They'll do you in, without remorse. They will make you end yourself, they'll just make the sign.

'Look where your friends have finished up, and they were amateurs. They went on trips with you ... where are they now? You're sweet and innocent, Petronia – but there's a shadow that you cast – and under it, there's nothing flourishes. Watch yourself, my dear. You've no protection, just your sentiments, that stand out like a porcupine's defence. Or maybe, thinking of the animals, the jungle that we're in ... an isolated creature, just like you, in black and white – you could well be, my dear: a skunk. A smell of big dead fish....

'And the innocents, if that is what they were – thrown overboard. If they knew what you know now, how would that change them?

'These questions – no one can answer them, and you expose yourself by asking. "Why? the universe. Why set it up, how does it work, and does it matter? An automaton? Or turbulences, gyres – and immense, unused unusable space?"

'The professionals – they stay clear of what they cannot give an answer to. What you ask – there is no satisfaction.

'You should have checked. If those were fish, and if they weren't – away, away – stay well away, and don't get on the ship, it's all been planned, where you'll end up, and who you'll meet, even the punishment's been set.... Don't touch the powerful, don't burn or bury them – stand well back.

'You are not trustworthy, Petronia. I keep you down, down where the dance takes place ... you should be out of sight, but you are not out of people's minds and their vendettas.... Whatever happens to you, don't let it touch my dancers....'

'What can I do, Camelia?' Petronia asks, aghast and trembling....

'If anything presents itself – a trip – keep off, unless you want to fall into the net, as you've already done, with no benefit that I can see....' Camelia says and hugs her.

'They can't silence me, Camelia – I haven't said anything yet,' Petronia says.

'That's of no account,' Camelia says. 'It's attitude. Disposition. As soon as someone sees you – they see you're gristle, and they'll have to spit you out.

'You're sour and shop-worn. You may understand the waves, the drift, when it's too late, but the sea, the sea! The force! The swell, the dominance – power that drives the planet....

'These strong precarious guys, no shame, playing their parts and trying to move everywhere, beat the others and resemble them – Russians, Americans, Chinese and Africans, and ... and – everyone who's not the waves. The waves, the surface – those are the ones you know because you saw them, lost on the sea, its force. Waves and people – they're the same, the people, waves of them, lost on the sea. The others, the big types – you flirted with them, their threats and wars, the interdictions and the plans ... the plots. You don't fear and distrust them, not enough, not nearly. They don't mean good, they won't do good for you, you see it over, over, you think you can fool them, have them adopt you – the fakes, and no, they are death for everyone, I know, I see them, Russians, and the rest, Americans – I see them when they try to dance. Monsters, like you say.'

There's silence, maybe a minute's.

'The "Takis" conspiracy – it's a good idea. It could cancel stupid boundaries; it promotes equality and lessens conflicts,' says Petronia. 'Conquer the continents! Unite, stand back – and wonder, hope.... The idea is Roman, that's for sure, but – it's a bad idea. It sets a massive overpowering power over, against, us all: there's massacres. In the heartlands – there forms a line of bosses who're psychotic, paranoid, ambitious, treacherous.... Besides, no one wants equality – a detail: everyone wants, expects, the wars.'

'They'll never tell if they eradicate the "Takis",' Camelia says. 'Nor what is happening after. The Takis plan, idea, will last, the people who promoted it – they won't. Another idea? – don't be sucked in, following its trail.

'Revenge will come, looking for you, Petronia – you're small.

'You're small, Petronia – so, you should be safe.'

'The fish,' Petronia says. 'They might come in – but now, it's all too late. I ought to understand why some things happen – but I don't. Can everything be a mistake, miscalculation? And does my Takis care about me, remember me? And if he does – is it a good? Or bad?

'The fish – an explanation is quite close. But all my other questions – unanswered, as before.'

'Conspiracies – they're quite banal,' Camelia says. 'And everybody knows about them. The curious thing is – if you're part of one, you stand to gain so little, and when you're fingered, then you end up dead.'

'Usually,' Petronia says. 'One of the sides you sympathised with abandons you. You end up like I do....'

'Yes,' Camelia says. 'You've been abandoned. Konrad was the proof. You, Petronia, can scarcely drop another floor, unless we dig it out for you.

'The only hope for you, your puzzlement, is guessing the identity of the fish. You might win points, be visible, and wait to be assassinated.

'Those Amazonian carp – 350 kilos, sweet white flesh ... abundance!

'Everyone competes, ideas don't count, and ideologies still less. Whole peoples are let go, lost, scattered in the deserts like grains of sand, waiting for the bombs, the truth, the faith, the test ... salvation. Is there one answer you've concocted, Petronia, in your life?'

'I realise,' Petronia says, 'you must not ask unanswered questions – "What's to be done, what ought I do?" Did I make anything happen, anything at all, to me, or did I just bring it on? By being – in the way?... Takis – does he make things happen, fiddling me, like I was a crochet on his score? Making history, making me? How and why? Is Lviv forever centre of a continent that purges its inhabitants, shifts them, enlists them, perpetual mandalas – devotions made of coloured sand, people believing they lost their paradise, that they were cheated of prosperity, thrown in the pit – responsible for nothing, then marched out to kill, enslave, the tables turning, always on the gyre. How does it work? What lifts Takis, fires him in the blue – a cheeky ball-bearing, shot from a sling, architect of a new world, dangling on a greasy rope, spluttering his final breath?

'My destiny: who thought that up? Yours, Camelia – have you wondered?

'Think. The world's "what happens in it". You are in it, to the death. Remember – you will be liable for the consequences of what you do, especially what you don't.'

*

This is not a movie

It doesn't end like you think it will.

*

Petronia thinks: Spying is quite difficult. People want to risk it when they're poor. If you've no money, you don't know anything, and so you can't be a spy. You're a casual – a bit of hearsay, eavesdropping.... It's all been filmed a hundred times, stock plots and silly movies.

Mock them, while you can. The bosses'll decide how and when you die. There's manuals on resistance; on asking for help; on not being framed and blackmailed ... on crossing to the happy lands. Skim through....

There's rules – don't walk, be trucked. Follow a water course. Don't go to jail, or land in court. Don't give up hope – people aren't interested in the depressed.

There's always bigger fish than you – you don't matter much, not like world's end – that *is* a concern. Make friends with families who will take your kids; salute the flag but keep your fingers crossed.

'None of us has kids, Camelia,' she says: 'It's not that we have given up....'

'No, no,' Camelia says. 'It's the clients. We get the wrong sort here. The hedonists!'

'We're sceptical,' Petronia says. 'I had to deal with the guy called Takis, and we saw "Takis", the conspiracy, close to.... I'm satisfied. There is an explanation! Many!'

*

'Ah, big ideas! France won the First World War,' Camelia says. 'That meant a lot to them.'

There's a pause. 'I was always on the left, Camelia,' Petronia says, 'though I never found anyone to share....'

'And the big river carp,' Camelia asks, 'do they swim out, into the sea? I've heard of the *arapaima,* known as the *pirarucù*; and there's those torpedo fish....'

'There's always bigger ones,' Petronia says. 'The heat swells them; most – inedible. It's true – we were superficial – 'fish? What kind?' We didn't think.

'Not fish? Then who? We didn't think.'

*

'There's two types, Petronia, came to look for you,' Camelia says. 'They went below, you didn't come. They danced, and didn't pay....'

'Not Konrad?' asks Petronia. 'Not Ivan? Not Takis, by any chance?'

'They didn't leave a name, nor anything. I didn't ask, you don't ask friends. They will be back – friends will,' Camelia says.

*

'I think it's time,' Petronia says. 'To take my trip. A long one, on my own. Home is always here for me, of course, and for my fellow-travellers, poor things.

'Watch what happens. Why it does. Is there an alternative? A cause, a purpose? Mystery revealed?

'Escape. Running down a different corridor? Disguise? Alas, I fear....

'Take care of my book, Camelia.'

The cover's pink, with flowers: 'Satyrs and Satires' on the title page. That's all.

'That's all?' Camelia asks. 'I guess you'll write it when you're back. We all love your stories, Petronia; no one tells them like you do.'

1

About the author

John Fraser lives near Rome. Previously, he worked in England and Canada.

www.ingramcontent.com/pod-product-compliance
Lightning Source LLC
Chambersburg PA
CBHW020550310726
48979CB00008B/1160/J

9781914938313